METEOR BITES

A S.N.A.F.U. Series

L. J. McKay

Order this book online at www.trafford.com
or email orders@trafford.com

Most Trafford titles are also available at major online book retailers.

Printed in the United States of America.

ISBN: 978-1-4269-6430-5 (sc)
ISBN: 978-1-4269-6431-2 (e)

Trafford rev. 09/13/2011

 www.trafford.com

North America & international
toll-free: 1 888 232 4444 (USA & Canada)
phone: 250 383 6864 ♦ fax: 812 355 4082

Acknowledgements

I want to thank my editing team (and the best payroll ladies in the trucking industry.)

Marylou, your awesome, but your bias and I can't believe the wonderful things you said about my book, but thank you. You encouraged me to keep going. Sharon, your just as bias as Marylou! Your tender-hearted nature and soft cheerleading style, kept my heart light while writing. Bonnie (the best travel agent a trucker could have) You are most definitely NOT bias! Your harsh judgments, helped me to make the book even better! Thank you.

Buddy and his sidekick Shooter, you set aside time to read even after driving 11 hours a day. You da MAN!

Book   1

By L.J. McKay

Meteor Bites

S.N.A.F.U   SERIES

To my family and friends. You have all been very supportive and I couldn't have done it with out you.

The Darkness Within

When I look in his eyes
I feel my blood rise
His skin glows white
Like lilies in the night
He walks with a dancers grace
Power, Strength, and evil smile on his face
Fire in his touch
Silky hair that flows
Centuries of knowledge on his face shows
All the while when you look at him
There is no doubt mistaking the Darkness Within

Author's Note

Dear Readers,

The color of my sky used to be blue. Now I see polka dots and stripes! Those readers, who are of the "McKay" clan, "Hopefully" will enjoy this book, and how I have twisted some "McKay" clan facts with the paranormal. I say "twisted" because I have a very twisted mind. I do not put anything in here to embarrass, or upset any member of the McKay clan intentionally. If I have then I apologize. My characters may have a slight resemblance to my family and friends… Mostly because they crack me up and they are as twisted as I am.

There is too much Damn DRAMA in my life! I love it!

As a Truck Driver, I have learned a lot, and seen even more. The amount of time we spend driving, is unbelievable.

There is always plenty of time to think, and plenty to think about. Most Long haul Drivers, have pretty much solved all the worlds problems in their own minds! Unfortunately, no one would listen to us, or take us seriously. There are always major political, social, economical, and sexual debates going on. Just turn your C.B. to channel 19 and listen for someone to say, "Shut up stupid" and you will know you are on the right channel!

Prologue

My name is Cassandra, Cassie to my friends and family. I am a five foot three and a half (dammit, I am claiming that half inch!) Truck Driver! I grew up a tomboy and it stuck. I also have a very prissy side, sometimes sweet, and caring, or I can get quite lippy. I have always had a small problem with the whole think before you speak thing. Oh well, your problem not mine right?

Just a little background on me... I am blah! Brown hair and eyes. I was very active as a teen, but always on the husky side. Three kids later, and a truck driver? Well, I am kind of squishy. Garfield's motto fits me perfectly. "I'm not over weight I'm under tall!" I love life in general. Something crazy is always happening at the house and I get to hear all about it... Then again, everyday on the road is an adventure!

As I am sure you have guessed, Truckers can be as bad as Sailors can. Usually only when someone does or says something stupid! Which unfortunately on the road is a lot! I always hoped I would win the lottery, or have my dream man swoop down and save me. Not gonna happen. I am a realist. I am also a hopeful romantic. Well, I do get to window shop a lot of men in this industry…(checking out pick up trucks as they pass me) .Haha you don't!

Bills to pay, miles to run, kids wanting money, and constant timeframes… Could it get any more hectic?

Chapter 1

This can NOT be happening. I was sitting in my truck, minding my own business, doing paperwork, trying to get ready for my next load, when "BOOM!" The ground was shaking as if we were having an earthquake, and debris, and dirt were flying everywhere. My truck was being pelted with asphalt, and god only knows what. The ground moved like a giant water wave. Everything on my dash hit the floor, *I* almost hit the floor! My truck finally quite rocking back and forth. I could barely see out of my windows, and then the dust and dirt started to settle. *WHAT THE FUCK???* I grabbed my mic "Break 19" I said into my Citizens band radio, both of my antennae's were still attached, but they were swinging like whips back and forth. Pushing the talk button, I tried again. "Somebody please tell me what the *FUCK* that is in front of my truck!" Small bits of dust were floating around the truck stop now. The parking lot was totally destroyed, and the radio was absolutely chaotic. Everyone was trying to talk at once, and all that could be heard was garbled voices because of it. Reminds me of the peanuts cartoon when they do that.

This thing was big! I mean really BIG! My truck is thirteen and a half feet tall at the roof. This thing was a couple of feet taller than my hood! "This is not good.." It looked like a big ass rock! I keyed up my mic again "Is that a meteorite?" still garbled noise on the radio. Speaking to inanimate objects is a good way to vent frustration. I have a bad habit of talking to myself and other people in their cars. They can't possibly hear me, but it still makes me feel better to tell them exactly how I feel. It's when I answer myself that my worries increase. Glaring at the radio, I mumbled "Big help you guys are." My eyes focused on the rock . "Oh this is soooo not good.. " It had a big crack in it, and it was spinning around. The meteorite landed about fifteen feet in front of my truck, so I had a front row seat. Would staying here be a good idea? With my luck, if I got out, the damn thing would spin out of the four foot hole it had made in the parking lot and chase me. Besides, the thought of having my Caterpillar motor between me and the rock, gave me a false sense of security.

Then true to form, my conspiracy theorist mind started spinning as fast as the rock. Questions were popping into my head left and right. What about Radiation poisoning? Are we being invaded? Am I going to glow in the dark now? My kids friends would think that was cool. Especially at Halloween. Me? Not so much. "Oh Shit!" The realization dawned, that if I didn't scramble my butt out of here, some government agency would have me quarantined! "Crap!" I wouldn't be able to get out of the area fast enough. Hell, my truck was blocked by the rock in front and another truck was parked behind me. What would I say anyway? *"No sir, officer, I wasn't in my truck. I was in the next state! I just decided to walk this load there…"* Nope. That wasn't gonna fly.

I looked around on the floor of the truck as fast as possible, trying to find my pouchie. *There!* My little pink pouchie was imperative for my survival. It carried my license, Mr. Visa, money, and my cell phone. Getting out of the truck was going to be tricky. My steps were covered with debris, and bent from where the parking lot had rippled under it. So I eased myself down and opted to try to get to the building. The rock was starting to slow down it's spin. I made it two whole trucks away when a sound like lightning hitting a transformer erupted behind me. Jumping between a couple of trucks, to hyperventilate, was not on my to do list for today. I poked my head around the front grille of the Freightliner that was doubling as my shield. Did the damn thing follow me? Nope! Still spinning like your favorite C.D., except the crack had gotten wider. Bright white light shot out of the crack and was turning with the meteor like a bright spot light circling the truck stop. "That can't be good." When the light flashed towards me I ducked back between the trucks again. I'm not stupid!

My momma taught me to get out of the line of fire. I firmly believe, meteorite light is the same thing. God only knows what could happen. Visions of Senator

Kelly from "X-Men" were going through my brain. Would the light melt me? Vaporize me? Would I wind up a jelly fish? Are segmented beasties with green acid blood gonna come out and get me?

My brain needed to quit thinking for just a few minutes. I scare myself more than anything else. It's a good thing I stay cool under pressure, well for the most part anyway. Looking around the grille again was something I really didn't want to do, but I needed to know if it was safe to run across the parking lot yet. It looked liked the light had passed over me so I poked my head around the hood of the truck again. I thought *okay this is my break*. The light had dimmed to a soft glow and the meteor had stopped spinning.

The crack was facing me though and I didn't like that. Being on the swim team in High school taught me how to prepare for extreme action, several deep breaths later prepared me to make a run for it. My flight response was in high gear. Eight feet into the parking lot, I heard the meteor turn, like it was starting to spin again. The sound was like fingernails on a chalk board.

Then, as if it had been waiting for me to come out of hiding, the light shot out of the meteor and straight for me. Trying to turn, run, scream, anything was impossible! I got a big fat nothing. Was this some kind of Alien tractor beam? An Alien spider web? The light had flashed over me and now held me. Sirens were coming closer, but I had the feeling they wouldn't be much help. The "Jaws of life" couldn't cut through a beam of light.

The opening to the rock was getting closer. No, I was getting closer to the rock. The light was getting brighter, like trying to look at the sun, I tried to close my eyes but nothing happened. The light went from being a blaze to a narrow beam and focused solely on my body now. The emergency personnel were in the parking lot now, and people were shouting, saying things like *"Lady, step away from the meteorite."* I thought, *NO shit why didn't I think of that?* my favorite one was *"Lady, I will come arrest you!"* If I could have rolled my eyes I would have. Last time I checked the mirror, the word dumbass was not tattooed on my forehead. Couldn't the cop see I was in trouble here?

Emergency personnel were pushing people back from the meteorite, trying to establish a perimeter, and were running back and forth. My peripheral vision caught movement. Fire fighters were pointing big grey hoses in the direction of me and the rock, then turned them on. Preparing myself for a blast of water was impossible, and apparently not necessary. The water never touched us. The light was hot and slowly increasing in temperature. Sweat was forming everywhere, and I could feel a migraine coming on. At least I thought it was a migraine. It felt like someone was digging into my skull with twenty ice picks, and an ice cream scoop. The pressure was so bad I wanted to scream. Then blessed blackness claimed me.

Chapter 2

Snippets of voices echoed around me *"pulse is still elevated....moving specimen to examine room 1 for more testing.... contamination affirmative, reaction negative.... Weight one hundred and twenty four pounds...."* that's when I relaxed. I knew they weren't talking about me. My last D.O.T. physical can prove I weigh in at two hundred and fifty two pounds. Remember muscle weighs more than fat, and I still have some muscle.

The smells in a hospital are unmistakable, once you've been in one you never forget. Everyone was muffled. It was like standing in thick fog, or wrapped in bubble wrap. My brain just felt foggy. My eyes felt like they were swollen, but I needed to see what was going on around me, so being very cautious of bright lights, I slowly opened my eyes. When my eyes finally focused, and my brain registered what I was seeing, I screamed. Steven Spielberg would have been proud. The "Exam room" I was being moved into looked like an operating room or part of some fancy lab.

The beeping of machines rang in my ears and the beeps got instantly faster. People were standing over me in white Haz-Mat suits, complete with air tanks on their backs. I tried to sit up, but that didn't happen. The spacemen had officially strapped me down to a hospital bed. Have I been abducted? Focusing my attention on one of the men in white suits I said "You can let me up now. I'm awake and I feel just fine." The good doctor did a double take and replied "I don't think so." and turned away from me. My panic was starting to make me shake and break out in goosebumps.

Sometime between passing out at the truck stop and waking up, someone had changed my clothes, I was now sporting a hospital gown. The fancy kind that had ventilation in the back and tied. What the Bloody Hell had happened to me? Where was I? This didn't look like a regular hospital, subtle clues gave that away, like the plain grey paint on the walls, instead of a nice soothing pastel. Too many questions, not enough answers. A nurse in a hazmat suit came at me with a needle. I hate needles! She didn't even acknowledge me, just tried to stab me to draw blood. Hell no! huh-uh! I wiggled as much as possible. "What the hell do you think your doing? Get away from me! You have no right! This is a violation! Get the hell away from me!" During my tirade, I got progressively louder. The rude doctor turned to me then and said "Hold still or we'll make you. You have no more rights. Your dead." Ice filled my veins and ran down my spine, effectively freezing me in place.

While I was absorbing what he said the damn nurse got me. My blood results had better come back normal, I wanted out of here. I was most certainly not dead! Doing a quick internal check told me so. Yep, my heart was trying to pound it's way out of my chest. Toes, legs, fingers, arms, lungs, it all seemed to work. Then a voice came from a speaker behind my head. "Doctor, the prognosis please." There wasn't a pillow under my head so I tipped my head back as far as I could, to see the speaker. I don't know why, I could tell it was a speaker, probably set in a wall somewhere.

The sight behind me blew my mind a little bit more.

At the top of the wall behind me was a bank of windows. Like an observation room. Upside down it looked weird. There were people at several different computer stations, and one really mean looking military dude.

He was in his late forties somewhere, and his scowl made him look older. Broad shoulders, military buzz cut, and the beginnings of a beer gut. He had what my grandma called a "bowl full of fruit" on his chest. I couldn't tell how tall he was from the angle of my bed, or see his sleeves or shoulders clearly. I wonder what rank he is. Jeez, this is probably not the time to be getting too curious about crap that doesn't matter.

The doc replied "The specimen has regained consciousness, we will run a new spectrum of tests for comparison. The last test results should be back within the hour, vitals are elevated, I would suggest a sedative, subject appears to be distressed." *no shit? I wonder why?* The military dude, said "Your call doctor, report when you have something." The doc nodded and turned away to read charts that were being printed out on the machines. Wires connected to small round stickers were attached to me in various places. "So am I a guinea pig or something? Maybe a lab rat?" Nothing, no response what so ever. Asshole. Since I opened my mouth to ask questions, doctor Kevorkian over there decided to shut me up so I wouldn't be a nuisance and bother him. He brought over a syringe and stuck me in the hip, then turned and walked away. Damn! That needle thing was getting old! Then nighty night me.

Not knowing how long I was knocked out for is a weird feeling, hours? A day? There were no windows to tell if it was day or night and I couldn't see or hear a clock ticking. I was alone in the room. Tilting my head back, allowed me to see if anyone was watching me from the glass gallery. Nope. I laid my head back against the bed and tried to grab the buckles on the straps at my wrists. No buckles, just huge Velcro straps. Double damn!

I looked down my body to try and see more of the room, when "Holy shit!" I could see my toes! My boobs used to get in the way and prevent that. All I had to do was bend just a bit. Then life happened and my belly kept me from seeing my toes. My belly was totally flat. I did a quick cursory visual on the rest of me. In a hospital gown it's easy. What did the doctor say? One hundred and twenty four pounds? *Holy Hell!* They *had* been talking about me. I tried to wiggle my hips. Nothing jiggled. AT ALL! I was skinny and solid. Did the meteorite do that to me? Was that why I had been sweating so much? Jeeez, it *did* try to melt me! There weren't any burns on my skin, that I could feel, nothing hurt anywhere. My only noticeable problem was my eyes, the people, whether they were in space suits or in the glass gallery, looked kind of funny. They were fuzzy around the edges, like I'd spent too much time in the pool. Maybe they put something in my eyes. Or maybe it's good drugs. What was in that syringe?

A female doctor came in, and checked my monitors. "Am I a prisoner doc?" she turned too abruptly, and wide eyed. I must have startled her. She came closer, and I noticed she was the same woman who stuck me to draw my blood. She said "Your supposed to be sedated." She grabbed my chart and checked something, then looked at her watch. "It's only been an hour since Doctor Hines gave you ten cc's of morphine. You should still be out." She eyed me like a specimen under a microscope. She walked to the door, and pushed a button. She paged a Dr. Hines to exam room one stat.

A few minutes later the door whooshed opened, and in came the male doctor who gave me the hip shot, spacesuit and all. I could hear the nurse clearly as she whispered to the doc. They had to be fifteen feet away. Ok, that's weird. Cool, but weird. Huh, good acoustics? What else has changed about me? It's a day of discoveries and fear. Doctor Hines came over to see if I was really awake, I thought about playing possum but decided against it. "I want to go home. NOW!" He grabbed my wrist and watched his watch. Yeah, I really need a pulse check with all these monitors on me, and how could he feel my pulse through the suit? "Am I allowed food in this joint? Even lab rats get fed." he was not amused. His reply was "See that tube in your arm? Your being fed." He was sooo not cooperating here! "How about something to drink? Or is that out of the question too?" My throat was scratchy and dry, my yelling earlier didn't help any. He didn't even glance at me just said "yes". Yes what? That I can have a drink or not? Since they didn't bring anything, I guess that was out too. Then Dr. Hines came at me with another needle. This time it looked full! I tried to wiggle away but it didn't help, he still stuck me. I am sooo gonna hurt him if I ever get free!

Chapter 3

I've heard that when you dream, is when your subconscious tries to solve your problems. Well, mine was apparently, on an Animal planet vacation. I had dreams of running wild in the forest, climbing tall trees, and flying through the air. Smelling prey, and chasing it down. The smell, and feel of tree bark beneath my paws. Paws? Huh? The smell of salty air and prairies full of wild flowers as I swooped towards them. What the Hell? I wasn't sure if I was wearing a fur coat or a leather suit of some kind. Everything was crystal clear, from the vines brushing against my whiskers, to the taste of fresh warm rabbit blood in my mouth, to basking under a hot sun on warm sandy beaches.

Now, I like to think I'm pretty open minded. Reading is a passion of mine, and I watch tons of movies, but what I was dreaming about seemed so real. When I woke up again, the smell and taste of some of the places in my dreams stayed with me. I didn't feel thirsty anymore or hungry! They didn't feel like dreams either they felt like memories. That can't be possible, I'm human, shifters and mystical stuff isn't real. My imagination was working overtime.

Besides, the physics never did add up to me. How does a two hundred pound man shift into a four hundred pound wolf? See what I mean? The whole train of thought is just bizarre. I've been all over this country, nights spent out in the middle of no where, full moon or not. If something like that existed, truckers would be the first to spot it. We'd see them darting across the roads at least. Besides, I didn't know how long I'd been here, long enough to loose half my body weight? That's a scary thought.

What did that damn rock do to me? Ok, quick room check. Yep, all alone again. Then the craziest idea I've ever had popped into my head. What if my dreams really were memories? The thought felt right, like I had just told my self a true fact. Somehow, even though I felt like the same person I also felt different inside. Alright, what do the books always say? Visualize and will the change? I looked at my straps holding me down. Was trying this a good idea? Am I just being stupid, thinking something dramatic was gonna happen? Probably. Were shape shifters real? God! I must have hit my head on something. Well, no one's here, so no one can laugh at my stupidity but me, besides it will give my mind something to do to pass time. But if it does work, will I bust the straps? Or will they hold? That would be bad. And what about all the wires that were stuck to me?

Now all I have to decide is what crazy thing do I try to change into? Hmmm, and would I be stuck that way if it worked?

Oh hell, are there cameras? I looked around the room again. Hell yes, there were cameras on every wall! Damn! They have to let me up sometime right? Soon?

The doctor came in again, and was muttering to himself now. "This can't be, you should be sedated for at least eight more hours." Well now I knew who'd been watching the cameras, Dr. Hines. He went to the intercom, pushed a button and started speaking. "Where's that blood report?" Another voice came back in the mechanical way a voice sounds through a speaker, and said "Everything in the blood screen appears normal sir. There's nothing out of normal perimeters. No toxins, viruses, diseases at all sir, cholesterol normal, white and red cells normal, metabolism normal. I think her blood is cleaner than mine, sir." The doc turned and looked at me. "We'll see about that." He grabbed a tray with tubes and those damned needles, thumped on my vein at the bend in my arm, with his fingers, and stuck me again! I was beginning to feel like a pin cushion.

He took his sample and left. He didn't bother to remove the needle out of my arm, just took the tube. Great, I'm going to bleed out all over the floor now. Then I heard a small pop. The needle casing wasn't in my arm anymore, it was gone. It had fallen out, that's what I heard. The tiny sound it made when the plastic hit the floor. Thank god! I tried to get a better look at my arm, there should have been bruises where they've been poking me. There was nothing, not even a red mark. Huh. That's odd.

After a while the doc came back in and looked at me. Just stood there and stared. "What?" I asked. "Your blood screen results came back normal *again!* They shouldn't have. They should have at least shown the sedatives, but they don't. Care to explain?" Now I just stared at him.

"Like I would know, you're the doctor." He let a long, deep breath out, walked to the wall, and took his spacesuit off. I guess I wasn't contagious anymore. He was bald on top with a ring of black hair around the bottom half of his head. "Do I get a potty break?" He walked back over, and looked at me and said one word "Catheter". I just can't get a break here.

"How about exercise? Is there a nice maze you want me run through?" He raised an eyebrow at me. "I'll take that as a NO! Do I eventually get a private room? Or am I on display for everybody?" He was visibly grinding his teeth together then he said "You are a specimen, nothing more. You are here for study." That really didn't sound good. "Does that mean you guys are eventually gonna dissect me?" The fucker just smiled at me, turned and walked over to a table. He picked up a tablet put his hand on the back of a chair with wheels on the bottom and pulled it close to the head of bed. He sat down, crossed his legs and poised his pen.

"Now that your awake you can answer some questions." He was sitting just far enough past the head of the bed, I'd have to strain my neck to see him. "Think you could move where I can see you, maybe raise the head of the bed?"

"How do you feel?" This whole not answering thing he had going on was seriously getting on my damn nerves. Turn about is fair play right? I started humming to myself "This is the song that doesn't end." The tune itself can get annoying after a while. "Answer my question please, you have knowledge we need." "Sorry, Charlie, if I can't see you, I can't hear you." We both waited for the other to respond, what do they call that? A Mexican stand-off ? He'd never met anyone like me, I'd bet money on it. My stubborn streak runs from one end of this country to the other. Trucking isn't just a job, it's a lifestyle. You have to be stubborn to stick with it for over thirteen years.

The head of my bed started to raise, imagine that, and he rolled his chair where I could see him. My humming ceased, and I responded to his question. "I feel with my fingers." Probably not the answer he wanted, he raised his eyebrows at me like he wanted me to continue my explanation, or give him the answer he wanted. If he wanted answers, he was gonna have to ask more questions, and trade info. "So, Where am I?" of course he ignored it, "Do you feel any pain?" pssshh "You're a very rude man." Turning my head away from him, I noticed the monitors were very interesting. High tech, digital displays, and reels of paper with printed out information pooling on the floor. Yeah yeah, I know it's an obvious ploy, but you work with what you got. Right? "You are property of the United States Government, you can answer the questions here and now, or later with someone else. I can assure you it will not be as pleasant." "Look, Dr. Hines?, I have questions too, ya know? In case you missed it, this is happening to me here." "So be it." He uncrossed his legs, stood up, rolled his chair out of sight and put my bed back the way it was prior to the questions. Completely flat. He walked over to me, gave me an anticipatory smile, and said "When they are through getting the answers from you, I'll conduct your autopsy for study and research." Then he walked out.

That is so NOT going to happen! His beady little eyes were so not going to be looking at my innards! Cameras or no, I need to know if I'm delusional about my dreams, and the sooner the better.

Okay, if I try this and succeed in shifting and get stuck, I want to be something sleek, so I guess I'll try something feline. Leopard? Panther? Lynx? Lion? Tabby cat? Huh… so many choices. Well, a house cat would easily be able to slip out of the restraints, and they are very pampered animals. If I got stuck as one at least I've have a good life. So, tabby cat it is. Closing my eyes, I thought of our family pet polydactyl, our six toed cat. He's the epitome of bonkers. I thought of the color of his fur, how soft he is, and his size. Concentrating and trying to will myself to change isn't as easy as you might think, especially when your scared. I tried to imagine shrinking into a cat. Hey, don't laugh, all the books say to do this. My head got a little fuzzy and then I felt really warm, and goose bumps rippled all over me. Well crap, now I'm just giving myself chills, wait that can't be right,

I'm warm not cold. Huh. I opened my eyes, and was now laying on my stomach, and everything was in black and white. Vertigo hit me then. It really freaking happened to me. Oh. My. God. I thought I said "HOLY SHIT" what came out was more like "RORYRI" I had white fur with cinnamon colored spots!

I checked to make sure none of the tubes were still in my arms. Unfortunately the stickers with wires do stick to fur. The machines were going haywire. Wow, this new vantage point was weird. The alarms on the machines apparently attracted some attention. The emergency lights came on as soon as I jumped off the bed and headed for the door. An automated alert was sounding throughout the whole place, it was set on repeat. I heard it echo through the door, down the hall. "WARNING, Contamination possibility in effect!" When that damn door opened I was out of here. With the cameras in place someone had to be watching. And they were, they knew I was by the door too. When the door opened a small crack I stayed on the floor looking lazy and content. *I'm an innocent little kitty here, nothing dangerous about me.* Dr. Hines opened the door wide enough to walk through, and I bolted. He was bent over like he was going to grab me when he came through the door. I jumped from the floor to the shoulder of the doctor in one leap. His shoulder was a spring board for me and then I ran the gauntlet of people in the halls. How the hell do you get out of this maze? Security must be pretty tight, there were keypads for office doors, and the elevator. Running around a corner, I lost traction on the plain white tile floors and used the wall for a backstop, Ye-ouch! Four legged running was way different than two legged. I needed to figure out the right synchronization between my front paws and my back paws. Then I was up and off again. There was a pa-ting behind me! Crap! I took a quick look back and saw a dart lying on the floor. Not good. A door opened to my left and I ran inside. Hot damn! The cafeteria! Food! I ran between peoples legs, and table legs. One man stood up and I jumped up onto his chair then onto his small round Formica table. Alarms were still going off everywhere and they were loud. Someone grabbed me by my belly and picked me up. I turned to look, and found a pissed off military dude. The same one I saw before. The one who had been watching me and asking questions. I also got a look at his shoulders. He had a spread eagle pin there. Isn't that a Colonel rank? *Dumb ass! Big mistake grabbing the kitty.* Turning my furry body toward him, I used my six toed foot to slice open his face. He let go real quick and started giving orders to shoot on sight.

Security guards, and doctors, who were chasing me came through the doors to the cafeteria, I ran between their legs and prayed no one stepped on me or my new tail. Three hallways later, I found a hallway with carpet. Traction! Woohoo! Digging in my claws was a small comfort. Another door opened at the end of the hall, and I put on a burst of speed and was through the door before it could shut.

If I hadn't been a cat, I would've gone head first into a wood crate. The agility of these little beasties is impressive! Scrambling my way around a couple of crates, I learned that cats could pretty much fold themselves in half. The door opened again. My instincts told me not to look back, to keep going forward, my ears picked up a lot of info like, when the Colonel growled out "Find, and shoot that Goddamned cat!" Must have pissed him off. Deep breath.

There were small gaps between some of the crates, and I squeezed in between one that read "Flammable" and one that read "Bio Hazard". *Oh Shit, Holy Mother of God!* I needed to be somewhere else, anywhere! Moving a few crates away, I read the crates again "Gas Masks" on one side and "Ordinance" on the other. *Crap! Not great but better.* I needed to be not so visible. A light colored cat in a dark warehouse? Not good. Our family house cat was white with cinnamon colored spots. Could I change just the color of my fur? Huh, only one way to find out. Concentrating on a spooky, Halloween black cat was easy. Then came the ripples and warmth. Opening my eyes, I looked at my paw. Yeah, still trying to get used to that idea. If someone got close enough they'd hear how happy I was that it worked. My motorboat noises worked. I was solid black, YES, I did it! I sooo wanted to do an "End Zone" dance. Maybe later.

Moving out from behind the crates, I ran for all I was worth across a warehouse. Distance was essential right now between me and the military. This place was packed, with crates of all different sizes and shapes. Some of the smells coming from the crates had me cringing. I recognized some smells, like gun oil, gas in barrels, and black powder.

Then the most amazing sound came to my ears. Vehicles approaching the building, and a garage door going up. Shouts were going out from several guards to "close the damn door!" Guess the drivers couldn't hear over their motors. My breathing was regulating even though I was freaked out. My kitty form was in better shape than my usual two legged form, and it was getting ready. My instincts were saying *Wait for it!* my mind was saying *Get out of Dodge!* My butt was rocking side to side preparing for launch as my leg muscles tensed, and my tail twitched. The door was six inches off the ground, bright sunlight was coming in, and freedom was about ten feet away. My instincts screamed *NOW!*, and away I went, didn't even question it. My instincts had saved my bacon so far, why stop now? Across the floor and out the garage door. I had to dart under the Hummer to get out, because there just wasn't enough room between the sides of the hummer and the sides of the garage door. Talk about a tight fit! Shots fired from somewhere, I heard them pelt the hummer with bullets, then boots were rhythmically slapping against the pavement.

I was running as fast as my paws could carry me, sunlight on my face, heart in my throat, and taking fast peeks from side to side, looking for bad guys, trying to find a hiding place, and trying to figure out where I was. Well, there wasn't anyplace to hide! It was all desert, and rock, not even a shrub, and the bad guys were still after me. Being a black cat in the desert is not a good idea. I was too easy to spot *Again!* Damn I need to figure out this whole camouflage thing.

In no time I was face to face with a fence that had to be twenty feet high. Not counting the razor wire at the top. *Shit!* I turned and ran down the fence line, keeping one eye out for guards, and one eye out for the exit. The guards were like ants crawling out of the woodworks. Where did they all come from?

All of the guards were wearing desert camo, and carrying big guns! I was getting winded , and still didn't see the exit. I am so not used to all this exercise! Where's a plane when you need one? *Wait! Plane, fly!* Crimeny, could I really do it? I was running fast enough I could take off if I had wings. What the hell? It's worked so far, right? I didn't want to stop and try to shift again, guards were closing in from all directions toward me and bullets were hitting the ground all around me. *Guess I'll have to try this on the run! Or would that be on the fly?* I pictured a Peregrine Falcon, they like the desert right? It's a fact they like road signs to perch on. Planting the image in my head of the small brown speckled bird, I jumped into the air as high as I could. Warmth and ripples, I was starting to get used to that feeling. This time my eyes stayed open, as soon as I saw feathers, I started flapping.

Let me tell you, it was not graceful by any means. How the Hell do birds stay level! The wind was hot against my face, and felt weird as it rustled tiny feathers around my beak. Scents were being filtered through my small feathers and through tiny holes in my beak.

Moving through the air was hard work, especially when flying against it. Dusty drafts and inexperience can make one very wobbly. Luckily that saved my life a few times, bullets kept buzzing by me, and I know I couldn't have intentionally dodged that many bullets on purpose.

The facility, base, whatever the hell you call that place, House of Terrors maybe, was getting smaller and smaller. *Thank god!* The view I had was breathtaking. Panoramic. Ok, now I just had to figure out where the heck I was. There were mountains, more desert, shrubs, cacti, rocks and an interstate, in the distance. Soaring in the sky is an adventure, total freedom. I flew around a mountain and saw a town up ahead. *Good that should tell me where I am!* The town mileage sign I saw read Socorro four miles. It was a familiar name but still didn't help me. Do you expect me to remember every town? Then Hello Mama! The interstate sign came into view. *Hot Damn! Interstate 25! Now I remember!* Pulling my left wing down and my right wing up allowed me to make a very wide left turn and started heading south.

What can I say? I'm a Trucker to the bones, we follow interstates when ever possible. You just can't get lost if you know the interstate system. Odd numbered roads go north and south, even numbered roads go east and west, simple.

When I flew over Las Cruces, I made another left hand turn and headed for El Paso, Texas. My poor wings felt like they were about to fall off. Getting the hang of flying wasn't too hard after I got out of the line of fire, for the most part. Got to watch out for wind drafts though, they can be brutal! *I have to make El Paso!* My new mantra.

When the truck stops came into view I felt a big wash of relief, they're a drivers best friend and they make great landmarks. Then again, so do repair shops, and dealerships. *Repair shop! Hell yes! Spare parts, spare sleepers*....Remembering there was one close by, I aimed for it. Oh, this landing was going to hurt. My wings, and the muscles in my back were cramping, and I was losing altitude fast. I tried to slow down, before my not-so-graceful crash landing, and mostly managed. Just so you know, when you roll head over tail in dirt a few times, IT FREAKING HURTS! Any landing you can walk away from is a good landing right? Does hobble away count? Doesn't matter, right now, I'm alive, and have no extra holes in my head except what I was born with. Slowly moving towards a white sleeper that was for sale, I gently hopped inside. This sleeper had the bed frame, cabinets, and a big hole on the front (where it would be accessible from the cab) along with the big leather curtains that divide the cab from the bunk. I couldn't close the curtains with my wings so I just hopped onto the bed frame and passed out.

Chapter 4

Well this is different. Everywhere I looked, no matter which way I turned was clouds. I wasn't dead, unless I died from exhaustion. There was a thick, heavy blanket of fog all around me. Suddenly a ball of light, the size of a soccer ball, floated out of the fog and straight for me. *Oh Crap! Again with the light.* Becoming nocturnal was sounding good right about now. In a hushed tone I heard the word *"Greetings"* in my head. I raised my eyebrows and asked "Are you talking to me?" again in my head I heard *"Yes"* "What are you?" *"I am you"* Cryptic much? "Uh. Could you be a bit more specific? Cause your freaking me out here. This is the weirdest dream I ever had." *"I am your guide to the power, you can learn from your dreams."* " You came from the meteor." I didn't ask I just knew it. *"Yes"* "What the Hell did you do to me? Do you know what I've been through?" *"You have taken our essence."* "Come again? I don't think you understand!" *"No, it is you who does not understand, all will be explained."* "Well, this should be worth an award, let's hear it. Explain, exactly what you did to me, and why the hell it was me!" I might have been a little testy. There was a long silence then I get this….

"My people were doomed, our sun went supernova. Our race was very special. Our essence gave us gifts. Before our destruction, my people decided to try and save our essence for another race. So they could prosper like we did. One of our people had a very unique, and special gift, he could collect and capture our essence. So, we built a safe place to house the gifts of my people. When our planet exploded, this sphere, was launched into space to find new life for our essence. The only ones we found who were compatible, were here on Earth." This sounded like it was gonna take a while, so I sat down on the fluffy clouds, and got comfortable. *"Our essence defines us. Some of my people could do extraordinary feats because of it. Some could shift into an animal, or heal others with a touch, or manipulate energy. Our ultimate goal was to find a new world and spread to the people there, so our essence could continue to grow, in harmony with the life we merged with."* "Am I possessed by the souls of your people?" I was totally dumbstruck. *"No. Not our souls just our essence, our gifts. We watched your people and waited for the appropriate time to merge. There was always a war, and strife somewhere. We were waiting for your people to grow more in their hearts, but that time didn't come. After centuries of waiting the different essences were inseparable, they merged together to form one. We were running out of time. We started searching for one person, who had the qualities needed to be able to except, and use our essence, the way it was meant. We found a ripple in the sea of humans. You were the rock that made the ripple."* "What the hell is so special about me?" Okay that sounded whiney. *"Everything that you are, that*

you think, act, feel, physical form, believe, is what we wanted, needed, and you still had a slight spark." Stunned, I asked "Spark? What does that mean? Have you been watching me? Spying on me? Following me?" *"Yes"* Dear God in heaven! Ewww peeping toms! I quickly ran through my memory to see if I had done anything I should, or would be embarrassed about. Hmmm. Yep. Crap. I'm celibate mostly in the truck, but I do have toys! I'm not usually one to blush, but I felt my face getting red hot! I looked at the pretty cloud I was sitting on, it was suddenly very interesting.

"Okay," I said with a pitiful note of resignation even I heard. "Tell me about this spark, what do you want me to do and how do I do it?"

"Your family line, carries the spark to shift shape. Though yours is diluted, it is still there. You are to protect, to give our essence meaning. You already know how." huh? I suddenly remembered some of my family history, my Ancestral Clan was termed "The Invincible Scotts" Back in like, eleven hundred and eight, when they fought with some Welsh guy, William of Orange? Well, I guess now I know how they did it, they were freaking shape shifters! "I think I figured out the whole shape shifting thing, unless this whole thing is some whacked out dream, but it's totally weird. In case I'm just getting lucky here, explain it all to me in detail. Please." *"There is a human saying that would apply. K.I.S.S. Keep It Simple Sweetie."* I thought it was keep it simple stupid. Shows you what I know. *"The essence took you, and burned your energy to help the merger. That is why you appear different than you were before. You*

should be able to shift into any known creature, real or imagined, current or extinct. You will be able to heal any type of creature, to the point of death, even the dead ones." "WHOA! Stop right there." I held up my hand towards him in the universal sign for "STOP". "Umm., Uh. Okay, I get the burning my energy part, I think. That made me skinny right?" *"Yes."* "But well, healing the dead ones? Like zombies? You said 'to the point of death.' Make up my mind! Cause that is just confusing as Hell!" *"The dead ones who walk at night, the Vampires."* Okay, enough sleep for me, time to wake up! Vampires? Hell NO! Do I look like an Anita? A Sookie? Nope. Trying to come to terms with the whole shape shifter thing was enough to deal with. The light had to be joking, had to be! Time for a subject change. Quick like and in a hurry. I could shift into any creature? Hmmm. Unicorns, and dragons, how about a T-Rex? I've met a few people I wouldn't mind scaring the piss out of. Movie pun intended. I refuse to shift into a cockroach though, no way in hell. "Okay, You said the "V" word. Their real? Seriously? Your not just yanking my chain?" I was hoping he was yanking my chain real hard. *"They are real, and walk among you. Don't discount them. One day you may be glad they are here."* "Why would I be glad to have a blood thirsty, blood drinking, moon bleached, leach here?" *"They are long lived, and so are you. Now."* "Beg your pardon? Am I immortal? Are you saying I'm gonna live forever?" Stunned didn't even cover what I felt now. *"You are technically not immortal, just extremely hard to kill, if you use your gifts correctly. You are going to live a very long time. That is an essence gift."* Okay, I'll deal with the vamp stuff later. I took a very long and deep breath and decided, to try to think of them as powerful humans on a liquid diet. Kind of like vegetarians. I rubbed both hands over my face trying to wipe away all that I'd heard. "Alright then K.I.S.S.," I took a very heavy sigh "do I just think of an animal and poof? Or what?" *"Visualize the creature you wish to change into and imagine yourself as that creature and it will be as you say "poof"."* Uh huh see? I was right, "I can handle that. What about the energy manipulation thing, what can I do, and how does it work?" There was a long pause before he answered. *"You can use energy in many ways, visualize a shield around your body, and the energy will repel whatever you want it to, thus making you hard to kill. Create small amounts of light, or fire. Hide yourself, by bending the light around you, and you will blend completely into your surroundings. Your senses are greater now, smell, hearing, taste, touch, sight, you have greater strength and speed. You can change the energy in your own eyes so you can see in pitch black, or find heat."* "Are you saying I'll have night vision eyes? Like the goggles? Heat seeking vision? What about x-ray vision? Do I get that?" *"Yes, but it is very limited, few had that essence, so it will not be nearly as powerful."* "Holy Shit! That is cool! I hope I don't accidentally use it on some big, corn fed, guy who decided to go commando that day." That's not even a mental picture I want in my head. Jeez, I'd need eye bleach! "So, I guess there are other shape shifters on the planet?" *"Yes, that is how we knew you were a compatible species, and even though you have the essence to see thru objects you may not be able to use it, very little essence."* "Can you tell me what is wrong with my eyes now? Are they adjusting or something? Everyone is kind of fuzzy." *"What you see is their essence, you call them "Aura's". You will be able to know what everyone is just by looking at them. Shape shifters will show their respective animal in their Aura's, just as Vampires will have none. I will be here in your dreams if you need me. Day has come, you should wake."* And just like that, I woke up. Man, this was just getting weirder, and weirder. I guess it falls under the S.N.A.F.U. category. Situation Normal All Fucked Up! Everyday is an adventure right? I may sound a bit whiney, but, I want my vacation.

Chapter 5

I woke up feeling completely overwhelmed, and sat up. The hard wood of the bed frame was not all that comfortable. Switching back and forth from animal to human was going to take some getting used to. Especially, when you go to sleep as one thing and wake up another. Sitting there trying to put things into perspective, and trying to take in all the information I was given was going to give me a headache. *Aliens? Essence? Shoooo! No, not essence. The Aliens Auras.*

Okay, it's time to start figuring this stuff out, if I plan to keep living that is. Oh yeah, I'm "long lived" now. My personal power trainer said to visualize my power wrapping itself around me. Like a cloak? I wanted it to repel everything! Feeling a slight warm ripple, I looked down at myself. Well, I was naked, good thing I'm skinny now, wouldn't want my old body hanging out all over the place. But where was my new shield? Shouldn't I be able to see it, or feel something unusual? Maybe it didn't work? I took a long, slow frustrated breath. Well, hmm, lets try to bend the light, I can't walk around in the buff. The mechanics around here might like it, but I wouldn't. Being husky most of my life made me a bit prudish I guess. Do I just think I'm invisible here or what? Warm ripples cascaded over me again, so I must be doing something. It may not be right, but something was going on.

I looked at my hand. It was gone! "What the ..?" It wasn't gone, it was clear. I saw right through my hand. Turning my hand back and forth, I noticed I couldn't see any edges to my hand at all. My eyes got huge as I remembered an "Arnold" movie, where he was chased by the "Predator". He had a force field but not like this! I was like a damn *ghost!* Does Fort Knox have enough security measures to keep out a ghost? Hmmm. Now, how long will this last. Well, supplies were needed for sure, food, clothes and transportation right now, so I guess I'll have to take my chances. Leaving the safety of the sleeper was nerve racking. There weren't any mechanics wandering around so I slipped off the property and headed for the truck stop.

My heart was pounding, my hands were sweating, my nerves, I think were about shot, and I was at the edge of the parking lot to the truck stop. Hell, I'd only gone about a half of a block. Deep breath, I ran across the parking area and up to the door. If *I* open it, they'll think they have a ghost, crap! It was a short wait for a driver to open the door, then I slipped in behind him. Waiting for a lady to go to the restroom, had me doing the pee-pee dance in the hall! As I came out I brushed up against a t-shirt, and did a double take. The shirt had disappeared. Oooo. I grabbed the shirt not caring what it said, and slipped it off the hanger and over my head, then I went after shorts! As soon as I touched them, the clothes disappeared, just like I had. Why? Was it because I just touched them?

The smell of coffee about undid me, so naturally that was my next stop. One fingertip touched a cup and it went poof, *Yeah Buddy!* Hot chocolate, French vanilla creamer, and the intense energy coffee. Yum! I had to dodge a couple of people to get to the hot dogs, but I got mine! This was pretty cool, walking around, and just helping my self. My conscience would kick my butt later but right now I was good, next stop shoes. Since it was a small truck stop they had a limited selection. Men's work boots, men's tennis shoes, men's socks, well that wont work. An attendant walked by me and went to the fuel desk with shower keys. *Oh, Yes! I have to get me one of those!* umm, umm, I need, I need, yes! Shower bag and goodies to go in it. Shampoo, soap, hairbrush, tooth brush, and tooth paste. Everything I needed was here, maybe not my favorite brands, but still… After I put my stolen goods into a small duffle bag, I swiped a shower key and headed towards the back of the building. The hot water did my muscles a world of good. My shower was great!

Before leaving the building I filled my duffle with some snacks, and drinks. Didn't know when mealtime was going to be, and girl scouts taught me to always be prepared. Leaving the building with my contraband was just as much of a hassle as getting in was. Now travel arrangements needed to be figured out. This is Texas, maybe a horse? What kind of horse, toting a duffle wouldn't stand out, crossing the city? A small giggle escaped me as the image flew through my mind. Becoming visible in the shower was a plus, it helps to see what your washing. Then I became clear again before exiting the shower area. Would the invisibility stay when I shifted? Ugh! I'm getting tired of testing theories. Pulling my clothes off and placing them in the duffle bag made me nervous. According to the books I'd read, they say that when a shifter changes, they rip the hell out of their clothes. Since I've recently acquired mine, I wanted to keep them. A horse is much larger than I am so that actually made sense. Since I'm short, am I going to turn into a Shetland pony? Placing the long strap of my duffle around my neck was an uncomfortable weight, and hoped it would stay there when I shifted. Picturing a Palomino was easy enough. After the warm ripples were through, I had four hooves, and a tail, and I was still invisible! Yee-Haw! Wow.

All day, I trotted across El Paso. On the east side of town were several larger truck stops. One I knew carried women's shoes. Now I'm the proud owner of a cute pair of blue Minnetonka slippers. Night was coming quickly, and my stomach was growling like I was starved! Slipping out the door, and heading for the back fence, I sat down and ate a whole po' boy, and drank a whole quart of milk. Wow! Even after my stomach was full it still growled! Those sandwiches are like a fully loaded foot long sub. The books also say a shifter eats twice as much. Maybe that was true too. Stripping, and changing again, my clear mane and tail fluttered in the Texas breeze as I took off across the field that borders the back of the truck stop. It was going to be a long walk home.

After about twenty minutes of walking across the desert, a Rattle snake just lunged at me, no warning rattle or anything. Using my powerful legs I jumped up and back to get away from it, but didn't land. Hovering there, the snake made another lunge for me and I drifted backwards further. Turning my head to look at my back I saw the clear vague shape of wings. *Holy Shit! I'm a flying horse, no I'm a Pegasus! Wow!* I looked for the snake again, it was still on the ground and making sure it's rattles were heard now. I have wings now, I'm not landing, there's no snakes up here! I tested the muscles in my back and my new wings lifted me higher.

Well, the Pegasus is infinitely better at this flying thing, much more stable, maybe because I'm bigger? More weight? The winds gusts didn't hardly bother me now, and my wings were fast! Before, I knew it, I was flying over the Alamo, then beautiful downtown Houston came into view. Altering my course I headed home. One thing bothered me the whole trip though, how did that snake see me?

My landing was much better as a Pegasus, and there was just enough room in my backyard to slow my trot to a stop. Before I could change to human form my faithful guard dog came running out of the house. She cocked her head at me, and decided to finally earn her keep and growl. I smiled to myself, she's such a part of the family she forgets she's a dog, but she was looking at me. A quick look showed my invisibility was still going strong. Real animals could see me? Taking a cautious step forward, she stepped back, I guess they could see me. Angel, was a mix between malamute, and border collie. She had a thick coat of salt and pepper fur, great for deep snow, and she was the size and shape of a border collie. She even had the floppy ears.

Picturing my two legged self in my head was easy. I just had to remember to picture my new and improved self. Then I became visible, and once she saw me, it was all good. There's nothing like the slobber of a loved one. After our reunion of scratches, kisses, hugs, and a shared po'boy, I got dressed, took a deep breath and made for the back door. The military or government agency that snatched me, probably had a satellite trained on the house watching for my return. Hell, they probably bugged the house, tapped the phones, *and* had people watching it! Quietly opening the door and stepping inside, I headed for the fridge and the quick leftovers I could find and scavenge.. then straight for my mom's bedroom. God only knew what my family had been told. Probably, the same thing I was, that I was dead. So, when mom see's me, most likely she's gonna flip out. Deep breath.

Angel, my goofy dog, jumped up onto the bed, made a few circles then laid down. Mom always leaves a lamp, or television on, sometimes both. So, there was plenty of light to see as I walked to the side of her bed. Very quietly, in case the house was bugged, I whispered "Mom" in her ear, while giving her shoulder a little shake. My mom never wakes up gently, she jerks like she's been startled every time, and this time was no different. The look on her face was priceless, that told me immediately that she had been told I was dead. Her brown eyes were the size of silver dollars, and her brown hair looked like it collected a few extra grey hairs in the last couple of days. My heart was heavy as I realized I had put them there. Before she could scream I closed my hand over her mouth and started shushing her. My mom is five foot six, and early sixties, but she doesn't look or act it, and her grip was like a vice around my ribs. I gently rocked her and whispered in her ear. "Mom, it's okay. I'm alive, calm down, be very quiet and listen. Get your smokes, grab a blanket, and meet me on the back porch. No questions here, I'm gonna get Yoda." My sister, Illiana, and I have different fathers, so she's my opposite. Where I have dark eyes, dark hair, and olive skin, she has light brown hair, blue eyes, and pale skin. She didn't learn from the screw ups my mother and I made, and got pregnant to young. When we found out about it I popped her with my palm (gently of course) in the middle of her forehead and said "That's yo' duh!" she's been yoda ever since.

I quietly opened her door so the noise wouldn't wake my nephew, and walked to the side of her bed, well, I get points for trying to anyway. I jammed my toes on her end table, stepped on a squeaky toy, tripped over a pile of clothes, and nearly landed on her. My sweet teenage, clothes hog sister, the imp! Well, she was awake now, I scrambled to her side and repeated the shushing, and instructions. She jumped up and followed me out the door, I don't know how she did it but she didn't trip at all.

Angel followed our procession outside, then I was attacked from two sides. Tears were flowing, hands were gripping me and questions were flying. "Whoa, slow down, it's okay, breathe people breathe. One question at a time." I tried to keeps things from spiraling out of control. We're a very dramatic, and theatrical family, and generally hold nothing back when our emotions are involved. Right now we needed to be practical.

My mom started the inquisition, "Cassie, what the hell is going on? We were told you were dead, they gave us a check for five million dollars and said it was your life insurance money, what happened?" My sister chimed in "Cass, how did you get so skinny?" We spread the blanket out on the porch and sat down, I said "First, as you can clearly see I'm alive, and not dead. Second, my life insurance policy is for two hundred and fifty thousand, and that would go to my kids, not you, third, I think what you got is "hush" money, so you wouldn't ask questions or look for me. Now, I'll give you the detailed version or the reader's digest version, which do you want?" Mom said " Reader's digest version." Yoda, said "I want details." I went with mom. "A meteor landed, I was exposed to meteor rays, taken to a military facility for study, escaped, and came home." Questions exploded around me again, I raised both hands and started shushing again, jeez, my family couldn't keep their voices down. "People please, keep quiet!" I blew out a long breath, and said "Look, I was exposed to power coming out of the meteor, and obviously it changed me." I gestured my hands up and down my new body. "I believe it changed me on like, a cellular level. I didn't stick around the military base, long enough to find out. Besides, their tests kept coming up normal, and right now they're looking for me. So keep the noise down. The house might be bugged, phones tapped, you name it. Right now, *I'm America's most wanted,* and BIG Brother *is* definitely looking for me! Didn't the meteor landing make the news?" My sister shook her head and said "There's been nothing on the news about a meteor" My mom asked, "Cassandra Justine, why are they looking for you, and where have you been for the last week and a half?" Awww jeez, here we go, she used my first and middle names, and the "Mother" tone, not good. "What? A week and a half?" My family looked at each other, my mom said "Cassie, we had your memorial service and funeral four days ago, we buried an empty coffin. It's been nine days since you disappeared."

Both of them were now on the verge of tears. Me too. She pleaded with me "Please tell me what the hell is going on? I'm having a break down as it is." I had hoped to avoid telling them about my new lifestyle. I didn't want to see disgust in their eyes, or have them think of me as a freak, guess that wasn't gonna happen. Maybe it will be alright, they read the same books I do. "Uh, well, you see, umm" Letting out a resigned breath, I let it rip. "Well, I might have, like shape shifted into a cat, and they might have possibly, got it on tape." Okay, so the let it rip, came out very grumbled. I didn't look at them, looked everywhere but at them, I was waiting for the blow to come. Yoda spoke first, "Are you for real? You've read to many books, and it's affected your brain, you've gone schizoid, maybe some good drugs will help. I love you and I'm glad your home and alive, don't worry, we can get you help." I gave her a dirty look then took a chance and looked at my mom, her face was very controlled like she didn't want to spook me, in case I was crazy.

Double Damn! Well, show and tell was always the best part of school. The neighbors flood light illuminated our back yard enough for them to see me clearly. A heavy sigh escaped from between my lips, Angel had plopped herself down onto my lap, so she needed to be moved. I didn't want to scare them or Angel, so picturing something non- threatening, was going to be a trick. I chose a snow white Unicorn, complete with iridescent horn, and thick wavy tail and mane.

I closed my eyes, and pictured the animal I wanted, feeling the warm ripples, and presto chango. Their jaws dropped to the ground, they were gonna start catching flies soon. I whinnied at them.

Yoda jumped up first, "Holy Crap! You're a Unicorn!" Then my mom slowly got up and walked over to me, I ducked my head. She slowly reached up and stroked my neck, in an awed voice, she said "God, your beautiful.

Do you want a carrot or something, Cassie?" I lifted my head and just looked at her. Mom's and their comfort food. Iliana was walking around my backside and I shifted back. "Hey! Your too close to my butt little sister!" Both had big grins on their faces, she said "Wow, I mean.. just WOW!, how did you do that?" I shrugged, "It's part of the new package, it came with the body." I looked at mom then, with raised eyebrows, "A carrot mom? Come on now." Leave it to my mother "Well, I didn't know what else to say, give me a break, I didn't know shifters were real, much less that my own daughter was one, that's not exactly something you see everyday!" She was very indignant at the end.

"Do I usually lie to you mom? The last two days have been stressful for all of us, but right now, we need to plan." My mom shook her head "No, Baby it's been nine days. And right now you need clothes." Ooops. I still couldn't get over that, it only felt like a couple of days to me. Over the next two hours they told me what they had planned to do with the money. I gave them a few more ideas, then we planned how to tell my kids, I was alive. It was agreed no one was to use phones, if it was important. My mom didn't like my idea, about me not sticking around, but it was safer that way.

Chapter 6

After leaving mom, and Yoda, I decided the block needed to be scouted, just in case. Was I paranoid? You betcha! My family would be in danger. More now that they new about me. Illiana gave me a few of her clothes since we were close to the same size now, and mom loaded a bigger duffle bag with all my usual bathroom stuff and food to go. The best invention to ever be made was Tupperware and leftovers.

Taking chances right now was NOT an option. Going out the side gate invisible was tough, Angel kept trying to squeeze out between my legs, but I finally made it through. She watched me till she couldn't see me anymore. Living someplace where all the neighbors are gossips is the best way to get to know who lived where, and what kinds of cars they drove. Mostly so you could avoid some of them. So, a running dark blue van on the block, a few houses from ours, was kind of a dead give away. I just shook my head, did they really think people were that stupid? Creeping closer to the van might not be the best idea but, I needed to see if anyone was home. Sure enough, there were two male voices. .. *"be home this soon." "Stop complaining, if she comes back here we'll get her." "This is nuts, we're Mercenaries, not babysitters!" "I'm going to step out for minute and stretch my legs."* I moved to the side of the van, I didn't know which door the man was coming out of, until it opened. My, mouth had dropped open. *Mercenaries? Holy Crap! What the hell were they doing in MY neighborhood?* Of course, he chose the side where I was. I jumped and scooted to the back of the van.

Ye-ouza! This guy was *BIG!* He was about six foot eight, with a very nicely muscled body. Trim waist, tight butt, and wavy sandy blonde hair, that came to his shoulders. He wore a tight black t-shirt, black jeans and black boots. But his aura was incredible! It was wild, like it didn't want to be contained on his body, and the ghost of an animal floated through it. I gasped, "Lion" I whispered, apparently, I wasn't quiet enough though, because he heard me. He whipped his head around, and started sniffing the air. That just looks strange on a human face. He started slowly walking towards me. My heart was beating so fast and hard, It's amazing he couldn't hear it. I thought about my shield, and tried to imagine, no sound coming out of it, unless I was speaking, and no bullets coming through it! I felt a slight warm ripple, God, please let it have worked. Taking a couple steps back kept the distance between us.

"Where are you? Who are you?" He growled. His eyes were brown with gold flakes in them, they were pretty, but they looked pissed. The other man climbed out of the van then. He was tall too, over six foot with light blonde hair, and green eyes. His aura was just as wild. He asked " Alex, who are you talking to?"

The guy closest to me "Alex" said, " Someone's here, I think it's her." Then Mr. nameless started sniffing the air. "I don't smell anything." Alex replied "I heard her Brett, I know I did, I'm not crazy, she's here." "Where?" Brett asked, "I don't know!" Alex replied. He was getting frustrated. "I know your here Cassandra, and I know you can hear me. Talk to us. We want to help you." *yeah right*. Again, no forehead tattoos'.

"Do you need medical attention?" *He was joking right?*

"Are you hurt? Can you speak?" This was just too much, finally I gave in and said, "Leave here!" Keeping myself moving, hopefully made it hard for them to pinpoint me and they wouldn't bump into me. I should have kept my damn mouth shut though. Both men abruptly turned towards me. "I heard that." Brett said. "I don't see her, but I heard her." I was at the front of the van now, hmm, can I manipulate the energy to short out the van, and their equipment? Did I just have to imagine a spark or something?

Placing my hands on the hood, and concentrating, made me nibble on my lower lip. A pulse of power tingled out of my hands and into the truck. My hands got really hot, then pops and fire cracker sounds came from inside the van. Since I was invisible, I finally did my "End Zone" dance. Yeah Me! The men opened the doors to the van and smoke poured out of it. Uh oh,

I might have over done it! The inside of the van was on fire! I was stunned but couldn't stop the giggle that erupted out of me. The men turned towards me again, both were now scowling. Alex took the lead, "Well I hope you're happy, that was about fifty grand worth of equipment. You have us at a disadvantage now, want to come out where we can see you?" I was still grinning "Not really, you still look pissed." I should be ashamed of myself, Bad Truck Driver! I kept moving around, didn't want them to get a bead on me, spy movies are a favorite of mine. "Well," Brett started "we have a bit of a right to be pissed, don't you think? We paid for that equipment with our own money. It won't be easy to replace." What could I say? I wasn't sorry I did it. Maybe, a little something for their time? Becoming visible, but behind them, I said "BOO!" both men turned. There I was, my grin just wouldn't go away. "Think your cute don't you?" Alex asked, then they both tried to pounce on me! In less that a second, I was like Casper. That skill has been totally mastered ! We all moved with incredible speed at the same time, so they didn't catch me. They did however, land on each other. Which was fine by me, the vertigo had a grip on me at the moment. My body has never moved that fast. I giggled again, Gosh!, these guys were fun! "SHIT!" One of them said. They rolled off each other and were upright instantly, looking for me.

"Do you know you have a bounty on your head? Twenty five million, to whoever brings you in, dead or alive." Well, thank you Alex for that little tid bit of info. He had managed to wipe the smile from my face. *25 million?* The van was turning into a nice big blaze, and the sirens of fire trucks was getting closer, I hope they are coming here. Alex gave me something to think about so I returned the favor. "How would you like to be put in a lab, caged, tested, and dissected? You are both Lion shifters, I'm sure they would like to get their hands on you, just as much as me."

I let that soak in for a few seconds, maybe they wouldn't like it. "I'm leaving the area, I'm not going to put my family in jeopardy, I just had to know they were alright." I kept moving around "I don't know where I'll go, but you can bet your next paycheck, you won't find me, unless I want to be found." Trying to divert them was the essential part. They didn't need any extra information about where I'd be, hell, I wasn't sure where I'd be.

Fire trucks pulled up the street, and the guys looked towards the fire trucks then bolted. Shifting into a Falcon, so I could keep my eyes on them, seemed like the best option. My duffle bag was in my claws. They used their super natural speed and ran down the block, around the corner, and towards our neighborhood park, and pool area. Finally, they stopped at one of the park benches. I actually managed to land in the grass without rolling head over tail. Brett, pulled out a cell phone from his pocket, and hit a speed dial number, before he sat down. He hit the speaker button, when the call connected. "Marcus, we have a problem, we need a pick up, we're at the park in the neighborhood." There was no response, just a growl, and a click. Twenty minutes later, two motorcycles pulled into the park. Brett, and Alex, climbed on the backs of the bikes without saying a word, and off they went. I followed them.

We headed out highway two-ninety, after about ten minutes at very high speeds, they took their exit, and headed further west. They slowed down and turned into the driveway of a *Huge* mansion. There was nothing but land, and trees for miles. It was very quiet, and very country. There were several house cats, roaming around, so I shifted into one that was tortoise shell colored, left my duffle on the ground and followed them in. Alex, actually held the door open for me. *Stupid man!* Since they were Lions, I guess they had a respect for all cats.

The guys walked down a hallway through a living room, that didn't have much in the way of furniture and into an library/ office. Jumping up onto a couch, I rolled around and got comfortable. From my current seat, everyone in the room was in view.

An older man, of about fifty, with dark brown hair, cut in a short business style, was sitting behind a beautiful hand carved desk. He looked like a wrestler, with a thick neck, and too many muscles. His suit was tailor cut and looked like fine silk. The desk had Lions, standing up on their hind paws, roaring, carved into the corners. Creepy, but beautiful.

Alex, and Brett, had taken straight back chairs, in front of the desk. "Report!" The man behind the desk growled.

Alex stood up, "Leander Marcus, we made contact with the mark, she was there tonight. We lost all of our equipment to a power surge of some kind. The van caught fire, emergency vehicles arrived at the scene. Briefly, we saw her, but for the most part, it's like she was invisible." Alex, sat down when Brett stood up. "No, not *like* she was invisible, sir. She *WAS* invisible." *Thank you Brett you big tattle tale.* he continued, "We couldn't have been more than, three to five feet from her, several times. She had no smell at all, unless she spoke, we couldn't hear her or pin point her." he sat back down.

I got up off the couch and walked over to Alex, looked up at him, and jumped up onto his lap. Yeah I know, way too close to the enemy. He started absently petting me, I got my purr on, and started kneading is very muscled thigh. Damn! Why did he have to be a bad guy?

Marcus was so mad his face almost turned purple. "You mean to tell me, you let twenty five million dollars get away from you? You couldn't even catch one little girl?" Neither man said a word for a long minute, then Brett said "I think we should try to recruit her. Imagine how close she could get to a mark, without ever being seen?" "It won't work, she won't do it." *Finally, a man with a brain! Thank you Alex!* "Look at her file. She's weak, unpredictable, and from what we saw tonight, I'm not sure she's even stable." I think I'm insulted, I might have dug my claws into his leg a little hard because he hissed at me, picked me up and put me on the floor. "I still say we should talk to her, as you said Alex, look at her file, you have to be pretty strong minded to thrive, in a man's industry. That takes courage, and strength of character. She's a single woman running around the country, she has to know how to defend herself." Alex was steadily shaking his head. I walked around the desk and jumped up onto the desk blotter, and stretched out. Marcus, started petting me then. *If only these men knew...*

"I don't care how you do it, or who you have to capture to get her attention. Bring me that girl! A.S.A.P!" Ohh, no he didn't! That did it! He's not going to threaten my family and get away with it! Since, I was on his desk blotter, and right in Marcus's face, I shifted from a house cat, to a Lioness and Roared! He jumped back so hard, his fancy leather chair hit the wall. "Who the Fuck are you?" Alex, and Brett had also jumped up, they were ready to pounce on me. Shifting into my human self right there on his desk, gave me the advantage. "The woman in question." You could almost see the light bulbs turning on over their heads.

Shifting Back to human form in front of strangers made me nervous. My clothes should have been ripped to shreds when I shifted to follow them, however, my mental picture of myself was clothed in what I had been wearing, and the clothes came back with me. No more nakedness! That is definitely something to remember later.

Marcus didn't ask but made the statement "You've been in here the whole time. Listening to everything we said." Then he threw his head back and laughed out loud. There was a sparkle to his eye I didn't trust. He pointed at me and said, "That gentleman is how you infiltrate the enemy, right under their noses." He held up his hand towards me and I let him help me off his desk. He has a very evil smile, that I didn't want to turn my back on. Sidling around to the side of his desk, put me in position to see all three men.

He turned to Brett, and ordered me a chair. The chair, another straight back chair, was placed between Brett and Alex. I reluctantly moved between the two men and sat down. Alex, looked like he wanted to string me up by the tail, Brett's eyes were smiling at me. Hmm. "Well, you've been listening to us, Cassandra. What do you say? Want to make millions of dollars a year? A mercenaries life is very profitable. We could train you in weapons, hand to hand combat, whatever you need." Marcus was back in his chair, with his arms resting on his desk. He still had an evil twinkle in his eye. "That depends, I thought you wanted to kill me." " Well, after what I just saw, I'm rethinking that. What do you say" "I'm practical enough, that I would kill anyone who tried to hurt me or mine, and not lose any sleep over it. There are of course some things I won't do. My weapons knowledge is just fine, I can handle myself, and as you have seen, I can be quit covert." Marcus leaned forward "Like what? What won't you do?" I had to think about that a minute, that's not something the average person thinks about everyday. "Well, I won't kill someone for petty bullshit causes, like, a corporate take over gone wrong, someone getting caught with the wrong persons spouse, because some one was embarrassed, no kids, things like that. I won't kill someone when a slap on the wrist, a little jail time or just a good scare will do. Now, Serial killers? Rapists? Terrorists? People like that? Okay, I'm game. I wouldn't lose sleep over them."

Apparently, he wanted more from me than that. I figured I didn't pass his qualifications, when he pulled out a gun, from   somewhere, and shot me in the heart.

My breath left my body in a harsh whoosh. I was dead, and just didn't have enough sense to know it. Both Alex, and Brett jumped up, and turned towards me. I looked down at my chest, and started breathing again, when I saw the bullet about an eighth of an inch away from me. It just hovered there. Then four more shots rang out. There was a small cluster of silver colored bullets right over my heart. Slowly, with very shaky hands, I grabbed the bullets out of my shield, that Thank God had worked, stood up, and dropped them onto Marcus's desk. The doors to the library/ office opened and people came rushing in. Shock was settling in, I could feel it. Cold was settling in and I began shaking all over. My legs were a little unsteady, the only option I could think of to keep my sanity, was to get down right pissed! "You missed you Son of a Bitch!" I said through gritted teeth. His eyes were very wide, and he fired again and again until his clip was empty. The cold was dissipating, I was starting to get hot. Very Hot! I reached across the desk and grabbed the barrel of his gun and squeezed. My fingers were melting the barrel, leaving finger grooves. I yanked his gun out of his hands and threw it at his head! He ducked just in time. I swatted the rest of the bullets off my chest. "Oh Shit!" Brett, said "Look at her hands." I did too. They were on fire, but there was no pain. The fire was on the outside of my shield, and slowing climbing up my arms to encase my whole body. My eyes met Alex's then. His eyes were like an owl's. "You ought to look at her eyes." My eyes could have looked like anything at that moment, Looking back at Marcus, he stepped back until he was against the wall. I've heard that when someone means to kill you, you can actually see your death in their eyes. I hoped he saw his. But now was not the time. I was too freaked out

Turning for the door, I started walking out. Getting the Hell out of there, was top priority at the moment. Everyone moved out of my way as I started searching for the front door. My adrenaline was pumping, my breathing was coming in fast and short . The need to calm down was a must, but not here, and not right now. A beautifully carved set of wooden doors came into view, raising my hands, the need to release power from my body was almost overwhelming. Without even thinking, fire shot out of my palms. The doors were incinerated in seconds. I didn't even stop to admire what had just happened, just kept walking. Walking across the front lawn, I became invisible again. Some of my brain cells had cooled enough for me to start thinking again, besides most people wouldn't like seeing a woman walking down the street on fire.

After an hour of fast walking trying to calm down, my adrenaline rush was wearing off, and I stopped on the side of the road, and sat down in the grass. The streets were vacant at this time of morning. That's when it all hit me. I don't like to cry, but the release was needed, *BAD!*

My crying lasted until the hiccupping stage, and there were no more tears. Sometime during my escape from reality, my body became visible again. Hunger pangs hit me, and the thought of a bed was real nice. The sun would be up soon, so gathering my strength and pulling both arms over my head for a good stretch, I stood up. First on the list was a restroom. I was thankful I had enough brains when I left to grab my duffle, unfortunately when I touched it, the damn thing caught on fire. No more food or spare clothes. Shifting into my Falcon form, was becoming comfortable. Raptors had excellent vision, but I never knew just how excellent. The landscape was clear for miles. I spotted a Whataburger and prepared for landing. Well at least my landings are getting better. Then back to human form.

Looking into the wall of windows showed the front counter area was empty. *They must be in back.* Sneaking inside, the restroom was my first stop. My eyes were red and puffy and my nose matched. Can anyone say Rudolph? I'm not even going to discuss my hair! After getting cleaned up, and going invisible, the only step left was getting out the restroom door.

Chapter 7

My sleepy time power trainer had said a "small amount of fire". What happened tonight, in my estimation, was anything but small! I'd stolen food from the Whataburger and it had revived me some, but exhaustion was still settling in.

Back off the main road, was a beautiful and very dark Victorian home. Was it dark because no one was home? Or because they were asleep? Remembering what the light had said about my eyes made my decision to see if it would work. Trying to focus my thoughts to change my eyes to see heat was strange. If someone was home, hopefully their body heat would show in a bedroom right? Doing a long slow blink, I opened my eyes again and saw outlines of the building, the inner walls, and a small red glowing blob, by the front porch. Nothing else glowed though, so maybe no one was home.

Twenty feet up the drive, I came face to face with a very strong, very big wrought iron fence. Most fences like this have a square rod about a half inch wide, and thick, that are set about five or six inches apart. These rods were two inches wide, and thick, and three inches apart. There were decorative spikes on top, but from the ground, they looked very sharp. Shifting to my Falcon form, allowed me to fly over the fence, and land on the railing, of the wrap around porch. The house was Gorgeous, butter yellow paint with dark green shutters and trim. The fence railing for the porch was bright white. There were big bay windows, round rooms on the corners and a widows walk on the roof. Back in human form again, I tried the handle on the front door. Locked. Darn it, figures it would be. I walked around the house and checked all the windows, and the back door. Muttering to myself. "Damn! Why couldn't the owner be nice enough to leave a door unlocked?" As I peeked into the window a low whistle escaped me.

The inside was more elegant than the outside. "I do *not* want to bust a window to this beautiful house." "I would appreciate it if you didn't, the windows are a special cut, and quite expensive."

A deep, sexy voice had me spinning around in place. He'd said it like we had been having a regular conversation. Six feet of Yummy was leaning against the stair rail of the back porch. He had thick, white blonde hair that came down to his hips, and eyes so blue they looked like neon. They practically glowed even in the dark. Broad shoulders were covered with a dark red silk shirt. He was a waking advertisement for his black leather pants. *I would have bought some!* He wore matching dark red suede, calf high boots. "Ooops!" I said. He cocked a well trimmed eyebrow at me and very casually asked, "Who are you? And what are you doing here?" I'd been caught, almost in the act of breaking and entering. I was definitely trespassing. What was I supposed to say? "Uhh, well, I was looking for a place to crash, and get a bath." Quickly I added, "I wasn't gonna steal anything! I swear!" Another voice came from right behind me, deep and a little bit raspy "There's no vehicle in sight." He scared me and I jumped and gave a very girlie eep! I eyed the two men now standing in front of me. The new guy was wearing all black. "Jesus, did I stumble across a secret playgirl mansion? Or something?" They both raised their eyebrows at me. I really hope I wasn't drooling on myself. The new guy was about six foot six, long black wavy hair that went to the middle of his back. The term "Built like a brick shit house" would apply here. His eyes were a silvery grey, very mesmerizing. Staring at them, I noticed something odd, they didn't have auras. Either one of them. My eyebrows drew together and realization dawned as my own personal light bulb clicked on what they were. Then my eyes got very big. They were Vampires. I panicked, and squeaked out, "Oh Shit!" turned and tried to run.

I got about three feet, before I was yanked back against a very large and very hard chest. My arms were pinned to my sides as I was picked up, my feet were dangling about two feet off the ground, so I figured the vamp with black hair had me. He turned us around and my suspicions were confirmed. Blondie, pulled out keys, opened the door turned on a few lights and ushered us in.

The house on the inside was breath taking. Beautiful gold plated wall sconces, wall paper with crushed gold velvet designs lined the hallway. At the moment I didn't care that big strong hands were carrying me. Actually, it might have been a good thing I was being carried. I'm a hands on person, the kind who likes to touch things and feel the texture of them. I would have picked up and inspected everything we passed. My mouth was hanging open as I took it all in. A *Huge* crystal chandelier was hanging in the foyer, we turned and went into the sitting area. *Oh My God!* I was in a dream house! *MY* dream house! Thick, heavy wine colored velvet drapes over shear curtains graced the windows. The furniture was all French Provincial! Every piece of it. The hand carved wood, the dark blue stripped damask silk fabric, the blue, and wine Persian rug. All of it was gorgeous. Gawking and drooling on myself is probably not very attractive, but it couldn't be helped.

The Blonde was watching me. "You can quit ooing, awwing, and moaning." I slowly shook my head "I don't think I can." He sat down on one of the beautiful chairs, which sent me into a frenzy "AWWW get up, get up!" My feet were kicking in the air trying to get free. What was I was going to do? Yank the man off his own furniture? He raised both eyebrows at me in question "You might snag the fabric! Do you see what your sitting on? That's an antique!" His reply? "So am I." His expression said he didn't know what to make of me. He nodded to the vamp holding me and then my feet hit the floor. My feet were cushioned sounds on

the beautiful rug "Get your fine ass out of that chair!"
I demanded "Have you no shame?" Gawd! What was
I doing? He was a vamp for cripes sake! He scowled at
me then and ordered "Sit." I gasped, and in the most
distinguished, British, indignant, snobby tone I could
muster, said, "I will not! What if I snag the fabric? Do
you know how much this thing costs?" He nodded to
the other vamp and motioned for the divan. Before I
could protest any more, the black haired vamp grabbed
my shoulders and pushed me down into a seated position
on to the antique. Was he the bodyguard?

I held my breath, waiting for something terrible to
happen. The big black haired Vampire went around
the room and started closing the drapes. Very carefully
readjusting myself so I *didn't* snag the fabric, I looked
at Blondie.

"Yes, I do know how much it cost, I bought it new
over one hundred and fifty years ago." My mouth fell
open at that "Now tell me who sent you? You play the
dumb, innocent quite well." I took a deep breath at that.
"Nobody sent me, I told you what I was doing here, and
depending on the topic, I'm far from innocent." Then I
thought about what I said, "That didn't come out right,
in *THIS* situation I am definitely innocent! I had NO
idea this was a vampire lair! If I had, I wouldn't have
stopped."   "What makes you think this is a Vampire's
lair?" "Uh, well, you guys don't have an aura. Either one
of you. You are a Vampire right?" He looked at me for
a minute and finally said "I believe you. And yes we are
definetly Vampires." A huge sigh of relief escaped me,

I was getting the hang of this mystical crap. "However, that doesn't change the fact that you can not leave here." "HUH?" Eloquence is not my strong suit sometimes. He smirked at me "Do you believe a vampire would want someone walking around with the knowledge of his resting place?"

I had had about as much paranormal attitude bullshit as a person could take for one night, first the Government, then the Lions, now this. I pointed my finger at him and stood up. The bodyguard guy moved behind me. "Now look, you arrogant jackass! You're not going to kill me, I'm not going to be your breakfast!" He raised both eyebrows at me "I do have something to bargain with though. I can protect your day resting place, if you let me stay." He chuckled at me, looked at the other vamp and asked "How many times have we heard that plea?" I turned my head, to see the bodyguard, he just shrugged. "I'm serious! Don't think I can't!" "You are a mere child, you can't even take care of yourself." he said. I went invisible then and walked towards Blondie, his eyes were scanning the room.

I moved behind him then faced the bodyguard and became visible again. The guards eyes snapped towards me. "There's a very good reason I'm in the situation I'm in right now." Blondie moved with vamp speed, towards his bodyguard, when I started talking. "I'm not as much of a child as you think I am. I'm a grown woman, born in nineteen seventy two, and I have enough power to do whatever the hell I want! As you can see." Flames erupted on my arms, but I was well away from the furniture. "I'm not exactly human. Or I'm more than human, however you want to think about it." They both stared at me with completely blank faces. Then I felt a tingle like vibration at the base of my skull. I doused the flames, reached back to rub my neck, and tried to figure out what it was. Is that a pinched nerve? I focused on the vibes and accidentally tuned into a silent telepathic communication. That's the only thing it could be. I was hearing their voices in my head. "*... think she might cause trouble?" "I believe she IS trouble." "Do you believe she is a threat to us?" "No, but I do think that gift of hers' could be quite valuable." "Which one?" "Both, give her a chance, you took a chance on me, I wasn't a bad gamble. I have a feeling about her." "No, you were the best chance I ever took. A feeling? Alright, a short trial period, if she doesn't work out, or if she tries anything you know what to do. There is something about her...*"

I walked forward, they were on the back side of the divan, while I was on the front. "Look, I've never met a vampire before tonight, I swear! Hell, I had never met a shape shifter until tonight. Seriously, no one sent me here, all I wanted was a place to sleep, bathe and maybe grab a bite to eat when I woke up. Uhh, I'm going to guess, there's no food here right?" They looked like Siamese twins when they both shook their heads. "If you don't want me to stay, that's understandable just point me to a barn, or something. Right now, I really don't care." I held out my hand hoping Blondie would shake it, "I'm Cassandra, by the way. And you are?" Blondie took my hand in his, then brought it to his mouth and kissed the back of it. Pure blatant old world charm. That

earned him a small smile, and a blush. He gave me a
small smile in return "Cassandra is a beautiful name,
I am Christian, and this is my bodyguard, Sebastian."
Ha! I was right, he is a body guard. I didn't try to shake
his hand, we shared nods with each other. See? Not so
stupid after all. "It's interesting to meet you, your much
more pleasant than the damn Lions." Christian, lost his
smile then, and let go of my hand.

"You know the Lions?" he asked. I made a disgusted
look then became wary and said "I hope they aren't
friends of yours, I think I'm gonna have to kill some of
them. They aren't friends are they?"

My voice held a hopeful tone. Christian replied "No,
they are not our friends. How do you know them?"
"Uhh, I ran into them in front of my mom's house.
They tried to recruit me. Marcus is not a happy camper
right now." Getting worked up again just thinking
about him, here and now might not be the best of ideas.
"After he unloaded his clip at my chest, I incinerated his
front doors." They both looked at my chest and gave me
questionable looks. I shrugged "For a merc he sucks,
he missed at four feet. What can I say?" I left it at that.
The guys both exchanged looks with each other, then
back to me. "Soooo, can I stay? Please? I won't be any
trouble. I swear!" " I believe you will be much trouble.
For now, you may use the room, up the stairs, first door
to your left." He got a genuine smile out of me then.
"Thank you!" I wanted to give the blonde stud a hug but
I didn't think that was appropriate. I raced up the stairs
in search of my room, and hopefully a bath.

The room was perfect, pale pink carpet and walls, mauve velvet curtains, dark furniture, complete with a four poster bed. An attached bathroom matched the bedroom. White marble tiles with pale pink veining throughout the whole bathroom. The separate shower had three shower heads! One on two walls, and one directly overhead. The garden tub had my complete attention though, for about forty-five minutes. After my wonderful bath, I climbed into Egyptian cotton comfort and finally got some well needed sleep.

Christian said to Sebastian "I have the strangest feeling our undead lives are going to become very interesting." Sebastian smiled at Christian and replied "We need interesting, it's been very boring lately, maybe she'll bring a little life back into these old bones of ours"

Chapter 8

A solid knock on the door woke me up. "Yes?" no reply. Rolling out of bed, I went to the door and opened it. Luckily there had been some old clothes hanging in the closet, and I'd swiped a clean t-shirt to sleep in. "Christian said to give this to you. You are to wear it tonight." Then Sebastian turned and went down the stairs. Closing the door, I looked at the garment bag I'd been handed, then draped it on the bed. *Bathroom first.* After my personals were done, I unzipped the garment bag, and gasped at what was in there. I stomped on the floor, and yelled "You sick Pervert!" From then on I just mumbled to myself. Inside the bag was a royal purple, leotard, with purple suede boots. Snatching the leotard out of the bag and pulling it on, my mumbling continued "I can't believe you want me to go out in public in this thing. Only a man would have picked this out. It leaves nothing to the imagination!" I stomped the floor again to make my point, they were vamps, I was pretty sure they heard me. According to all the fiction books I'd read, vamps were supposed to have exceptional hearing. I do like the boots, though. One inch heels, and they came almost up to my knees. Instead of long sleeves, the full body leotard had one inch straps over the shoulders. Before leaving the room I went invisible, going out in public, looking like a skanky tramp was not at the top of my to do list!

My boots made a lot of racket as I stomped down the stairs, and both vampires looked my way. "How can one little girl make so much noise? Does your attire fit?" Christian had a small smile on his face when he asked. I replied. "Like a second skin." he said "Good, we need to prepare." When I got to the bottom step I asked "Prepare for what?" Then Sebastian opened the front door and out they went. If I wanted to know I'd have to follow. Curiosity is my new middle name. Besides, what else have I got to do right now? I pulled the door closed behind me and followed them to a big stretched black Escalade. Sebastian opened the door and we got in. Sebastian's second job is chauffer. After we were on our way I was enlightened to tonight's events. "Make yourself visible please, that is disconcerting." "I'd rather not." I did though, with my legs crossed and my arms crossed *over* my chest. The leotard had a low scoop neck. "I have a meeting with the local leaders, it will be a closed meeting, which means no one but us will be attending. No guards are allowed, not all of the leaders are trustworthy. I want you to come with me." He gave me a very pointed look then "I want you to be my bodyguard for the meeting." "Your bodyguard?

You don't even know me or trust me! And your willing to put your life in my hands?" He paused and looked a bit uncomfortable. "At this juncture I have little choice. The timing of your arrival, is still questionable, but your gift to be unseen could be very beneficial. I have some reservations about this meeting, not counting the ones I have about you. Hence the skin tight clothes. I now know your not hiding any weapons," I crossed my arms *under* my chest, thought a minute, took a deep breath and smiled at him "Okay, if you're willing, then I'm willing, but I'm gonna need supplies if I'm to guard that body of yours." I got a suspicious look from him then, maybe because of the satisfied glimmer in my eyes. "What kind of supplies do you require?" Sebastian was watching us in the rearview, I turned to him and said "The Galleria please." We didn't change course until Christian nodded agreement. Oh boy! I'm taking men shopping. Better yet, Blondie's buying! Even as we entered the mall, they were both suspicious. Did they still think I was sent to kill them? Maybe. In their eyes, I guess this could have been a set up.

The mall map was close to the door which was convenient. A woman not knowing where the stores were is just sad, but that's okay. The look on the guys faces as we entered Victoria's Secrets was priceless.

The lady behind the counter saw both vampires, and nearly tripped over her own feet to get to us. She was the perfect person to work in a store like this. She looked like a swimsuit model, it made me want to hit her. She was almost six feet tall with long wavy dark blonde hair and green eyes. "Good evening, how may *I* help *you*?" Woo! She works fast, and Christian worked it. "Anything the lady wants." He nodded towards me and the salesclerk acted like she hadn't seen me. Well the guys were HOT! Couldn't blame her for her lack of attention. She turned to me then, with a very small smile and looked me up and down. I don't think I passed inspection. "I need a black half corset, no boobie cups, fastening in the front." She looked down her nose at me and said "This way, please." We all followed her out of the main showroom and into a smaller private showroom. I never knew VS carried BDSM stuff! She found exactly what I was looking for on the first try. She helped me put on a black leather corset, and it fit perfectly, but I needed it to be bigger. "I need to adjust the sides, it needs to be bigger." She looked at me like I was an idiot, but I knew what I wanted. We got it loosened until there was a one inch gap in it. "That will work!" She led us to the check out and flirted the whole time, Christian was trying to pay. I stood there and shook my head, and mumbled "A woman that pretty can not be that desperate." Sebastian was standing with me and asked "Do you not find Christian attractive?" DUH! "Well yes, but if we don't get him out of here, it looks like she's gonna start stripping."

Sebastian rescued him and we were able to move on. Next stop, Asian Art Gallery. According to my books, the best way to kill a vamp, is beheading, fire, or stakes. Well, if I'm gonna have to behead someone, I need the right tools. At least I wouldn't need to tote around a

Zippo. When we walked into the Asian gallery, a petite older oriental woman, came around the counter gave a little bow and asked if she could help us. Her eyes were dark and soft around the edges. She was about the same height as I was, five foot three. I gave a respectful bow back and said "I would like to see a Katana please." This store has REAL Asian stuff in it, none of the cheap, fake, dull swords, you can't put an edge on. She pulled one off the wall behind her with a braided black and blue silk grip, and handed it to me. I took it and pulled the handle about four inches exposing a little blade. Very nice. Then used my raised eyebrows to ask a question to her, she bowed again, turned, walked to the back of the store and we followed. She motioned me, with a very petite hand wave towards a big rubber block. It's said if you pull out a blade, completely from it's sheath and don't cut something with it, you insult the blade. I had a double handed grip on the handle and gave the rubber block a good slice, all the way through it. I wasn't the first one to cut the block, but I think I was the first to cut all the way through it. She looked at me with big eyes. Giving her a big smile and a bow , I said "I'll take two."

We all went back up front. She handed me a second one, and I looked to Sebastian for help. "What do you want me to do?" he asked "Criss-cross them on my back inside my corset." While he was putting in the sword and sheath, I hadn't cut the block with in my corset, I turned the blade I was holding away from us, and ran a line of fire down the blade to get the rubber dust off it. I had pictured in my mind what I wanted, but didn't actually think it would happen. It did. Surprise. Surprise. The Asian lady gasped and hit the floor, calling out to someone in Chinese or Mandarin. A little Asian man came running from the back, and knelt down, on the floor in front of me. "Um, excuse me, I didn't mean to frighten anyone." I had a worried look on my face now. The Asian man said "You frighten no one, and honor us with your visit Longwei. Anything you want is yours." Huh? Are these people nuts? I put the sword back into it's sheath. "Thank you, I think, but uh, my name is Cassandra not Longwei." I turned to find both vampires with questions on their faces, I gave a wide eyed shrug. Sebastian got the other sword in my corset and I tried to pull it out of is sheath. My damn arms were too short! "Excuse me, uh I'd like to trade these for two Di-Katana instead." The Lady jumped up like she'd been stung, grabbed the two smaller swords, ran around the counter, came in front of me, and bowed, holding the swords out in front of her. This was getting weird. Must be another S.N.A.F.U day. We changed out the swords in my corset, and I tried pulling one out of it's sheath again. I got it! Short sword, but oh well.

"These, will work perfectly." My grin went from ear to ear. "Would you by chance have any Sai?" The Asian man stood up, backed up five feet, bowed then turned and ran into the back. We heard several crashes, and definitely heard something glass breaking. Then he came running back out with two boxes. They were both about a foot and a half long, about eight inches wide, and four inches thick. The first box he held out, with another bow, was light wood, probably bamboo, and very simple. He held it up in front of me like he was presenting it to me. Then opened it. Inside were two very shiny, silver colored, Sai. The tips of the prongs were needle point sharp. "Perfect!" They slid down the outsides of my boots, long prong inside, and short prongs outside. It had the paperclip effect.

Again the Asian man said, "Please take this, is for you only Longwei." Why did he keep calling me that? He handed me the other box. It was gorgeous. Black lacquered, with a dragon on the top, all inlaid mother of pearl. I looked At the guys, now they shrugged. I opened the box and inside were ten silver finger claws. Each one had joints so, you could bend your fingers. The claws on the end were two inches long and serrated. Freddie Kruger would have been envious. I slid one on a finger and sighed, it was too big. The Asian man saw me take it off with regret and disappointment, and waved both hands at me and said "Wait wait, I fix, I make to fit you! Pwease, put back on. Put all on." So I put them all on and he pulled out a small wooden tool with what looked like a tiny belt on it. He slid it over each knuckle and squeezed, until all the joints were snug. "See? I fix!" "Wow!, these are great." I turned to show the guys and they both took a step back, and both had suspicious looks again. My smile faded and I just shook my head.

I took off the claws and put them back in the beautiful box, then turned to the Asian couple, who were still bowing, and asked how much we owed. "You,

Longwei, owe nothing, you honor us by coming to store. If you need anything else. We here, we help." They both started bobbing up and down. "Thank you. Why do you keep calling me Longwei?" "Because you are Longwei, you are the great Dragon!" My forehead wrinkled and Christian and Sebastian shared a look with each other. "Uh, excuse me, but I'm not a Dragon." The Asian couple looked up at me smiled and stood up. They gave me a conspiratorial look, bowed several more times and the lady said "Okay, we keep secret, you no Longwei. Except here in our store." These two just wouldn't let it go. I noticed a white candle on a shelf. It was a pretty good size, about six inches in diameter and eight inches tall, with a gold colored Chinese dragon on the front. A great idea popped into my head. I grabbed the candle and put it on the counter by the register. "Look up." the couple did. Then I lit just one finger on fire, reached out and lit the wick on the candle. The couple was grinning, and the lady had tears in her eyes, as I grabbed my new boxes and we walked out.

"Well, that was weird." I said. We made a quick stop in the food court then headed back to the car, when Christian asked. "Why did you light the candle?" I shrugged "It seemed like the right thing to do, you know? They acted like I was some big wig dragon, I just thought having a candle lit by a big wig dragon would please them." Christian wasn't through with his questions "Are you a Dragon?" I snorted then "Ha! No!" "Do you know how to use those weapons?" "Oh yeah, I've seen all the kung fu movies, and I even own the movie 'Crouching Tiger hidden Dragon' , and I learned a lot from 'Kung fu Panda' " I just looked at him then, it took everything I had not to laugh at my own joke.

We left the galleria, and headed up highway fifty nine. "You will need to be invisible when we get there." My eyes involuntarily rolled in my head. My new black box kept drawing my attention, "If I wear these, is it gonna freak you out?" "Very much so." Heavy sigh, they were cool as hell. I looked at him again straight in the eye. "Get over it, I wasn't sent here to kill you." I pulled them out and put them on. The box was on my lap, but I didn't want to touch it with the claws on, I might scratch it. "Will you please move the box so I don't mess it up?" With vampire speed he reached over and grabbed the box, and moved back "Thank you." When we pulled into the parking lot, I turned into Casper. Sebastian pulled us up by the other limo's that were already there. He parked us, got out and opened our door. I stayed right on Christian's heels.

There were more shape shifters here, it's a good thing no one could see me, cause my mouth was practically dragging on the ground. Their aura's were all wild with different animals ghosting through them. Seeing them all around like that was a trip. The intensity of each aura varied. The colors were different, some were brighter than others, some flared out more. The smells in the air caught my attention too. All the smells were confusing though. Sharp acrid odors, or the smell of green fresh cut grass. Too many to try to figure out right now.

Chapter 9

Christian and I passed through double glass doors and entered a big dark hallway. Sebastian had to wait outside with the other bodyguards. The hallway in front of us was pitch black. *"Wait!"* I hoped the telepathy thing worked right. He stopped in his tracks, so I guess it did. *"I'll go first, playing bodyguard is my gig tonight, remember?"* I pulled off the claws on my left hand and tucked them into the top, front of my corset. Claws out of course. I reached back and took his hand, adjusting my eyes so I could see in the pitch black, then we proceeded onward.

We walked about ten feet then stopped. *"There's a trip wire about a foot off the floor."* I guided him past *two* trip wires. Then we went about ten more feet. In front of us the carpet looked like it was just barely sagging, the edges didn't look like they had even attempted to try and tuck them in. I motioned for Christian to stop, pulled out a sword and sliced the carpet from left to right. It fell away and revealed a fifteen foot gap. I looked down and gasped. *"What do you see Cassandra?"* I took a deep breath and said *"Don't ask, you don't really want to know."* The bottom of the pit was covered in pikes. Wooden pikes. Crap! How were we going to get past this? I looked up, no convenient pipes to use, only in the movies right? *"Be patient, I need to check something. And for God's sake don't move!"* I hate testing theories in situations like this. Why can't I test them when no one's life depends on it?

I thought about my shield, and tried to picture it expanding around my feet, and going flat. We needed a solid floor we could walk on. Using my shield was chancy, but an idea is an idea, so the theory needed to be tested. First I turned away from the pit, so I didn't accidentally fall in, and tried to imagine stairs. I picked up my foot and tried to step up. To my amazement it worked. YEAH! Ok, now could I do it with another person? *"Don't panic, I'm going to back up completely against you and I want you to follow me exactly. Don't deviate. Move your feet with mine. This is just a test, if we screw up, were still ok. Okay?"* *"I understand."* I took my left hand and gripped his butt, to keep us close. GAWD! His ass was tight! And in his silk suit his ass felt expensive. Yum! He wrapped his arms around my neck. I wasn't sure if that was a precaution, or a threat. I lifted my foot and he followed, we both stepped up. *"Ha! We did it! It works! Were walking on air!"* *"Will it hold us both?"* *"Uh, sure, no problem."* That didn't sound very convincing even to me. We turned toward the pit and we slowly walked over the pikes, to the other side. I held my breath the whole way there.

"Okay, were here. You can let go now." We separated and he said *"Have you ever done that before?"* *"Nope, first time for everything. There's a door about ten more feet ahead."* How do you like that for a subject change? The last ten feet were obstacle clear. Besides, now was not the time to debate my gifts. Who puts that kind of shit in a hallway?

I showed Christian were the doorknob was and stepped in front of him, good thing too. As soon as he opened the door and was in view, two arrows came flying out of no where. As I've said, I'm short, and he's about six foot. The arrows landed in the middle of my forehead. I grabbed them out of my shield and pulled him to a safe hiding place. Then examined the arrows. Good god, they were wicked! Aluminum shafts held razor blades for arrowheads, except for the very tip which was a very thin glass. As I squinted my eyes to look at it I noticed a needle inside the glass. I unscrewed a tip and pulled it off the shaft, and saw a small vial of mercury attached to the needle. *"Hold out your hand."* I placed the tip into Christians hand. *"Mercury injection in the tips. That's liquid silver."* I saw him take a breath he didn't need to take. A female voice rang out through the warehouse "That must be Christian I hear, you're the only one left." I grabbed the tip out of his hand, and reattached it to the shaft, and kept them close so they would stay invisible too.

"Come out, come out, wherever you are." She taunted, in a sing song voice. *"Who's that?"* He gave me back my own words *"You don't want to know."* "If you won't come to me Christian, then we'll come to you." Two seconds later, three vampires with machine guns, came around to where we were hiding. Vamps with guns is just redundant isn't it? They grabbed Christian by the arms and hauled him away. *"What do you want me to do?"* *"Nothing. Let us wait and see what Rochelle wants."*

They pulled him into the middle of the warehouse and I followed. I did NOT like what I saw. There were six big cages, all suspended from the ceiling with big chains. As soon as Christian was added to his cage, they'd all be full. The cages all faced each other in a big circle. The other peoples Auras were all wild, all shifters, and three of them were butt naked! I tried not to look, really I did! There was eye candy just staring me in the face. Okay, so it was swinging in my face, which made it worse. The men were standing proud, and defiant, there was a lot to take in, on them and with the building. Broken windows along the ceiling, Vampires along the cat walks, six vamps on the floor with machine guns guarding the cages, and one red headed vamp I assumed was Rochelle. They none too gently placed Christian inside that last empty cage.

"Awww look at my new collection of toys. Aren't they pretty? I always liked pretty toys." Okay it's official, this Bitch is insane! I'll bet she decorated the entrance too. She was about five foot six, slender frame, with short, spiked, dyed electric red hair. The hair only made her look more pale. She wore the proverbial vamp type garb. A long flowing, white gauzy dress, that pretty much showed everything. As she walked around her

"Toys" inspecting the goods of each man, she would aimlessly spin the cage.

I saw Marcus in one of the cages, that made me feel good. He was a Lion leader? Good to know. Thankfully, he was one of the three that were dressed. Besides Christian, and Marco, the other man dressed was a Wolf shifter. That left the Leopard, Snake, and the Eagle shifter naked. I was getting real good at this Aura reading thing. So, what? One flew into the meeting, one slithered, and one padded in?

The Eagle shifter, had snow white hair that came to his shoulders, he had the very slim body, of a long distance runner, about five foot eleven, and grey eyes. He spoke then "What do you want Vampire?" He said "Vampire" like it was a cuss word, or something vile. Rochelle snapped her head towards him and said "We want everything. You are the leaders in this Domain, you control all the shifters" She looked at Christian then "and the Vampires. As long as WE control you, WE control this state, and the country. We want your money, assets, all of it! We'll settle for nothing less." Christian asked "We? Who?" "WE being me and mine. Did you think I would take on an endeavor such as this alone? You must think very highly of me Christian." Something started pushing against my shield, like waves at the ocean. I was looking around, but didn't see anything. Rochelle spoke like she was bored "Your power can't hurt me, your not that good people, I'm protected." Huh, that was what I felt pushing me? Their power? Then the Wolf shifter had to open his mouth, get his two cents in. He was about six foot three, wavy light brown hair, complete with professional highlights. You could see how is suit was tailored, that he was well built, with a great tan. "A witch helped you. Put a protective shield over you? You don't think we actually followed the meeting mandate to come alone do you?" My eyebrows flew to my hairline as my eyes started scanning the place, looking for anyone other than the vamps, and saw no one, he was bluffing. Rochelle announced "The only ones here, are your drivers, who are outside, me, and my people, who are inside." Christian asked "Are you sure about that?" "I'm more than sure," she purred "if someone else were here I'd know it. As you so sweetly put it Wolfman, I had help from a witch. Now, let's get on with this. I have here, contracts for you to sign. These will give me ninety percent of all your holdings. Who wants to sign first?" Her eyes were alight with excitement. *"Let her know we're not alone in here."* I was just given my first official order, Hot Damn! *"Something dramatic? Perhaps?"* *"VERY dramatic."* What does a Vampire consider dramatic? Ideas of how I was going to use their arrows against them came flying into my head. I walked up behind two vamps that were standing together, watching an exit, and slammed the arrows into their backs. Effectively breaking the glass tips.

They screamed and went to their knees. Almost instantly, they started to turn to ash. The blood vessels turned black, and looked like spider webs across their faces. Rochelle turned at the noise and screamed "NO! Find who ever did this and bring them to me NOW!"

She moved a cage and walked inside the circle of cages. She was going to use them to shield herself. *"Dramatic enough?"* *"Very well done."*

The men in the cages looked smug now, ALL of them, like it was their idea, and their people who did it. "Which one of you did it? How did you get someone in here past the wards and my guards? TELL ME!" No one answered her. *"Want me to take out a few more? You could always start a bidding war."* I grinned to myself at that. I thought it was funny, Christian however, took me seriously. He spoke very loud and very clear. "I will give five million dollars for every vampire killed in this warehouse, who works for Rochelle." The other leaders were NOT going to be outdone by a vamp. They all agreed to the verbal contracts.

Five million per bad guy. Hmm, Marcus was right, a mercenary can make good money. Vampires were searching the warehouse, moving all around. I pulled my claws out of the front of my corset, covered my left hand, and started hunting bad guys. I took out another guard on the main floor, in plain view of everyone, by shoving a clawed hand through his back, and out his chest. The blood clung to my shield for a few seconds, so it looked like a big red animal hand had just ripped out the vamps heart. My hand slid through his chest a lot easier than it should have. There should have been some resistance right? My hand slid in his back like I was playing with Jell-o. Maybe it was because of the silver. Damn, how the hell much stronger have I gotten?

When I pulled my hand back, bullets showered the area. My shield held. Within seconds the blood had evaporated away and I was completely invisible again. Shield or no shield, being shot at is NOT cool! The remaining three vamps on the main floor moved so their backs were to the cages. I rammed my clawed hand through one of the vamp's chest and out his back. He tried to bring up his gun to shoot me but the silver got to him before he could fire. Him missing his heart might have had a little something to do with it too. The other two were now standing back to back, I pulled a sword out and sliced their heads off in a single move. It's hard to dodge what you can't see coming for you. This was too easy.

Then up the stairs to the catwalk. The vamps up there had gotten together, backs against the wall, guns facing out along the catwalk. "What the Fuck have you people brought in here?" Rochelle was a bit hysterical at this point. I pulled my other sword out, and opened my arms wide. One good slice, bringing both swords together in front of me, and following through, took off four of the bad vampire's heads. They didn't even try to fire their guns. I kicked the heads off the catwalk for Rochelle to see before they became dust. Several people were taunting her now. "When it gets through with your people it will come after you!" "Doesn't look like we'll be making any deals with you Rochelle." She was starting to freak out, "SHUT UP ALL OF YOU OR I'LL KILL YOU MYSELF RIGHT NOW!" That was a dumb thing to say. The taunts kept up as I worked my way to the other side of the warehouse. The other vamps were gone. *"I don't see anymore, I think they tucked tail and ran." "Open our cages, mine first!"* I didn't know you could hiss, and growl in someone's head. Christian was pissed!

Once back on the main floor, I walked around the outside of the cages, and started spinning them. Rochelle didn't know which way to go. Which ever way she moved, that was the cage I spun. She stayed in the middle, not moving. As Christians' cage door spun to the outside I said *"Back up"* Sheathing one sword, I timed the cage, so when it came around, I could swing down on the cage lock. It just made sense. Christian pushed open his door when it swung back to the middle and pounced on Rochelle. His fangs were extended and even though he was fine as hell, at this moment, he was scary as hell too. Everyone saw what happened to Christian's cage and they moved back from their doors. Systematically each cage was opened. Marcus was the last one out.

By the time the group of leaders were freed, Rochelle was pinned to the floor. She was staring death in the eye. Six pairs of eyes as a matter of fact. Since Christian had a grip on her he got to asked the questions. "Tell me what I want to know and you'll die quickly, who are you working with, how many more vampires are here with you, and where can I find them?" "You wont catch us all, there's over sixty of us!" She let out a very evil laugh "My people are placing bombs around the city at strategic points, and YOU are all fools!!!" She truly needs a padded white room. "I'll never tell you who my partner is, or exact details, besides, he'll save me, I'm too important to him. He needs me!" I wasn't sure who she was trying to convince at that point. Christian stood up, pulling Rochelle with him, in one graceful move, no strings attached.

He pushed through the group of leaders, and the cages, but was stopped. The leaders all started protesting at once. "Wait! She hasn't given us her partner... Torture her!!! We need more information!!! Where's the bombs???" He turned around and looked at them. "We have enough information, go see to your people, and territories, we'll reconvene at a later time." *"Cassandra, I promised her a quick death, if you please." "She'll make eleven bad guys tonight. Hold her out and hold her still."* One of my swords was still out, I positioned it at her neck, then swung it back like a baseball bat and lopped off her head. The questions came flying at Christian again, no one had left yet. They wanted to see her dead. "What is it?? What's in here?? You brought it here to kill us didn't you? Are you Rochelle's partner?" Christian held up a hand and they waited. "I did Not bring it here to kill you, only extra protection for myself. You all benefited by it as well. Eleven vampires were slain, we agreed five million apiece, we will split that six ways. Get your portions to me, I will see to it they go where they need to. I would advise *not* using the front entrance."

The snake shifter spoke up then, he was Hispanic, about five foot eight, with a slim build, black hair and black eyes, and a thin mustache that trailed down to his chin. "How do we know you didn't plan this to get money from us? How will we know you will pay your assassin?" Christian replied "Would you want to upset what took out the vampires here tonight? I assure you, I have seen it, and would never think of not paying. You have no idea how it can be." *"Hey! Now! I'm not that bad! Sheesh, you make me sound like some vicious, crazy, bloodthirsty monster!"* We were headed out a side door of the building at this point, ALL of us. *"If that is how they choose to take it then so be it, I was genuinely speaking of your tantrum with your clothes, I would hate to see how much worse you can be, you are a woman." "WOW! Was that? Was that a joke? From you?"* I was laughing in my head at him. The leaders were still trailing behind us talking amongst themselves, I stretched out my arm, at shoulder level, and let my new silver claws dig into the outside brick of the warehouse. They were protected by my shield, so I knew they wouldn't be hurt. The other leaders just stopped and stared at the four claw marks, that came out of no where, and how close they were. They didn't realize I had been walking with them, or they didn't think. "I will see you in three days Christian, with my payment." said the leopard. He was another hottie, he looked like "The Big Sexy" Kevin Nash on wrestling, only a younger version.

Six foot eight inches of yummy. He even had the long wavy blonde hair, and a perfect goatee.

As soon as we got back into the Limo, there was a very sharp tingle through out my neck, and shoulders. Christian's eyes were closed like he was concentrating.

I opened myself up to the harsh buzzing in the back of my head, and heard him giving orders. *"...gather every resource, and find those bombs, supposedly they have been placed in strategic locations, start searching the businesses, we're are not sure of the number. There is also an estimated fifty unauthorized vampires, in our territory , if you find them, destroy them without prejudice."* The buzzing stopped and he opened his eyes. After the message went out to all the vamps, Sebastian pulled out of the parking lot of the warehouse.

As we were heading back it gave me time to think about what had just happened. I spent part of my childhood around men who like to hunt and they believed if you shoot it, eat it. Well we weren't going to put anything on the spit tonight. I've killed a man before, and felt no guilt over it. But he did have it coming. When I did Security work back in my younger days, I patrolled the complex I lived in. Easy work right? I made sure all the kids knew where I lived in case they needed me. They thought they were cool because they knew the security guard. Whoopee. One day the kids knocked on my door. I was ready for the pool, ya know? Shorts, swimsuit, tennis shoes and a towel. The kids had talked very fast about a guy hitting the other kids with a window frame. I grabbed my security guard shirt, zipped it up, and my holster which held my Taurus 9mm, then followed the kids back to where the problem was. A man about five foot eight was swinging the window frame around in the air and threatening a group of kids. I stepped in between the kids and the crazy man. He was early twenties with greasy brown hair and wild eyes. His eyes were very wide and bloodshot. My first thought was drugs. Dude was high. He dropped the window frame and tried for my gun. We wrestled about two seconds then I pulled the trigger. He fell to the ground looked up at me as he held his stomach and said "It hurts". The police had been called and showed up right after that. They took my statement, and my gun for ballistics. Standard stuff, but I didn't like not having my gun.

Later when I was called to come pick up my gun, the detective in charge of the case, gave me details since I was the one who took him down. The detective didn't have to give me any info, but I'm glad he did. The crazy guy was D.O.A. to the hospital. Dead On Arrival. According to the forensics report from the Medical Examiner, the man was dead before I shot him. He just didn't know it. Approximately twelve small baggies of cocaine were found in his stomach. The baggies were already dissolving and large amounts of cocaine had already been dumped into his blood stream. My bullet had ripped through a few more baggies, and his stomach lining. I never lost one nights sleep over it. It had never bothered me killing a human being.

Even at the time of the shooting, and I was putting pressure on his wound for the E.M.T.'s , it didn't bother me. He was a bad guy. I was supposed to be the good guy. The kids are safe and the bad guy is no longer a threat to anyone. Tonight I killed eleven more people. Vampires or not, they are truly dead. By my own hand. I know I should feel bad for taking eleven lives. I checked my conscious. Nope. No guilt. Does that make me a closet sociopath? I don't think so. My job was to be the bodyguard tonight. Okay so yeah, it started out as a game for me, going through the hall of traps. I felt like a super hero or something. It was fun. The adrenaline rush, and excitement was a thrill for me. I may not be a perfect little Christian, but I do believe if it had been wrong for me to kill the human or the vampires, my conscious would let me know. Maybe it's the old "God is busy" theory.

If you don't know GOD, don't make stupid remarks!!!

A U.S. Marine was taking some college courses between

assignments. He had completed 20 missions in Iraq and Afghanistan. One of the courses had a professor who was an avowed atheist, and a member of the A.C.L.U.

One day the professor shocked the class when he came in. He looked to the ceiling a flatly stated, "GOD, if you are real, then I want you to knock me off this platform. I'll give you exactly 15 minutes." The lecture room fell silent. You could hear a pin drop.

Ten minutes went by and the professor proclaimed "Here I am GOD, I'm still waiting."

It got down to the last couple of minutes when the Marine got out of his chair, went up to the professor, and cold-cocked him, knocking him off the platform. The professor was out cold.

The Marine went back to his seat and sat there silently.

The other students were shocked and stunned, and sat there looking on in silence. The professor eventually came to, noticeably shaken, looked at the Marie and asked "What In the world is the matter with you? Why did you do that?" The Marine calmly replied, "GOD was too busy today protecting America's soldiers who are protecting your right to say stupid stuff and act like an asshole. So he sent me."

The classroom erupted in cheers.

Maybe that's what happened the day I killed the drugged crazed idiot. Maybe it's because I have a cold spot in me. A quiet spot. Growing up I figured I'd be a great Ninja Assassin, or a Surgeon. Blood doesn't bother me. It's ironic really if you think about it. Marcus offered to make me an Assassin and I didn't meet his qualifications. Yet here I am. Is that what I've become? Is a bodyguard a glorified way of saying someone is an assassin?

"Your body and face are calm, but your eyes look deep in thought. What are you thinking?" I turned from the window and looked at Christian "Just thinking about what I did tonight."

"Have you ever killed before tonight?" "Yes, actually. Once."

"They deserved what happened to them. If you had not been there, and the Leaders of the shifters and myself had not been able to escape, what do you think would have happened?" "Ya'll would probably be dead." "Exactly. You didn't hesitate to protect me. Or anyone else for that matter. They benefited by proxy. You did what you said you would do. And I for one, am glad you keep your word. I rule this country. If I had died, the Vampires in this country would have retaliated and there would have been a war like this country has never seen." "Who would they have retaliated against? Not the shifters, they would be in the same boat. Besides the Vampires started it. Wouldn't they have tried for other vamps? " "The relationship between shifters and Vampires is tenuous at best. Someone would have been blamed for it. Count on it. It may not have been vampires who started it either." I didn't know what to say to that. A war between all of the super naturals would be very very bad.

Christian chased that thought away with the next question "What is your sign?" "Huh? Why?" "I was just wondering." "Libra" He nodded "That explains a few things." "Like what?" "About your temperament." "What is that supposed to mean?" He smiled at me and said "Calm down, I'm just trying to learn about you. I would say you are very much the Libra too." "Is that good or bad?" He shrugged "Both, I too was born a Libra. So I have a little insight as to how you will react to certain situations." "Well, that goes both ways you know?" he nodded "Indeed it does."

Chapter 10

We arrived at a very large strip mall. The kind where all the stores are in a straight line. Not the stripping business kind. On the far left was a Red doorway, well lit with a big red glowing sign, that read "The **Blood Sport** Bar and Grille". On the far right was a set of Black double doors, with guards posted out side. Again, that entrance was well lit too. A long line of people were waiting to get in. The music coming out of it told me it was an Alternative Rock club. The glowing sign above the club read "The **PANIC** Room". Cool.

We got out of the limo and started walking straight up the middle of the parking lot, to a section of the building that wasn't lit. Light draws the eyes attention. It's a subconscious thing, it's safer in the light, you know? Only a single grey door was in the middle of the building, painted the same grey as the building. I was invisible when we entered.

We walked down a long hallway, then turned left down another hallway. Christian finally picked a door and went inside. Another man was waiting for us, he was in a grey wing back chair in front of the desk. The desk was cool as hell! Solid glass! The top was a pale smoky grey with beveled edges. Then the closer you looked to the floor the darker it got. Where the bottom of the desk met the carpet, the desk was solid black. I had never seen anything remotely like it.

The man sitting in front of it had short black hair, dark eyes, with slightly feminine features. Christian acknowledged him with a nod, and said "Tell me Peyton, what have we found." Peyton, pulled out a piece of paper and read it. "So far, we have found three bombs in our area, search continues for a fourth. Were finding "unauthorized" renegades all over. So far the count is ten, but we also have reports coming in just past the hour of how the shifters are fairing. We'll have a higher renegade count by then." "Good, Sebastian, go with Peyton, I'm going hunting." Sebastian didn't like the thought of Christian going alone. "This could be a trap to get you out there. You aren't going alone. We'll go with you." Christian held up a hand to stop the protests "Fine, Sebastian you and I will go together, Peyton, you and Cassandra will team up." Peyton hadn't met me, so he was a bit confused. "Who is Cassandra?" I became visible, and looked at him. His eyes were wide, my smile was innocent.

We left Christian's office first. Christian wanted to arm himself. As we were walking down the hall I checked my finger claws and asked, "Are you any good at riding horses?" He didn't look at me at all, he acted like he just got stuck babysitting the lackey and didn't seem to happy about it, but he did answer "Yes". I wanted information on if he would freak out if I shifted. He's around shifters all the time. Probably feeds on them too, but he'd never seen a shifter like me. "Can you levitate? Are you afraid to fly?" big talker this one. "No, and No." "Good" We exited the back of the strip center, I smiled, and said "Climb on board." I shifted into a solid black Pegasus, my hooves though were sterling silver. I looked totally cool! My silver claws conformed to my hooves. He just gawked at me for a minute then he gathered his composure, and climbed on.

A few running strides and we were airborne. I could send messages to Christian telepathically, so why not try with Peyton? I concentrated on sending my thoughts to him, and he was very receptive. He talks to me more now too. *"Any place in particular you want to start?" "Yes, the Masters house." "You'll have to give me directions to it."* I didn't know if he knew where it was or not. That's not information I was going to give out. He did give me directions, right to it. We landed, I shifted, and we both searched the grounds, all the way around and under the house, as far as we could. To my relief, my dream house was clean. When we were done, we took off again, flying patterns over Houston. Peyton spotted some bad guys in an alley, pointed me towards them and we landed right behind ten renegades, who had four of the good guys, two vamps and two shifters backed up to a wall.

We had them pinned between us. As soon as my shifting was over I said "Well guys, it doesn't look so good for you. The odds are in our favor." One of the bad vampire's sneered and said "I guess your to stupid to count, it's ten against six. The odds are in our favor." I smiled at him them pulled both swords, and tossed one to Peyton. "You know how to use this?" He enthusiastically said "Yes!" "Good, let's see if these turkeys can fight on two fronts, and maybe sometime you can teach me to sword fight." We both launched at the bad guys. I decapitated the one who was ugly to me, right off the bat.

I've never had any kind of professional sword training. I figured keeping a good grip and swinging for their necks or anything else that came close to me would work. I wasn't worried about my form, I could mimic what I'd seen in movies though. I also knew aim past where you want to hit and follow through. I learned that playing tennis in high school. Always follow through!

When I spun around to find my next victim, a vamp was flying through the air at me. As he came down on top of me, I slammed my clawed hand into his chest. We both hit the ground hard, but I got up and walked away, spitting out ash. I looked for my third target, he was coming up behind Peyton. He was too far away to get to him in time, so I pulled out one of my Sai, and hoped like hell, it would fly straight. A feeling came over me, that's hard to describe, it felt like I had been pushed back to a corner of my mind. I could still see out my eyes, but something took over my body, and threw the Sai like I'd been trained by every Martial arts expert on the planet. It hit the back of the vampire coming up behind Peyton with deadly accuracy. He collapsed in mid strike of Peyton. One of our shifters was getting double teamed so I ran my fist through one vampire's back, as I brought my sword up to spear the other one. I started looking for another target but they were all dead. Fun time was over. For now.

Peyton got three, and the other four got two. Ten bad guys to add to the total. Peyton looked at me then, but he wasn't looking at me like I was a lackey, but a fellow warrior. We had a moment of complete understanding. I'm not sure what had happened to me, but when the fighting was over, I was completely back in my head again. Peyton turned to the others, and said "Dispose of this." Then a thought occurred to me. "Peyton, let them go, we can take care of this." I'm not sure what I looked like but he decided to give me this one. There was blood and gore galore! I have to admit, I felt a little green around the edges. The gore was starting to ash. Some turned to ash a lot faster than the rest, leaving splotches on the ground. I guess newer Vampires don't ash as quickly as the older ones.

He nodded to them to take off, and with preternatural speed they were gone. "What do you have in mind?" He handed me my sword and I sheathed both. I'm glad Vamp blood ashes so quickly. My sai was across the alley and I went for it. "Just get on and don't panic." I shifted into my Pegasus, and he climbed on. Once he was situated I pictured a big black Dragon, with sterling silver claws. The ripples were warmer than they usually are. I could hear Peyton taking breaths he didn't need to take. *"Are you okay? How ya doing?" "You're a Dragon." "Your observation skills are amazing! Are you like the second in command or something?" "Yes" "Oh."*

Well that explains a few things.

I took a big breathe and slowly let it out, extreme heat came out of my mouth, I looked at my passenger and grinned. *"Hehehehe, this is gonna be cool!"* Taking another deep breath and forcing it out this time, white hot fire shot out of my mouth. I aimed for the vampire remains, and blood stains. In seconds the whole area was wiped clean. *"Just call me the Cleaner!" "Please don't smile at me again, if that is what that was."* I shifted back to the Pegasus and launched us out of the alley. It's smaller so I didn't think it would show up on any radar. But a big ass Dragon? Shoot, I didn't want to be shot out of the sky, for being a U.F.O.

Peyton spotted one then on a roof top and pointed him out. *"I'll come in low and you can jump on him, sound good?" "Excellent"*

I stayed in the air circling the area while Peyton, dispatched another one. Then hovered next to the building, and Peyton jumped on my back, again. My wings were getting tired from the extra weight. I was about to give up and go home, we hadn't seen anymore bad guys, until we crossed over into Marcus's area. Peyton had been giving me the territory markers as we flew around town. Five Vampires were standing in a dark parking lot. *"Are those guys ours?"* I asked, as soon as Peyton could see them he said *"No"* *"Hold on then."* I swooped down towards them, shifted back to my dragon form, in mid downward swoop, took a deep breath and lit them on fire as I passed about three feet over their heads. When they saw me they were too stunned to move, they had been sitting ducks. I pulled hard on my wings and took us back up into the air and headed for HQ. When did I start thinking of the Vampires as mine or someone else's? The Dragon form is better if you have a rider. Bigger and more powerful wings.

I got a buzzing in my head again and tuned in, *"...are you?" "We are just coming back."* Peyton was communicating with Christian *"Good, meet us in the alley."* He was going to rat me out! The Fink! I shifted back to a Pegasus, I didn't want everyone to know I could shift into a Dragon. *"You changed back." "No Shit!, if I wanted everyone to know, I'd tell them myself! I don't appreciate you putting me in this position. You're lucky I don't knock your ass off right here! It's my business, not yours, so keep your mouth shut!" "Your right, it's your secret. I will keep it, until I'm told otherwise." "Too late bonehead! They'll see I'm a shifter anyway!" "They didn't know?" "NO!"*

Christian and Sebastian were both waiting for us when I landed. Both of them looked astonished. I guess they had never seen a Pegasus before. Peyton dismounted and I shifted back. I calmly took my finger claws off, and tucked them into my corset, walked up to him and stole a line out of one of my favorite movies. "Head or stomach?" I believe he got my intentions because he gave me a nod and said "Stomach." I nearly knocked his head clean off his shoulders. Asshole.

God! That felt good though. The playgirl twins, both had questions in their eyes. I looked at Christian "I'm going to go find food." I left Peyton dazed and confused to update the guys. Following my nose down the hall to a door that had the best smells coming out it, I opened it and walked into the kitchen of the Blood sport bar and Grille.

Chapter 11

I was yelled at the moment I walked through the door. "What do you think you are doing in MY Kitchen??? OUT! Out out out!" I looked at this guy like he just grew a second head. "You!" He pointed at me "Remove yourself from my kitchen, and do it NOW!" I doubled over laughing it couldn't be helped. Damn, the man looked and sounded like Dom DeLuise! He used to crack me up as a kid, and this guy was doing the same thing. It's almost like watching Dom in action… "Whoa! There big guy, ease up, or you'll hurt yourself." I was still grinning like I was star struck. "What's your name?" I stunned him when my composure flew out the window. "I am the Great Chef Antony. Who are you? And what do you want here?" I smiled and stuck out my hand. "Thank you Antony, I really needed that. Call me Cassie, and as far as what I'm doing here, well, it's kind of obvious. I'm in search of food. Christian is running me ragged, I need sustenance." His eyes got big "We don't serve" He dropped his voice to a whisper "vampires in here." His tone went back to loud and proud. "So you should leave!" Huh, he thought I was a vamp. I could tell by his aura that he was totally human, so maybe he just couldn't tell. "Uh, well I'm not a vamp, just a hungry human. Is that Chicken Bella- vitano I smell?"

I started walking towards one of the many food prep areas leaving Chef Antony to follow me. He followed me and asked "You know Italian food?" "I know food period. I love to eat! May I taste?" "Well, since you asked I guess it's okay." He scooted the other cook out of the way, grabbed a big spoon and let me taste the cheese sauce. Oh it was heaven. "Mmmm, oh Antony, please let me have some. I'll eat in the back and won't bother anyone I swear! But I gotta have some of this!" He looked like a proud papa. "Okay, I give you some, and you eat every bite!" "YESSIR!!!" I gave a mock salute, there'd be no problem eating it all, I was starved. He fixed me a big plate and handed me a fork. Grilled chicken on a bed of rice, covered in the bella-vitano sauce and sautéed mushrooms, mixed veggies, and garlic bread. This was truly heaven, my plate was scrapped clean. He noticed, smiled really big and walked over "Leave the enamel on the plate Cassie. Did you enjoy?" "How could I not? That was the best I've ever had. But umm just out of curiosity, what the hell is that ticking? Whatever is it you should get it fixed, it's annoying as all get out."

There was a very faint ticking, and it was driving me nuts. "I don't hear anything, maybe your heart has fallen in love and it is beating harder." "I have to say, I think I love you Antony, but this is different." A bad feeling had settled in the pit of my stomach, and I don't think it was the food. Maneuvering, slowly around to the back part of the kitchen, proved nerve racking, the closer I got, the louder the ticking got. A regular human, might not have heard it, I barely heard it. In front of me sat a turkey pan. One of those great big ones with a lid. Pulling it off the bottom shelf, the ticking vibrated through my hands. Very gently, I set it on the counter. Antony was right there with me when I opened the lid. There was another bomb. "OH, mama mia, we must leave at once!" "Wait!" I grabbed his arm. "Calm down we still have time. If someone can disarm it before anyone finds out, then no one will freak out. If we yell "Bomb" people will run screaming in hysterics, and someone will get hurt. Just stay calm, I'm sure Christian can fix this." Very few people were here this late, mostly just the staff. I sent a mental knock knock to Christian. He answered, *"Yes?" "Are you busy at the moment?" "Yes, why?" "Could you come to the kitchen for a few minutes please?" "Cassandra, now is not the time. I do have important business to attend to." "Okay, handle your business, no problem. Just let me know one thing. Where do you want me to put this bomb I found? Should I just bring it to your office?"* Our mental connection was severed. Christian, Sebastian, and Peyton were at the kitchen door five seconds later.

They walked in and looked into the turkey pan. The timer was ticking away, the LCD screen showed:

00 26:24 13

We had just over twenty six minutes to disarm this thing. I waved to it. "Okay superman, do your thing." They all looked at me with blank expressions. I whispered "Disarm the damn thing already." Christian said "We do not possess the knowledge. Our bomb experts are currently at the Snake colony. They will not be here in the next twenty six minutes." Great. Just great. I looked to the ceiling sending a mental prayer upwards. *Please God, just one day where shit doesn't go haywire.* I held out my hand "Someone give me a damn phone." I don't know who it belonged to, but it was really fancy. One of those Titanium numbers. I dialed a good friend of mine, who would be able to talk me through this. I hoped.

He's an Ex- Army E.O.D. turned Trucker. There are a lot of ex-military on the roads. As soon as the call connected, I put it on speaker and set the phone down. *"Hello?"* he sounded asleep, oops, I woke him up "Hey Allen, what's up?" *"Cassie? Oh shit girl, I've been freaking out since your mom told me, where are you?"* "I'm safe for now, mostly, but I do have a small problem and I need your help." *"Name it, you know I'll do anything I can for you."* "Alright you asked for it, I need you to put your thinking cap on. This problem of mine is your area of expertise. You ready?" His tone became very business like, *"Yeah, hit me."* "I have a bomb here, a block of C-4 with a black box attached to it. There are two wires coming out of the box and going into what looks like a long shaft, and that is shoved down into C-4. The box also has a little rubber ducky antennae on it. I'm guessing it has a remote failsafe. How do I disarm it? We have twenty five minutes." *"Okay we have time, don't panic. And your right, if there is an antenna then it can be remote detonated"* "I'm not panicking yet." *"That's why I love you, is there any covering on the C-4?"* " Yes, it's like a green waxy plastic." *"Good, that's what it's shipped in, so it may not be tampered with more than just the detonator. Get some dental floss, or fishing line."* "Okay hold on." I turned to my small crowd of four and rotated my hands in circles to get them moving. "Dental floss? Fishing line? Hello?" A minute later I had the dental floss. "Okay I have floss what do I do with it?" *"Is there any kind of plate, or anything between the box and the C-4?"* "Uh, I don't see one." *"Take the floss, and slide it under the box slowly and gently, this will check to see if there are any other wires attached that you don't see."* I did as directed and the floss came away easily, I relayed that.

"Good, now gently pull on the two wires and pull the detonator out of the C-4." I did that "Okay I got it." *"Good, wipe off the detonator, and turn the box over. You should see a small door on it like you find on a TV remote, or game controller."* "Yep" *"Okay, open it, there should be a nine volt, or maybe a couple of C size batteries. Take them out."* "Alright, I see a nine volt, and it is now unplugged." I turned the box back over and the timer screen was off. *"It should be off now is it?"* "Yes, thank you Allen!" Relief washed over the whole group "Hey do you want me to save this for you?" He collected all kinds of neat toys *"Are you kidding? Yes! With a little checking, I can let you know where it came from depending on chemical composition…"* I cut him off, my best friend was a total military nerd, he lived and breathed it still. "Allen, we don't care where it came from, we know

who set the bomb. But thanks anyway." *"Not a problem, are you sure your doing okay?"* I could tell by his voice he was worried about me. "Yeah, I'm fine. I've got to go though, I'll save this for you. Next time you come thru call this number and let whoever answers know who you are. This isn't my phone." *"I understand, no worries. Be careful."* "I will, you too. Bye." *"Bye"*

I handed the detonator and the battery to Peyton. Put the lid back on the turkey pot, and handed that to Sebastian. I held up the phone, and Christian took it, I should have known it was his, then turned to Antony, "Mind if I sit down for a minute?" He took my arm and led me to a stool and pushed me onto it. "You can have anything you want anytime you want it, no questions asked. Sit, stay, I bring mama's cure all for you. You no look so good." Huh I wonder why? Maybe because I was just playing with a bomb? I've had to many adrenaline rushes in too short a time in my opinion. I allow myself one a day, I've gone over my daily quota. Antony handed me a steaming cup of Roasted chicken soup broth. I sipped on it until it was cool enough to drink. Thanked Antony then went looking for Christian.

I found him with Peyton, and Sebastian in his office. When I walked in he looked up, and I asked "Are we spending the day here? Or going to the playgirl mansion?" he replied "Sebastian will show you to a room, thank you for what you did." I shrugged, "I figured my friend could help, I've heard some of his war stories." he nodded and said "You saved a lot of lives, no one got hurt, and the building is safe. I owe you." I shook my head at that "Don't worry about it, Antony's got your back." My smile was ear to ear "I get free food!"

He gave Sebastian a nod and I was escorted to an elevator. He used a magnetic key card to access it. I got the two cent tour of the buttons. "Sublevel one is storage, private conference rooms, offices, etcetera. Sublevel two is living quarters, sublevel three is private living quarters." Sebastian pushed the number two button. When we reached the "living quarters" floor, I was a bit amazed. From the elevator, was a very long hallway with other halls coming off it at different intervals. Along the top of each hall we passed was a plaque with a big letter on it, I noticed all the doors were numbered too. "You are assigned E6" He showed me to my door and used a master key card in the slot. This was just like a fancy hotel. He opened the door for me and we walked in. "There should be an entry card for your room on the top of the TV, you might want to also walk to the double doors at the end of the main hall. I believe you will find it interesting. Good day." "Thanks Sebastian" then he was gone.

The room was set up like a very nice hotel room. Closet to the front, bathroom at the back, queen size bed with night tables, a small table with two chairs, an armoire with the TV inside, and a very long dresser with a mirror attached to the wall. The colors were very neutral, all shades of tan, and beige. It was nice though. I sat on the bed and laid back, undid the clasps on my corset, and sat back up. My corset, swords, sai and claws got shoved into a drawer.

The bed was calling my name, but my curiosity was peaked now about the double doors. Strolling down the hallway, it hit me then, damn these people do a lot of walking, a golf cart would be good or maybe a scooter. The double doors were plain white painted doors. Opening one and looking around showed the room was Huge! There were overstuffed couches and chairs, bean bags, and thick fluffy body pillows everywhere. The furniture was all a variety of colors, and technically nothing matched, but somehow it all went together. There were about thirty different shifters in here, of different species, lounging all over. On the far left was an expansive kitchen area. All industrial appliances, and an island with stools under the edges about thirty feet long. I walked over to the kitchen area and said "Hi! What are you making?" I'm comfortable in a kitchen, so I had thought this would be the best place to start.

The whole place got quiet, like they had been invaded and weren't sure what to do. A big werewolf who could easily be a WWF wrestler stood up and said, "You don't belong here, this is a members only area, get out." He was around the six foot five mark, with black hair in a buzz cut. He had on black jeans and a tight red t-shirt that read "BOUNCER". I believed it, he looked like one. Thick neck, barrel chest, and arms thicker than my waist. I took a breath and sighed. "This looks like a gathering room for shifters, a place to come at the end of the day and just chill, what other kind of member do I need to be?" "Well, for one, you need to be a shifter. Now LEAVE!" The door opened before I could respond again. I met the greenish brown eyes of one of the men from the alley. His grin spread across his face when he saw me and jogged over. He was almost six feet tall, slim and trim with light brown hair that was just a little shaggy. He wore faded jeans and a green t-shirt. He wrapped his arms around me and very enthusiastically hugged me and said "Thank you for saving my ass tonight! Those two vamps were crazy. If you hadn't gutted them, I'd be dead. I know it. Peyton was kicking ass too, but you came to my rescue, so that makes you my Hero! Allow me to introduce you everyone. I'm Travis by the way. The big black wolf down there, the one who's growling is Bryce." Bryce spoke up "Travis, no humans allowed. You know the rules." Travis was bug eyed "Dude, she's no more human than you are, you should see her animal. She's freaking awesome!" I touched Travis's hand "Travis, don't, if they can't except someone for who they are, then Fuck Them!" Travis wouldn't let up "NO! You have just as much right to be in here as anyone else. Ok I admit she doesn't smell, or feel like a shifter, and her aura isn't wild, which is really weird" he crinkled his forehead at me "But I saw her shift. She's the most beautiful P…" I clamped my hand over his mouth before he good spit it out. And shook my head at him. "Please don't, it's private. My business. If I want someone to know then I'll tell them okay?" He nodded at me, and I removed my hand. Travis glared at the room "SHE STAYS!!" Another woman looked at Travis, and said "Travis do you swear she's a shifter?" he grinned "Like you wouldn't believe. I totally swear!"

I was introduced around at that point and told they were trying to make pizza. There were two women both blondes, with blue eyes, and the same height and size. They were almost twins. Slight facial differences, and hairstyles. Randy (Miranda) had a long pony tail that was put up high on her head. Candy (Candice) had hair about an inch long, that stuck up like a porcupine with blue tips. It was a cute style on her. They were fighting with biscuits. Randy asked "Can you make these things stay flat?" I laughed "Nope, but I can make pizza dough." the RC twins looked at each other, grabbed the beat up dough and threw it away. Turned to me and begged "Show us, please?" I smiled again and set folks to getting supplies. Forty five minutes later, pizza's were coming out of the ovens. We made a lot of extra dough, Candy was folding the extra dough and putting it in wax paper for later.

The RC twins, Travis and I walked back to my room when they were through eating. We were all cutting up together, it was a real nice, normal thing. It felt good, I seriously needed that.

Once in the door of my new room, Randy made the comment "Wow you are new here, you haven't even unpacked yet." "Huh?" There was a large suitcase on the dresser. It wasn't there when I left, so someone had been in my room. It was probably a wanna be playgirl model. As soon as I opened it up, the room was instantly vacuum sealed. We all sucked in air when we saw what was inside. It was a fancy suitcase with the netting in it that holds your clothes in place on both halves, but it wasn't holding clothes. It held stacks of one hundred dollar bills. There was a black silk bag in the middle of it. I picked up the bag, heard jingling and paper. I looked inside and pulled out a note. It read

C,
This is a first installment for you, enjoy.
                                                    C

A set of keys fell out of the silk bag as well. I turned to my new friends. "Any one want to go shopping?" We weren't tired anymore. Everyone said yes. I put five stacks of money into the silk pouch and we left the building. When we got outside I held up the keychain and pushed the remote button until a car beeped at us. This was going to be a day for bug eyed expressions for all of us. A blue Mercedes was waiting for us, and we climbed in. Travis started the questioning. "What's all the money for?" Not wanting to scare them away by telling them what I did to earn it, I shrugged, and said "I'm Sebastian's counterpart, I was just at the right place at the right time." The RC twins were in the backseat staring at me with their mouths hanging open. Randy and Candy both asked at the same time "Are you serious?" then only one asked "Your Sebastian's counterpart? Christian's other bodyguard?" I was driving down the freeway and looked into the rearview mirror to see them, "Yeah, why?" Travis filled me in then "Some of the shifters have been trying to get that job for a long time, and here you come along and get it the first day. Some of them may resent you because of that. Be careful." I wasn't trying to be arrogant or anything when I replied "Well, I didn't apply for the job, per se. I just sort of stumbled upon it. If I couldn't do the job, I wouldn't have it. Christian wouldn't let someone get that close to him who wasn't capable of handling business, ya know what I mean?" They all nodded and got quiet. I didn't like it, it felt like they were pulling away from me. "Look, I'm not some asshole, out to prove who's bigger, badder or anything else I just have a gift that Christian can use to his advantage. I'd show you but the other motorists might flip out." Picturing it in my head made me giggle out loud. Travis asked "What's so funny?" The giggles got the better of me, and I went invisible. The windows were tinted, so other motorists might not see. Travis grabbed for the wheel in a panic. "I'm still here, I got it! Let go!" He reached out to touch me, and felt up my shoulder. "Wow, I feel you, your solid, but I can't see you." I became visible again. And said "Think about it from Christians point of view. Someone who has no smell, no wild aura, who can basically turn into a ghost. I'm nothing but an asset to him. I can get behind an enemy before they know I'm there." "Don't forget, you can turn into a Pegasus too."

Oh shit! The girls went bonkers! I was glaring at Travis and he was slouching down in his seat as far as his seatbelt would let him. He was hiding behind his hand when I heard over the squeals coming from the backseat. "I'm sorry, I forgot. Please don't hate me or kill me. I'm soooo sorry." I reached over and gave him a pat on the thigh, "It's okay, when the twins calm down and our ears quit ringing, THEN it will be okay." The twins were regaling each other with stories, of castles, and princes, and dragons and such, and they kept on until we got to Bed, Bath and Beyond.

No one wanted to go in. Randy said "You know shifters have sensitive noses, and the flowery stuff makes me sneeze." I looked at them. "None of you have ever been in here have you?" I was astonished to say the least. They all shook their heads, and I laughed "No worries, you'll love the place. Trust me." I gave them a wink and went for the door. They forced themselves to follow, but when we got inside, everything changed. If you've never been there, you have to go!

Jaws dropped three feet in the door, all the "As Seen On TV" stuff lined the walls, then isles of very kitchen gadget you can think of, and some you never knew existed. I had to stop them from running through the store like kids. "HEY! You guys, grab a buggy!" Two hours later, we left the store with more crap than we knew where to put it. The trunk was full, and the backseat was piled to the roof. Candy was in the backseat under the bags somewhere, and Randy was up front with me and Travis. We went back to HQ and unloaded everything. There was one more place I wanted to go. Wal-mart. I needed clothes, personal stuff, well everything. Between the four of us, we got everything down to the Playpen in one trip. Randy had told me it was called that because "We can't call it a pig pen, the others would get offended, and throw tantrums like babies, so we call it the Playpen." It sounded good to me.

We all hit Wal-mart together, and wound up filling up the trunk and backseat again.

Once back in my room with all our loot, we separated it all, pulled tags, and wrappers off and went our separate ways for the day. I climbed into the shower and let the nights stress wash off of me. Once out and dressed there was a very light knock on the door. I opened it. Travis was standing there in a pair of snug blue boxer briefs and a white tank top. I waved him in, and asked "What's wrong? Can't sleep?" I noticed he had a very nice body.

He shrugged and asked "Can I sleep in here with you?" He had an innocent look on his face, like a little kid. "Uh, why do you want to sleep in my room? Don't you have a room?" "Well, yeah we all do. I just thought maybe I could stay in here with you. You know cause of the shifter thing. Your new here, I just thought maybe you might like some company." I didn't know what the hell he was talking about. "What shifter thing?" "You know, the touching and cuddling thing?" I knew what I'd read in my books, but they were fiction. Or supposed to be, most of what I'd read seem to be coming true. I sat down on the bed and patted next to me for him to sit. So far I hadn't been overwhelmed with any need to cuddle. "Travis, I've been a shifter less than a week, I have no idea what your talking about." "Oh," he sighed "WAIT! Wait just a damn minute, I saw you shift." "Yeah, so?" "So? What do you mean so? I saw you shift. Our next full moon isn't for another week. You can't have been a shifter for less than a week. It doesn't work that way, I'm not stupid." I wasn't sure what to say. Travis was shaking his head and had a disgusted look on his face "Look, if you don't want me to stay just say so, you don't have to lie to me." He got up and started for the door, I jumped up and grabbed his arm. "Wait, please listen to me for a minute." He stopped walking and turned to me. "What?" Ok I had his attention now, pulling him back to the bed we sat down again. "I'm not lying to you, I've really been a shifter for only a few days. Four days, and three nights. Well, four days if you count today. Wait that's not right either, I was unconscious a week and a half before that" thinking things out loud here "I swear I'm not a normal shifter, I'm not making this up, please tell me about shifters so I'll know what to expect."

He gave me a very critical look, trying to decide if I was lying or not, his nostrils flared as he took in a deep breath. I guess he decided I wasn't "Your serious aren't you?" I nodded "OH boy!" He said, he ran his fingers through his hair "I'm not sure where to begin, I've never had to teach someone who knows how to shift to be a shifter." Several emotions ran across his face then he jumped straight up like a bee had snuck into his pants "OH MY GOD!" "What?" He was bug eyed again and starring at me "You can shift!" I rolled my eyes   "Yeah we already established that." "NO, you don't understand. Less than a week? Right? Wait you were unconscious for a week and a half so it's like almost two weeks right?" "Yeah." I was getting worried now. He wasn't saying much. "Ok, here's the thing." Finally some info "most shifters can only shift on the full moon. Only the most powerful can shift between the moons, like I saw you do." I was waving my hand in circles, motioning him to get to the point. "The point is only very powerful Alphas can do a partial shift, but only the Elite of the Alphas can shift when ever they want. Take the Colony of snakes for example. The only one in the whole colony who can shift anytime is Javier, he's their leader, their Viper. No one else can. Everyone else has to wait for the moon. Marcus is the only Lion in his Pride, he's the Leander. David, the only Bird of Prey, Gage, the only Leopard in his Cat Coalition, not even the few Tigers he's taken in can do it. Max, he's our Tamaska. And his brother Matt, our Bodolf. They are the only one's in the Wolf Pack. And you haven't even had a full moon yet." I was a bit stunned by this little bit of news. "Okay what else, don't stop now." I said, you could almost see the smoke coming out of his ears he was thinking so fast. "I need to correct something first, shifters can shift between the moons if their Alpha helps them, but you don't have one. Shifters naturally have a need for touch, kind of like our animal counter parts. Higher body temps, faster metabolism, heck, faster everything. Our reflexes are incredible, better senses, and of course we get to hunt once a month. Can you partial shift too?" "I don't know" "Go ahead and try." I closed my eyes to concentrate, thought of my dragon claws and felt a warm ripple from my elbows to my fingertips. Travis gasped and I looked and smiled "Hey! It worked!" Travis looked like he was ready to bolt out the door. "Yeah, okay it worked but I was expecting a hoof or two, not claws." Ooops! I forgot he'd only seen me as a Pegasus. Travis reached for my wrist to inspect it with me. "What the hell has scales, and four and a half inch serrated claws like that?" "Uh, well, if I tell you, do you promise not to run screaming?" Suddenly a smell like sour vomit started coming off of him in waves. Was that fear? He swallowed hard and nodded, then shook his head, paused then nodded again. "Travis, are you sure you want to know?" "Please just tell me you're not a demon or something like that." He was genuinely scared. I shifted my claws back to hands, looked him in the eyes and said "I'm not a demon or anything like that." He took a deep breath and released some of his fear. "Okay tell me." There really wasn't an easy way to tell him "I'm sort of a dragon." He laid back on the bed, closed his eyes and muttered "Like a fire breathing dragon? A Komodo dragon? A Chinese dragon? What kind of dragon?" "Uh, the fire breathing kind?" I wasn't sure what his response was going to be. He sat back up looked at me again and asked "Are you serious?" I nodded he started muttering again, this time to himself. "This isn't possible, you can't be more than one kind of shifter at a time, the genetics don't work that way. One would cancel out the other, no not cancel out, but override it." He looked at me the way the scientists did at the lab. "How is this possible?" "That's a story there." "There's a story? Can I hear it?" He could tell I didn't know if I could trust him to keep my secret, just by the look that crossed my face. "Do you swear not to ever tell a living soul? Travis, I have a HUGE secret. You can't just say later, "Oops! I forgot" Not with this. Can you keep this kind of secret? The life or death kind?" I know his curiosity was about to kill him but he gave it legitimate thought and said "Yes, I swear." So for the next thirty minutes, I told him every detail for the last few days up to the present. The poor guy was awash with emotions, sometimes he laughed at me, sometimes he was in awe of me. He seemed to be taking it well though. "So, you can shift into anything. That is cool. Sometimes I wish I could shift into something else. Do you think maybe someday I can go for a ride when you shift into a Pegasus? Or a Dragon?" Now he looked like an eager kid. I smiled "Yeah someday" After that we both climbed into bed, it felt good knowing someone else knew my secret. Like I didn't have to shoulder it alone anymore.

Chapter 12

That afternoon we woke up about four thirty. I hadn't slept with anyone in my bed, other than my dog Angel, for a long time. I wasn't real sure I would be able too. Angel made it her own duty to keep my feet warm, it would probably be an insult to ask Travis to shift, and scoot to the bottom of the bed. Anyway, I awoke cuddled up next to Travis, and if felt very comfortable. Everything was right, his smell, the warmth of the two of us together, all of it.

Travis, turned over to face me, gave a lazy smile and said "Good morning glow worm." "Good morning, What? What was that you called me?" "I called you a glow worm. When you sleep your whole body lights up, you glow in the dark. Like a soft night light." *HOLY SHIT!!!!!!!!!!* The meteorite tried to melt me, when I merged with the auras. Now I'm glowing in the damn dark! And I still hadn't heard a peep from my personal power trainer.

"Hey, don't say anything okay? That's just way to freaky for me right now." "Don't worry, I promised not to say anything, and I won't." He left after that so we could both shower and get dressed for the day. Dark blue stretch jeans, and a royal blue peasant top, with my purple boots. I'd have to go somewhere other than Wal-mart, for some good boots. I adjusted my Sai, and dug through my plastic bags of Wally world goodies until I found my new hip purse. It's like a fanny pack but much more stylish. My finger claws fit into the big zipper pocket, my room card fit into the smaller zippered pocket, then off for the playpen. I was the only one in there so far. That would soon change though. There's nothing like the smell of food to bring people running. I just hope the sniffers on the shifters, didn't work too well. Randy, Candy, Travis and I decided to have Belgium waffles for breakfast. We had bought five double sided waffle makers for the occasion. We would have bought more, but BB and B ran out, we got them all. I also made sure, we had everything we needed to make waffles while we were at Wally world, including big freezer bags of blueberries. First things first, coffee, then out came the bowls to start mixing ingredients. In no time (thanks to the big box of pancake mix) the batter was ready, and I was spraying the heated irons. The girls showed up while I was filling the waffle irons, Randy is so observant it's scary. She leaned over the batter bowl to smell and dip her fingers in it, and laughed "It's Blurple!" We were all smiling when I said

"It's because of the blueberries, goofy." Candy said "I don't care what it looks like, it smells good and it's still raw." We got our waffles first then reloaded the irons. Travis bounced into the room leaving the doors wide open. Travis said "Wow, I could smell them outside the doors. Couldn't wait for me huh?" We all smiled and got him a plate. It only takes about two and a half minutes to cook the waffles. We were loading them onto a big cookie sheet when people started filling the room following their noses. They were all making comments on the smell, either waking them up, or getting them going. They couldn't believe they were fresh, and not burned. Leaving the RC twins and Travis in charge of the waffles irons, I went to check in for the evening and ask Christian a few important questions.

When I got to his office, he was being updated by Peyton on the previous nights events, work tallies, orders, bad guys killed, the usual stuff. I knocked on the door, and was told to "Enter". I came in a took a seat in one of Christian's wing back chairs. He nodded to Peyton to continue. "So far the total renegades come to thirty seven, and five bombs. I suggest we contact the other area leaders then recalculate our totals." Christian nodded to him, "I had planned on that, thank you. Let me know if there are any changes." Peyton was effectively dismissed.

Once he was out of the room Christian turned to me, "Is there something you need?" I smiled then, "Uh, Yes as a matter of fact there are several things I need. First, do I have a set schedule? Or just when you need me? Am I on call? Please tell me so I'll know what we're working with here." He thought about it for about three seconds "You will be on call, if I need you I'll call for you. When I call,(he tapped his temple) you get to me as soon as possible. If I call you, there will most likely be a situation, and you will need to use your talents. Anything else?" Cool, I could pretty much do whatever I wanted then. I doubt he'd be in very many situations the two of them couldn't handle. Sebastian was practically glued to Christian's hip. "Yes. Second do you know someone I could talk to about getting another identity? Possibly how much it will cost?" Christian asked. "Why do you need another identity?" He got a look from me that said I wasn't going to talk about it, continuing like he hadn't asked anything "And do you know how long it will take?"

He got my point, good thing I found a smart Vampire. He nodded to me and said "Sebastian will show you the way." "Thank you very much, that's all my questions for now." Sebastian led us out the door, down the hall and around another corner. As we were walking down one of the halls, a horrific odor stopped me in my tracks. It smelled like sour vomit. I looked at Sebastian and asked through my pinched nose "What the hell is that smell?" he replied "That would be the man you are going to see." *OH HELL NO!* "Hold that thought!" Holding out my hand, I demanded "Elevator card!" He handed me his card with a raised eyebrow. It didn't take long to get back to my room. Rummaging through my bags until a spray can of Moroccan flavored Febreze finally appeared, then back to Sebastian. I was spraying the hall before I got to him though. He took his card back, and had a small smile on his face as he watched me spray the hall, the walls and the floor. We stopped in front of a door, I sprayed extra here. Sebastian opened it for me but didn't enter. I didn't blame him, I didn't want to enter. The stench got instantly worse. He eyed the man sitting behind a computer desk and said "Take good care of her, whatever she wants, and give her the employee package." Then he was gone in a blur. Holding your nose, looks ridiculous and makes you sound very funny. I looked at the guy behind the desk and asked "Is that smell coming from you?" Was that really rude of me? He looked very sheepish and nodded. He was trembling in his seat. I sprayed the room (still holding my nose) walked over to the man behind the desk and said "UP!" He stood up on shaky legs, he got sprayed too. "TURN!" I sprayed him all over and his chair before I was done. I let go of my nose and took a very tentative breath. It wasn't great, but it was better.

The guy was still standing when I took a seat in front of his desk. "You can sit down now." He sat, jeez this guy had issues. His aura showed he was a wolf shifter, I would *think* the smell would be driving him nuts. He was a *Very* nice looking man. Late twenties, about five foot ten, with light brown hair and soft brown eyes. His eyes were the same color as warm milk chocolate. He wore small gold plated wire rimmed glasses, and he looked very trim under his brown plaid button up shirt. At least he matched, his pants were brown corduroy. Huh, shifters needed glasses?

He started out with "Wwwa wa wa what cc can I dddo for yyyou?" Oh lord! He was pulling out a hanky and wiping sweat from his forehead, he looked terrified. "Uh are you okay? You look like a scared rabbit." It wasn't meant to be an insult, more an observation. "Yyyyeah I'm ffine." Ooookay, "I'm curious, why are you wearing glasses? You're a shifter, shouldn't your eyes be great?" "Hhhabit, I I I gguess, I'm uused tto them." "Oh, Well, I need a new identity. License, social security card, the works, how much is it, and how long will it take?" I didn't think they were hard questions but I could be wrong. He gathered himself and replied "Wwwell, it it it depends." How could he stand it? This guy was about to rattle himself out of his own chair. I got up and walked around to the backside of his chair. He was instantly stiff, like he was waiting for me to beat him. Gently putting my hands on his shoulders, I started massaging them, and spoke very softly in his ear. He looked spooked, it would only take a good loud "Boo" and he'd pee his pants "Breathe, calm down, I'm not gonna hurt you, I only do stuff like that in life or death situations, now just relax, everything is okay, your safe here." His shoulders were very tight, and knotted. But, he was relaxing into my hands. Working my way up his neck, and into his hair, then back down, just like a good masseuse. Sometime during the process, he'd closed his eyes. The sharp stinky smell was going away too. "There, does that feel better?" He turned to look at me and said "Yes, thank you." Huh, what do you know, no stutter, imagine that. He cleared his throat, and started speaking. I still hadn't stopped rubbing on him. Under that butt ugly shirt was a nice set of broad muscled shoulders. "A new identity is usually about fifty grand and can take a week." Crap! I wanted it now. Me? Impatient? "But for the right price I can have them done tonight." hmm I asked "What's the price for tonight?" he replied "One fifty" I might have gotten a little loud and scared him. "WHAT? LIKE ONE HUNDRED AND FIFTY THOUSAND DOLLARS?" He hunched his shoulders, and pulled forward like he was dodging a blow and the acrid smell of vomit started up again. Damn! I took a breath and slowly let it out. I pulled him back into his chair and tried to think of calming thoughts, then I figured he could use those thoughts too. "Relax, I'm sorry I yelled, it was just a bit of a shock. I told you I wasn't gonna hurt you. Close your eyes and think of white beaches with clear blue water, soft ocean breeze blowing through your hair, the soothing sounds of the waves. Imagine sand between your toes." He relaxed into my hands again, we were both calming down. "Tell me about the employee package." He faced his computer screen and pulled up a file. I dropped my hands and walked back to the front of his desk. The sound of his stomach growling echoed through the room. "The employee package, gives you a cell phone already activated with direct connect, elevator card, room card, and access to certain parts of the building. I'll have to know what new name you want so I can put it in the system." I had thought about that. Not wanting to stray too far from my real name, I chose Casey for my first name. My last name is Scotch Irish, since the government was looking for me I couldn't keep it either. My highland ancestors protected, and lived with another clan in Scotland, that would still let me feel close to the family roots. "My new name is Casey Ross. And I already have a room card." He looked at me then, and very quietly asked "Aare yyou a Vvampire?" He's a shifter, shouldn't he be able to tell? "No, does it matter what I am?" "Wwell, I need to put in my computer what you are. Please don't be offended." I wasn't. What could I tell him, without freaking him out more? Hmm ha! I GOT IT. "Promise not to laugh too long or too hard if I tell you?" He just looked at me then like I'd lost my mind. Placing the sweetest smile on my face ever invented, "I'm a very sweet lizard." Hey a Dragon was just a big Lizard right? Was there a Pegasus category? Probably not. His mouth was twitching like he was trying to grin but had forgotten how. "Go ahead, you can laugh, everyone does." Since he was the 'everyone' I hope I didn't lie. He chuckled, then giggled, then that turned into a repetitive giggle. Maybe he was picturing a famous little green Gecko. I raised my eyebrows and waited. He finally cut loose a bit, and laughed. Good, that was the point. "SSssorry, sorry. Uh, I don't have a category for a lizard." "That's okay, just stick me in anywhere." "You're really a lizard?" "Yeah, why? Do you have something against lizards?" "Nnno! I've just never heard of one. It doesn't sound so scary. I'm glad your not one of the big predators, they really scare me." Oh great! Just what I need. I have the potential to be the biggest predator here, he'd probably piss all over himself if he knew exactly what I could change into. "I'll need a picture of you for your license and passport, if you just stand against the wall there please." He pointed to a blank wall, well actually all the walls were blank. The room was desolate. Getting a new name should have certain requirements right? Like a disguise? The big thing that needed to change was my eye color. Changing the color of my eyes to a blue green mix, was my goal. I hoped they would look turquoise when I was done. "Do you by chance have a mirror?" He pulled out a compact from a drawer and handed it to me. Eye inspection time, small shards of sky blue and lime green were shot thru them. Just a little more adjusting on my eyes, while I watched them change in the mirror, and perfection. It probably looked really weird. When my eyes were the color of a tropical ocean, I handed the mirror back.

The guy was staring at me. "So, what's your name?" he swallowed real hard, and very quietly said "Pppeter" "Well Peter, it's nice to meet you. I'm Casey Ross." "Hhow did yyou ddo thththat wwith your eyes?" "Well, it's a lizard thing, these are my lizard eyes, I figured I'd need a new look, right?" He nodded to me and motioned me to the wall. He took several pictures of me. "Um, is it extra to get endorsements on the license?" He shook his head at me. "Great, can I get a motorcycle endorsement added to it?" He was starting to get nervous again "Yyyou ride mmmotorcycles?" "Well, I've ridden a scooter once, you know like a mo-ped? But someday I'd like to learn. I understand it's a lot of fun. It looks cool!"

He grinned at my experience and nodded. "How hard would it be to get a new identity for a teenager? I may need one for a fourteen year old boy." "It's the same rate for any age." I nodded. He handed me a magnetic card for the elevators, and a cell phone. I tried to tease him to keep the mood light. "Is *your* number in here?" With a smile on my face, I still don't think he got it. "Wwhy do yyou want mmy number?" "Maybe I like having phone numbers of good looking guys in my phone." He didn't look convinced. "Can I have your number? Please?" My puppy dog eyes and pouty lips were at full begging potential. He was watching me for any sign I was toying with him I think. He also had a look on his face between scared and hopeful. He reached out his hand and I handed him the phone. He programmed his number in, then he handed the phone back. "Aaall right, you have it. Oh, and the direct connect feature works on all the phones." Cool I tried it out on his number -beep beep- "OH Peter," I said in a sing song tone "I have you right under my fingers where I want you." He was absolutely adorable when he blushed. "I have an errand to run too, if you like I'll beep you before I get here so I don't startle you." He looked good in red "You'd do that?" "Yeah sure, no biggie." I was still smiling "That would be good, thanks, bye Casey." "Uh uh, it's later babe."

I went back to my room using my new elevator card, picked up a couple of plastic wally world bags and put fifteen stacks of money in one then rolled it up and put it in another bag. Then headed for the playpen, Peter's stomach growled the whole time I was in his office, it was distracting and needed to be fixed.

I whipped up some more waffles and headed back to Peter's office. As soon as the elevator doors opened on his floor I used the direct connect feature. - Beep beep - "I'm almost there." After walking through the door to his office, he smiled up at me. I gave him his waffles. He was stunned. "Wwwhat's this?" "Um, take a good look sweetie it's called food, technically it's waffles." "I uh, I can see that but why?" "Because you need to eat, of course, your inner wolf sounds hungry." I waved my hand to stop any more protests or questions, pointed to the plate and said "Eat it!" He skipped the chewing part and just inhaled it. When he was done I removed the plate from in front of him, he was grateful "Thank you for breakfast, it was good."   "Your welcome. You inhaled it so fast I'm surprised you could taste it. You should come down to the playpen during meals so you can eat with the rest of us." "Uh, I'm not allowed in there." "What? Why not, you're a shifter."   "They say they don't want people like me in there making the place smell." He was ashamed of that I could tell, and being shunned made him sad. "Well, they won't talk shit if your with me. I'll stomp them into the floor! How's that sound?" Trying to lighten the mood again, wasn't going to be easy "It it it won't matter who I'm with, they said if I show my face in there, they were going to show me what true fear was. I don't want to find out." He looked me straight in the eyes when he said that. Okay, I'll fix their wagons "Okay, no problem, we'll just hang out in my room or we'll make our own hangout. What do you say?"

"You wouldn't do that for me, I'm not stupid. I've been a shifter for five months now, I don't mind." He wouldn't look at me now, I never knew sorrow had a smell. "You're my new friend Pete, you'll learn over time, I go to great lengths for my friends, and no matter how bad they screw up, I try to stand beside them. Can you give me a few numbers from your nifty computer to put into my phone?" he looked suspicious "Who's number do you want?" I told him and he very politely complied. My new phone was about to get it's first real work out. -beep beep- "Yo Trav! I need you!" "Hey Chickie! You got my number! That's cool, what do you need?" "Will you come up to Peter's office so we can talk?" "Uh sure, be right there." He was a bit hesitant but I knew he'd come. Peter wasn't so sure. "He won't come up here, shifters avoid my office." "Have faith Peter, I usually pick good people for friends." A couple minutes later Travis knocked on the door and came in.

"Hey, Peter, hey Chickie, Wassup!" I chuckled, Travis just has a way of making people smile. He was like a happy puppy. He took a seat in the other chair in the room next to me. "Is it true folks don't want Pete in the playpen?" He lost his smile and said "Uh yeah, sorry man." he said to Peter. I took a breath and said "Okay then we need another room to hang out in, Pete's my new friend and I'm not going to exclude him. What they're doing is wrong, and you know it." Travis thought about it for a minute, and said "I think there's an old living area with a kitchen still on this floor, it hasn't been used for a while, I'll have to check it out see what's in there. It may just be a storage room now." There might be hope yet "Let's go do that now, we have time, and if we need to we can go shopping to get what we need. Oh and Pete? Here's your money honey." I grabbed Travis by the arm and hauled him out of his chair and out the door. The look on Pete's face had been worth it. Travis lead us down a hallway on the back side of the elevator to the third door down on the right. The door was unlocked, so we went in. It was empty except for the dust bunnies, the kitchen area was smaller than in the playpen. The whole room was smaller. That was okay though since there wouldn't be as many people in it. We checked all the appliances, and they still worked, plugged in the fridge and went for cleaning supplies. We could decorate this room the way we wanted to. Two hours later, the room was vacuumed, counters wiped down, and we'd brought up the stuff I'd bought for the playpen to the new living room. We needed to name our hangout. We decided to wait for the girls, so we could all put it to a vote.

Midnight rolled around, and Pete was through with my new identity, I looked over my new license, and passport. It all looked totally legit. A moment of depression hit me, I wasn't me anymore. Now I was someone else, something else. Mourn later, time to collect the girls -beep beep- "Hey Randy, Catch Candy and meet us by the elevator on sublevel one" beep beep- "Okay, you got it!"

Five minutes later, I was making introductions. Travis and I had brought Peter with us. Everyone new each other, but it was awkward. Travis told the girls about our new room and the plans for it. We all walked down, so everyone could see it. The girls gushed all over it, talking over each other and us, about how it should look. Me and the guys just stood back by the door out of harms way. I put my thumb and middle finger in my mouth and blew out a loud whistle. The chatter stopped instantly. Laughing I said "Ladies, we all get to add our own touches to the room, so the room is all of ours to enjoy. Tomorrow we can go shopping for furniture, but tonight we go back to Wally world for essentials, like a T.V., food, stuff like that. Any objections?" The girls didn't hardly let me finish before they were pushing us all out the door.

Three hours later we came back, neither the guys nor I was looking forward to furniture shopping after the sun came up. The girls spent forty five minutes arguing over paint versus wallpaper or stencils. They had volunteered to stay up tonight and paint the room so it would be ready tomorrow. Me and the guys were glad to leave them to it.

I'm not going to go into the fiasco of shopping for furniture, but it got done. God Bless IKEA!! Our new living room was now pale blue, with lavender trim. We had a cream colored overstuffed sectional couch. There were five recliners built in, so we all got our own recliner. End tables and coffee table, and a sixty inch big, flat screen T.V.. The fridge was full and I was cooking lunch for us the next day, and so far Pete wasn't having any anxiety attacks. He was good, no stinky or anything. I think he just needed to belong somewhere, to fit in and have friends. Now he has four more. The girls were all over him, rearranging his clothes, styling his hair. He was their own living Ken doll, and he was starting to come out of his shell. Everyone seemed real happy with each other, they'd excepted Pete right into the fold. I was so proud.

Since I had time during the afternoon, Travis took me to buy a new vehicle. The Mercedes was nice and all, but not my style. A new blue Honda Ridgeline was in my future. Besides we needed the extra hauling room. One of the main reasons I'd opted for the Ridgeline is there's a hidey hole in the bed of the truck. It's big enough to be a cooler, or double as a money hole. Right now it's holding a small black duffle bag full of money. The extra that I'd brought with us.

The evening was uneventful, so we all got good sleep. The next day was gonna be a biggie. My first stop was to see my youngest son. Being a worried mom is one thing. Being a worried mom on the run and wanted by the Government was another. Needing to see him was essential for my sanity.

I Pulled up to his dad's apartment, and did a quick eye check to make sure my baby browns were back again, wouldn't want to freak anyone out more than I was already going to. Travis stayed in the truck as I went to the door. My son was inside moping around and being a typical pissed off fourteen year old. Pushing open the door and walking inside, his eyes lit up, and we caught each other in a tight, never let you go, kind of hug. I wanted to take him back with me. We were both crying, even his dad came over and joined our hug. My sweet baby boy was taller than I was. He was nearly six feet tall. His almost black curly hair was slicked back with gel and his brown eyes were red rimmed from crying no doubt. "Mom, Oh my God Mom! Take me with you, I don't care where we have to go, just take me with you." God, my baby was breaking my heart. "Baby, listen to me okay?" "NO!, take me with you!" Our eyes were both filled with joyous reunion tears. "Baby, where I'm going can be very dangerous. The Government is after me, because I was exposed to a meteor, they're looking for me. You need to be enrolled in school, right now you need to stay here." He cut me off "Mom, I'm going with you!" "Son, listen to me, I have to get us new identities, that takes time." That appeased him some, but not much, because he knew I was trying, and not leaving him forever. "As soon as I can get everything in place, then we'll be together." "That will never happen, you don't have a job now. How are you gonna get the money?" I smiled "I have a new job right now, and it pays a lot more than my old job." Pulling out a stack of money for him to see, I pulled out a few bills and handed it to him. I know giving money to a teenager might not be the wisest of things to do, but he needed to know what I was saying was true. "I have the money, what I need right now is time, and patients. Let me do what I can to get the Government off my back a little bit, and get established. I have the money baby, I swear, I just need time, okay?" "Hurry up mom, please hurry." His father who is definitely an older version of my son, put his two cents in then "Your not going to take him off somewhere and disappear. You're a wanted woman. Living on the run is no life for a kid. Why don't you give me some money since you seem to have plenty?" I looked at my son's father, his shoulder length curly black hair was in perfect place, as usual, and I said "We'll talk later, I can't stay. I just wanted my son to know I was alive." I gave my son a kiss, and another very emotional hug, and made promises to hurry. Damn, walking out the door, and watching my son watch me was hard. I also made sure I had current pictures of him in my phone for Peter.

Next stop, back to HQ, I wanted to go online and find information on the Bank of the Cayman's. If my understanding is correct, that is the place to bank. Especially if you didn't want the American Government to know your business. I also wanted to start searching for property and houses. With a new name I could get us a house where we'd be safe. I hope.

Chapter 13

When we got back to HQ, I went straight for our new living room, names were to be drawn tonight on what we wanted to call it. It was an anonymous draw, all the names would go into a hat and one would be pulled out. I was thinking very mundane things like "The Crash Pad" or "The End Zone" mostly cause we ended up there. My mind just was not caring right now what we called it. I put my two votes in, cause that's what we decided. Everyone got two votes. Christian was mentally telling me about a meeting and giving me descriptions of who was to attend. I was sitting by myself when the door opened, and Travis and Peter walked in. They came in, sat down beside me, and put their arms around my shoulders. Apparently feeling like shit makes you look like shit. Travis started "What's wrong Casey? You look like you just lost your whole world." I looked at him "I'm having a pity party, I want my life back, I want my kids back, everything. My oldest kids have left the coop. All I have left is my youngest boy. I'll be okay

I just need to feel sorry for my self for a while." Then the girls walked in and they were their usual chattering selves. My pity party was over.

Candy said "We're all here lets vote!" Randy grabbed the hat that had our votes in it, shook it up, and held it up in the air. "Okay, since this was your idea Casey, you get to draw the name." I really didn't want to. "Pete? Will you draw the name?" He looked unsure "I guess so." He stood up and reached into the hat and pulled out a folded piece of paper. Before he read it, I reminded everyone "No matter what is on that paper, the name sticks. We all agreed, no matter how corny, or stupid. Okay Pete, let's have it. What are we naming the room?"

He smiled and unfolded the paper, went bug eyed, then swallowed hard as he said "Uh, it's officially called the Dragon's Lair" My head instantly jerked to Travis, with a very pointed look. He shrank a bit into the couch. The girls were oooing and aweing, they thought it was a cool name. "Well, the Dragon's Lair it is!" I looked at Pete, "Are you okay with that? It sounds really tough." "It sounds really cool, I like it." He smiled then, there wasn't any strange odors coming from him, so I guess he was ok with it. The RC twins had broke out the stencils. They were applying them to the outer door, to mark it as ours. Then I got a mental buzz. "*I need you in conference room one.*" I sent back "*on my way*" "Sorry ya'll I just got paged I gotta go." Peter said "I didn't hear anything." I tapped my temple as I headed out the door. They all had an OH! expression on their faces.

Conference room one, was down the hall and around two corners from MY LAIR! God I can't believe Travis put that in there. I'm gonna kick his ass later. I changed my eyes, back to turquoise, pulled out my claws and put them on, and went invisible.

When I walked around a corner, and felt a buzzing in my head again. I tuned in to tell Christian I was on my damn way, but it wasn't him I tuned into. Peyton and another female vampire were in a deep mental conversation. *"… I need to stress three vampires were killed Peyton?"* *"No, Brenna you don't. Do not be concerned…"* I tuned back out, as second in command here, he would need to consol those who were scared or worried. There were two vampires standing guard outside the open door. One was big, bald and tattooed, the other was a red headed female who was about five foot ten. They both looked like weight lifters. I drifted inside and took up a position that mirrored Sebastian next to Christian. *"I'm here."* Most of the local leaders were sitting around a big conference table. I remembered the names Travis had given me during our shifter lesson. It helped that Christian had also told me about them. Max, the wolf leader was closest to the door on Christians right with Gage, the Leopard leader, in between them. Javier was the snake leader and closest to the door on Christians left with David, the bird leader between them, and Christian was at the head of the table facing the door, with the room to our backs. Every leader there had two body guards standing behind them.

Max was getting antsy, "Well, we're all here, where is it? You said if we brought the explosives and the cash to pay our debt, we'd be allowed to see your new monster. So let's see it." My jaw was hanging down to my knees, I knew it was. Against one wall, were duffle bags, suitcases and those big metal sided brief cases. Popping Christian upside the back of his head for what I just heard Max say might not be kosher but I'm betting it would make me feel better. *"I can NOT believe you did that! I am NOT going to show my self with all these people in here. Are you Crazy? The guards at the very least will have to go!"* Christian replied in a very diplomatic, and calm manner out loud. "I do not believe they will agree to that." Javier asked "Are you speaking to it?" Christian nodded to him. *"Christian, I have a bounty on my head, I don't want this many people knowing what I look like. Hell, I don't want them to know what I look like! The guards leave or I don't show myself!"* "There has been a request for all your guards to leave the room." The room erupted in complaints and protests, the guards didn't want to leave their leaders unprotected, and the leaders weren't keen on the idea of *being* unprotected. The noise in here could wake the dead, oh wait, the dead were in here with us! I reached over the highly polished dark wood table and slammed my clawed hand down as far out into the middle as I could reach, dug in my claws and slowly pulled back toward the edge.

The room went completely silent. When deep gouges appear out of nowhere it's a good bet someone will take notice. "I really liked this table, I'm sure there was another way to get everyone's attention besides defacing my antique, hand carved, cherry wood table." Christian kind of growled out the comment *"Hey, it worked didn't it?"* Christian looked to the other leaders, collected his composure, and said "I assure you no harm will come to anyone in this room, Sebastian can wait outside with your people." There were several more protests, but the guards were finally ordered out.

The curiosity of the leaders out weighed the guards votes. Once the door was closed, I hesitated, I didn't want to show myself. My feet were shoulder width apart, my hands clasped behind my back, and a small innocent smile was on my face. Then I gave in and basically materialized in front of everybody. It was all very anti-climatic I'm sure. Max slammed his fist against the table and growled "Is this some kind of joke?" he pointed at me "THAT little girl can not possibly be what did all that damage in the warehouse." Gage smiled at me and said, "Don't worry, no one will blame you for the game Christian is playing." I spoke on my own behalf then "Dynamite, Nitro, it all comes in small packages, do you *MEN usually* underestimate women?" The sarcasm flowed like thick molasses. David said, "You are human, you couldn't possibly be responsible." My eyebrows nearly hit my hairline "Oh no? Why on Earth would you say that? NO! wait, I know why, you where expecting a big bad monster, and all you got was me." I placed both clawed hands on the table so they could get a good look at them "Well, guess what? I'm not exactly human anymore. Can you smell me? Sense my power? I'll answer for you, NO you can't." Shifting my fingernails only into claws, was very intimidating. Javier smiled at me and said "I have brought your due, are those silver claws you have?" "YES, want to see one?" He shook his head and said "Shifters can not touch silver without being burned." My smile wasn't pretty "I can, see?" Then just shifting my lower arms and hands at that, warm ripples erupted into a wolfs paws. Max jumped up and said, "If you're a wolf then you fall under my jurisdiction not a Vampires." Shifting them to a leopards paws, I looked at Gage. "Are you going to try to claim me too?" Max scoffed, "That's not possible." I glanced at him and rolled my eyes. "Yeah yeah I know, I've heard it all before. I've only been a shifter less than a month, but I have someone teaching me the in's and out's. A wolf actually, you know Travis? He was freaked out when I showed him too." There was a knock at the door then, I went invisible. Sebastian opened the door and came in with all the guards, and Peyton and announced "The Leander is here."

We heard the outer doors open and Marcus and his people marching down the hall. The other leaders were wearing tailored suits, Marcus and his men breezed in wearing jungle fatigues, combat boots and a side arm each. He also had a manila folder under his left arm. He stood behind a black leather chair at the end of the table and very sarcastically said "Well well, it looks like my invitation to this little party got lost in the mail." Christian looked bored and said "These gracious leaders called me and requested a time to meet to pay off a debt, I never heard from you, so you didn't get an invitation." Oooo that was a slam! The Vampire did have style. Marcus on the other hand didn't, he was starting to get mad. Through gritted teeth he growled out "I have determined your guard to be a Wraith, they don't need money. They don't eat, or buy things. Essentially they are nothing but ghosts, that can sometimes manifest a small portion of their bodies. Hell, a Wraith doesn't even have a body! I'm not going to pay for a ghost!" I really wanted to hurt him. Christian stood up then and faced Marcus. "My guard is not a Wraith, and I'm advising you here and now not to piss off my guard, you have no concept of the temper my guard can have." Several of the other shifters chuckled at that. Were they picturing me on the rag and in a rage?

I also noticed how Christian never referred to me as he or she. He was keeping me anonymous, in his own way protecting me. Marcus still wasn't convinced "I don't believe you, you'll say anything to get your hands on more money. It's nothing but a Vampire ploy, and if any of you" he looked at the other leaders then "fall for it your fools!" He pulled the chair out to sit down in it, but before he could, I zipped around the table and grabbed him by the throat. My sliver claws instantly started burning his skin as I tightened my grip. Christian's eyebrows shot up and said "I warned you, I believe you owe my guard an apology." Marcus was starting to turn an ugly shade of red. Small wisps of smoke were coming from his neck where my claws met his skin. Alex and Brett were his chosen guards, Alex took a step forward to try to pry away whatever had a hold of Marcus, and I squeezed harder. Alex stopped in his tracks as Marcus started making choking sounds. Brett called out "Stop this, you can't kill him, he's our Leander. Take me instead."   *"Will you please tell Brett, HIS Leander is the one who Fucked up? And HIS Leander is the one who will apologize, or HIS Leander will look like the headless horseman?"* Christian relayed what I said verbatim. Max, and Gage were covering chuckles with coughs. It wasn't very convincing. Marcus got the hint I believe, he opened his mouth and whispered "I apologize" I instantly let go of him and backed away. Brett pulled open a small bag he had with him, and rushed to attend Marcus's wounds. *"He keeps a med kit with him?"* Christian responded *"He is their medic, he always has that kit."* Huh, good to know. Brett was sniffing the wounds around Marcus's neck as he tended the wounds, and said "These burns were caused by silver, I can smell it." Marcus pushed Brett aside and sat down. His voice was strained when he asked. "Is there any other business anyone wishes to bring forth, if not there is something I'd like to discuss." Christian sat back down and replied "Actually, I'd like to discuss what everyone has found while we are all here, get an account on the number of bombs found and how many "Unauthorized" vampires were found and destroyed."

Gage opened the discussion with "We found five bombs total, and three of the renegades, I wanted to thank you for sending someone to help disarm the bombs." Christian nodded to him and Max went next "We found five bombs too. Luckily, we have people who could disarm them. We caught four of the renegades in our territory and hunted them down." Marcus had a bottle of water that Brett handed him, waved his hand in the air in a dismissive gesture and said "My people disarmed the bombs we found, I didn't get a tally of them, and we killed three bloodsuckers." I didn't like his wording, it made me uncomfortable. Javier went next and said "There were five bombs in the Colonies, we found four before the time was up, thank you Christian, and Max for what your people did for us, it is greatly appreciated. The last bomb blew up one of my Colonies, luckily everyone had already been evacuated. We also found two renegades and took great pleasure in killing them." Then was David's turn "I believe there is definitely a pattern here, we found five bombs too. All located around the Aeries. My people disarmed four of them and Christians' Vampire disarmed the last. We also found two renegades in our area that we dispatched." Christian nodded to Peyton to give their report. "We found five bombs in our area, Christians new guard disarmed one of them" aww he was giving me brownie points "and total we destroyed thirty seven renegades." Christian commented "That is sixty two renegades, total. Our people are still searching in case some escaped notice." Javier asked "Why were there so many in your area Christian?" "We believe they were trying to hide in plain sight. As it were." All the leaders seemed to agree with that.

Marcus was so impatient is was funny "Now, that that is cleared up," He opened his folder and pulled out flyers with my picture on them, and passed them around the table. I got a good look at the one Christian held. It had a picture of me, a general description, and the amount of my bounty. Well, if that didn't tempt them nothing would. CRAP! "Have any of you ever seen this woman? Her name is Cassandra. She's a wanted criminal. Wanted by the Government dead or alive. She is extremely dangerous, and unstable. She has been spotted in the area several times over the past few days. We don't think she left it. Her family is here, I don't think she'll stray too far away from them."

Javier asked "What is she wanted for?" Marcus shrugged "It doesn't really matter does it? Look at that bounty, anyone who locates her will get a finders fee of course." Smacking Christian was sounding better and better. Javier folded his flyer in half, ripped it up and gave it back to Marcus in a small pile of confetti. Marcus was turning a bright shade of red. Javier said in a thick Mexican accent "I have not seen this woman, and we are not going to help you search for her. I have too many other things to worry about right now." Max, Gage, David, and Christian followed Javier's lead, and gave the flyers back either rolled up in a ball, or ripped up. I had to smile, they had my back, and I didn't know why, but I'd find out. Marcus was livid, the veins in his neck looked like they were going to burst right there. "FINE! I would have shared the reward, we'll get her with out your help. But I should warn you, I don't like being lied to." He gathered his envelope up, stood up so fast his chair went careening into the door frame, and stormed out of the building. Christian asked that all the guards step outside once more, and they did. As soon as the doors were shut I became visible again.

Why had they lied for me? "Why did you guys lie for me?" Javier spoke up "I didn't lie for you, the description said brown eyes, yours aren't brown." He smiled at me and continued "Besides, I like the way Marcus had to apologize. I would bet that was a new experience for him." I didn't even think about my eyes not matching the description on the flyer. Everyone got a good laugh at Marcus's expense. My relief loosened a knot that had formed in my gut. I turned to Christian and Max, "Is it okay with you guys if I call Travis and some others to help me carry bags back to my room?" No one objected. I pulled my phone off my hip where it was clipped -beep beep- "Hey Travis?" -beep beep- "Yeah Chickie what do you need my lady?" Eyebrows shot up around the room, I ducked my head and smiled. -Beep beep- "Could you snag some folks and come to conference room one?" -beep beep- "Your wish is my command my lady." Okay I knew he was sucking up for the room name thing, but no one else did. Max asked "My wolf follows your commands?" Embarrassed me? The tips of my ears felt hot. "He screwed up earlier, he's just sucking up, well that and I feed him. He doesn't want to mess that up either." A few more chuckles went through the room then, -beep beep- "Casey! Quick get out here!"

Travis was yelling into the phone and sounded hysterical, I bolted out the door with everyone on my heels. The scene was nuts, shifters and vampires were everywhere, Travis grabbed me by the arm and pointed to the glass doors that led outside. Well, I guess trying to hide my face was pointless now, everybody was staring at me and the carnage outside the doors.

Chapter 14

A wolf shifter was shot and lying on the stairs, outside the glass doors, bleeding all over the steps. It was one of Max's guards. Max went to get him, and several sets of hands stopped him. His other guard said "You can't get to him, we tried. Someone shot him as soon as he stepped outside. When we tried to go outside to get him, they shot him again. If we get anywhere near those doors they'll shoot him." Max was about to lose it, "THAT'S MY BROTHER OUT THERE LET ME GO!" I stopped him then and he growled at me, his eyes were turning amber right there "Wait, think a moment, smell the air, they used silver shot on him, if you go out there, then you'll be next. It's a trap Max." "Matt is my brother. I can't stand here and watch him die and do nothing." There had to be something I could do. Matt didn't have very long with the silver bullets in his body slowly killing him. He was lying on the stairs, writhing from the pain.

Travis, my cheerleader, said "It'll be okay, Casey will get him, she'll figure it out." Then he looked at me "Won't you Casey?" he was very hopeful. He had a lot of confidence in me. He had brought Peter, and the girls down to help carry bags, I had an audience. Great, no pressure here. My mind was racing trying to figure out what in the hell to do. I looked at Christian and asked "The docks are on this level right?" he nodded "Okay, the stairs are well lit, are the docks?" He thought for a moment and said "No, the lights should be off on them right now, we accept deliveries during the day." I nodding then, "Good, take me to them." I turned to Max "Listen and don't freak out" I looked at my group of friends too so they would be included in the not freaking out part. "I'm going to block the gunfire so they can't hit him, or you. When I do Max, then it'll be safe for you to get him in here." "How will I know when it's safe?" "You'll know, you won't be able to miss me." Now I get to be cryptic. It's kind of fun.

I followed Christian down a long corridor thru two divider doors then to a dock door, and laid down on the nasty dock plate. We had planned what we were going to do on the way to the docks. I became invisible, Christian used his vampiric speed to pull up the dock door, just enough for me to roll under it. The door was once again shut by the time my feet hit the ground. If anyone noticed, it would just be a blip on their peripheral vision. I jogged to the stairs, taking in my surroundings, and smelling the air trying to get used to all the new stuff my brain registered. I did a quick look around to find whoever shot Matt. Then dropped down to my knees to talk to Matt. "Hey Matt, don't panic, I'm gonna block the gunfire and Max will come out and get you. When I shift I don't want you to be afraid, I'm kind of big and scary, maybe I should say big and scaly but I wont hurt you okay?" He was looking up trying to see me and nodded.

He had beautiful brown eyes with cinnamon colored flecks in them, and his dark brown hair had blonde streaks in it from being out in the sun. I backed up a few feet, and shifted into my Dragon form. My wings stretched out and wrapped around the sides of the stairs, then I became visible. Several exclamations of "Oh shit!" "Oh my god!" and things like that could be heard from the other side of the glass doors. Instantly shots were fired right at me, bullets were hitting my shield on my back and wings.

I looked to the doors and nodded my big head. Max watched me with trepidation and grabbed Matt by the under arms and pulled him inside. Several people were standing at the doors still holding them open. They were waiting for me to shift and come back inside, but as long as they stood there I wouldn't move. No one else needed to be shot. A small roar from me vacated the hallway with lightning speed. I went invisible, shifted back to my normal self, then I shook off the bullets that had stuck to my shield, and walked through the doors.

The smell of blood and silver was thick in the hallway. Max had laid Matt down on the big conference table. Once back in the conference room, it looked like the only way for anyone to get near Matt was going to be the hard way. Short people get picked on all the time, but sometimes it's a good thing. Crouching, and nearly crawling on the floor was the best way through the crowd. "Move it, move it, coming through, look out." I finally reached Matt, he wasn't looking so good. He had a silver bullet in his very muscular right shoulder and one in his left chest. His breath had a wet bubbly sound to it. He was about the same height as Max, around six foot three, and had the body of someone who did hard physical labor for a living.

Max was almost hysterical "Someone get the healer. NOW!" I nudged Max. "I think I can help him if you scoot over and let me get close enough." There was fear in his eyes. Fear of me and fear of losing his brother. "Max, I'm not gonna eat him, Damn!" He let out a shaky breath and moved over just enough so I could get to Matt.

My silver claws slipped off easily and fit right in my hip purse. Placing my hands just over the wounds, but not quit touching them, I thought about my power and visualized it going into the wounds and wrapping around the bullets. Here we go again with the whole testing theories in the line of battle. The power wouldn't do exactly what was needed. My personal power trainer's voice floated through my mind *"Manipulate energy, move them with your thoughts."* Move them with my thoughts? Telekinesis? Matt was breathing slow and heavy now, dropping my hands to my sides, I closed my eyes and concentrated on the bullets rising up and out of the wounds. Max said "If your gonna do something then do it faster."

Several gasps caught my attention. My eyes opened and the bullets were hovering about six inches over Matt. The bullets slowly moved over the table then fell. The wounds were seeping blood and liquid silver. Max was losing patients "Hurry, please." I turned my head and looked at him, I was doing my best so it wasn't a pleasant look. One of annoyance.

Placing my hands over the wounds allowed my aura to directly touch Matt. The power pushed into the wounds to heal him. I thought about flesh mending and the bleeding slowed, but how did I get out the silver? A memory came into my head in a flash showing me what was needed to do. And it wasn't my memory. Tilting my head to the side in concentration and letting my power locate the silver as it moved through Matt's body seemed easy. Once I had figured out the difference between the blood and the silver toxin I manipulated the compounds in the silver to be something else, something non lethal. The whole process took about thirty seconds, and the wounds were closed, healed, and the silver was gone.

Matt tried to sit up after that and I pushed him back down, he scowled at me and said "Thanks, you fixed me, now let me up." I raised my eyebrows at him and said "NO, just stay there for a few minutes." He tried to sit up again, and I pushed him down again. "Matt, you said I fixed you, well then that makes me the doctor, and I say you should follow doctors orders and stay down for a few minutes, let your body relax and build up some blood, you lost enough of it. You were just shot with Silver bullets and Mercury for God's sake."

He tried to sit up again and I turned to Max "There are two choices here Max. Either order your brother to stay flat or I'll knock him out." I looked at Matt with an evil grin "He'll stay down then." Max gave Matt's leg a pat and said "She's right just rest for a bit." Matt argued "I feel good enough to sit up, and this table is hard." I scowled at Matt "Looky here boy! I learned I was a shifter about five days ago, I just saved your ass, and at least thirty bullets hit me while I was covering for you." I was getting worked up a bit, and I wasn't going to count the days I'd been asleep "so you can damn well keep your ass on this table for a few minutes. I may be new at the whole shifter thing, and I haven't seen a full moon yet, but from what I've been told I'm pretty goddamn powerful, so I would suggest you don't piss off the rookie shape shifting doctor." I shook my head and turned around to leave the room, but the looks on the faces that surrounded me caught my attention.

Looks of shock, surprise and awe not to mention they were all leaning slightly to see my back. "What?" I asked. Gage stepped forward "Five days? You expect us to believe you've only been a shifter for five days? The way you shift, and use your power is quite remarkable for a five day old. Most shifters would have passed out after shifting back so soon." His tone told me he didn't believe a word I said "Buddy, you have no idea. It seems everyday is another test." I pushed my way past the crowd. Once out in the hall my friends surrounded me. Travis was grinning from ear to ear "That was scary as hell, and Awesome at the same time. I knew you'd fix everything. My god you have to do that Roar for Halloween!" The girls were gushing about now being the most popular people here. I was definitely in-crowd material, and they were my friends, so they were in-crowd too, now. I snorted at that, and looked at Peter. "You said you were a sweet lizard." "I am a very sweet lizard, dragons are just big lizards right?" I gave him a hopeful smile, and got a very small smile in return. I reached for him and he jerked away from me. My hand fell, before we could discuss it further we were interrupted. One of Javier's guards was sent to fetch me.

Back in the room again, and folks were staring at me. "Take a picture it'll last longer! Jeez people you act like you've never seen a Dragon before." Javier kindly said "We haven't, there is no such thing as Dragon shifters." My self control was failing, I get pretty snarky when I get defensive "Well, now you have." Eyebrows went up into hairlines around the room. Gage turned to Christian and asked "Is she always like this?" Christian replied "I've only known her for a few days, but I believe so." Gage chuckled "It's no wonder you advised us to pay this debt." Gage gave me a smile and a wink at that. That deflated my anger some. Christian had a brain like an Elephant, he asked me "You said you were shot at least thirty times, yet you don't seem to be hurt or have any blood on you for that matter. Care to explain?" "Uh" Curious faces were waiting for my answer "NOPE!"

Max chimed in "Tell us anyway, I want to know how you were able to cover me and my brother and not acquire any damage." My eyeballs were bouncing around the room at everyone as they waited expectantly. "Too bad, a girl needs to have some secrets." Christian was eyeing me very hard, hard enough to make me damned uncomfortable. There just weren't words for the look on his face.

David pushed to get the proceedings moving again. "How are we going to get out, if there are snipers outside waiting for us?" Whew! I owe the man a cookie for deflecting attention away from me. Everyone started asking questions at the same time. Since nobody could hear answers or questions of anybody else, I put my fingers in my mouth and blew a very loud ear piercing whistle. Everyone shut up at that, and looked at me. "Those are Marcus's snipers out there I'm sure of it." Max stated "Marcus was just here, of course you smelled Lion." "No, Max I smelled Lion on the breeze," I had a confused look on my face and mumbled "which was weird," I looked back at the room "not just in the doorway and for your information I have damn good eyesight. I saw them too." Christian asked "Your positive it is the Lions?" "Yes, I know Alex, and Brett. I've unfortunately met them before. I recognized them out there along with another Lion I haven't met."

Christian walked over to a wall and pushed down on one of the wood panels. A section of wall about five feet long and four feet high flipped over with a detailed map of the block on it. It showed the whole strip center, the parking areas out front and back, the apartment complex back on the left side of the center, and a neighborhood on the right. It was very precise.

He held out a dry erase marker to me and said "Show us were they are positioned" I walked up, took the marker from his hands and drew three big X's on the map. "Alex is on the third floor in an apartment. I figure he has a pretty good angle shot to anywhere in the parking lot from there. Brett is in a tree at the far right corner, again open territory for a good shot. The Lion I don't know is perched on a rooftop almost directly across from the double doors. He can see right into and down the hall." Christian looked to me and said "Go invisible to the doors, there is a door cover like what you'd find over a small shop. Pull it down and lock it. That will prevent them from seeing inside." David said "That will also ensure us staying here. We'll be trapped."

Sebastian began snapping his fingers, had a very thoughtful look on his face, and started slowly shaking his head and quietly said "Maybe not" everyone turned to him at that. You could almost see the wheels turning in his head. Javier asked "You have an idea?" Sebastian gave a slow smile and replied "I just might, but we will definitely need that door covered so no one is the wiser." He looked at me, I rolled my eyes, huffed out loud and left.

It really was like a small garage door, with a chain on the side and everything. As soon as I started pulling the chain the metal door started unrolling out of it's case at the ceiling and bullet holes began redecorating the door.

I pulled on the chain as fast as the thing would go. Then locked it in place. Turning to go back to the conference room, the new silver décor had me stopped in my tracks. The walls were now sporting holes that looked like they were bleeding silver, it was really spooky.

Sebastian came out of the conference room first, with Christian and everyone else on their heels. They saw what I was looking at, then turned and walked away. No one wanted to look at the bleeding holes. I caught Travis, the RC twins, and Peter, "You guys should go downstairs, it's safer there." They all got good looks at the bleeding wall and gave wide eyed nods. I ushered them into the elevator and waited until it closed, then followed the rest of the procession down the hall.

We went through the kitchen of "The Blood Sport" and I got a good look at the customer side. TV's were mounted all along the top of the room. The dining area was divided into different sections with different sports memorabilia and there was a bar in the middle of the room that customers could get access to drinks from both sides. Peanut shells, and crushed popcorn kernels littered the floor. On one side were dart boards and pool tables. It looked like a fun place to hang out. We walked through a set of swinging double doors with small windows at the top, down another freaking hall and into a store room.

It was big enough to hold a ton of supplies, there were pallets of napkins, different types of beer (foreign and domestic) huge burlap bags of peanuts, pretzels and all kinds of stuff for the kitchen. When we got to the end of the isle we were on, we all stopped. Sebastian pointed to a dock door and said "That door has a ramp for the forklift to exit out of and take trash to the dumpsters, all we need to do is move the pallets blocking the door, and have Casey drive your vehicles inside. I believe all of your vehicles are armored, yes?" Everyone nodded and mumbled their affirmatives. He asked "Who has experience with a forklift?" I'll be damned if everyone looked to everyone else waiting for someone to speak up.

I said "You've got to be fucking kidding me. All the men in this room and none of you know how to operate a lift?" I was the only woman here, and apparently the only one with an inkling of what to do. Rubbing my eyes, and shaking my head, I started moving forward then Gage asked "You know how to drive that thing?" I just looked at him and said "I've seen it done a time or two." That was all there was to say. Thirteen years as a truck driver ensured I've been on a lot of docks, counted a lot of freight, and used a motorized pallet jack more than once. I've actually operated a forklift about three times, which doesn't make me good at it, but I had a good idea how to do it, and having a bigger title than a man (woman) means I can do anything.

Once on board with my seatbelt fastened, like your supposed to, a quick look at the small dash was all it took to locate the on button. It fired right up. The evil grin on my face as I looked over our little crowd must have been priceless "You'd better back up boys, this may not be very pretty, but it will be effective!" They all moved back away from the area as I started playing with the controls for the forks. Familiarizing myself with the up and down, and the tilt only took a minute. I actually knew how to make it go forward and backward, that was easy. The lift was compact and easy to turn and maneuver. The forks slid into the holes built into the bottom of the pallet, pull a lever and the pallet tilts back. Lift it up off the floor about six inches, then all you have to do is drive. I took the pallet to the far side of the store room and set it down, then I repeated the process eleven more times. All the pallets were double stacked, meaning one on top of another. They were wobbly, but they moved. When I was done I was graced with a standing ovation from the group. Since we were in a store room and there was no place to sit, it had to be standing. Gage was smiling and placed a hand on Christian's shoulder. "She is a very handy asset to have, would you be willing to loan her out? She seems to be knowledgeable with a great many things." Christian replied "You should speak to her agent if you wish her services." Max asked "Who would that be?" Christian smiled at them all and said "She is her own agent." I laughed at that, the looks on their faces were just too funny. We needed to get this show moving. "Okay people, first does anyone here have a Limo? Cause a car will fit right in here. But a Limo will only fit about three fourths of the way in here." Gage held up his hand "We have a Limo." Somehow out of all the people here, he would be the one with a limo. "Okay, I'll back it in and your driver can climb through the privacy window from the back to the front." Gage nodded turned to one of his guards and held out his hand. The keys were turned over to him, then to me.

I took a deep breath, went invisible and slipped out the driver check in door. I ran top speed to the middle of the parking area and pushed the alarm button on the keychain. I'm sure that got everyone's attention, I opened the door and climbed in. As soon as the door was shut bullets began pelting the Limo. What was it with these people? Was there a bullet sale somewhere? Wasn't there some kind of limit for being shot at? Wasn't that liquid silver mercury stuff expensive?

No holes appeared in the hood, which meant the armor plating must be some really good shit. Think they'd mind the new silver polka dot paint job? It was kind of funny. Out of the parking spot and to the dock door, then turn around and back up the ramp, simple right? I was almost to the door when it began to open up just enough for me to drive under. Bullets were still being fired, at the Limo, the door, and the building. The car was about three fourths of the way inside when I put it in park, left it running and got out. Once inside Gage handed me a business card with a smile and said "Call me, we'll do lunch, talk business, maybe come to an arrangement." I couldn't help but smile back at him, he was a hottie after all. The Leopards climbed into the Limo and left.

The garage door went down right behind them, I turned to the group raised my eyebrows and asked "Who's next?" Javier approached me with his keys in his hand and handed them to me. His car was also graced with the new fancy spring color paint job. Once I was all the way back into the store room, he shook his head and mumbled. "Chinga tu madre', I'm going to teach those Gato's a lesson." The regular sized cars would completely fit inside and the garage door could be shut while they casually got in. Everybody there made sure a business card got into my hands. Some wanting to hire me for my services, others, I'm not so sure about. I wasn't sure if that was something I would like to do, but we'll see. Max was the last to go. After his car was inside and the door was shut, he came over to me "I owe you a great deal, you saved my brother's life, if you ever need anything no matter how big or how small, call me." He handed me his card and Matt came over and gave me a small hug. He felt kind of stiff like he didn't really want to hug me "I owe you a life debt, since you're a new shifter, I'll let Travis explain what that means. I need to take care of a few things, then I'll be in touch. Thank you." He kissed me on the cheek then turned and got into the car. Sebastian raised the garage door and they left too.

Chapter 15

Christian, Sebastian and I walked back to his office, but something was missing. No, not something per se but someone. "Hey, where's Peyton?" Both men looked at each other then turned their faces forward again. The slight tingle in my head was going off, letting me know a telepathic communication was going on. So I tuned in. *"Peyton, where are you?" "I'm on my way." "I asked where you were. Tell me."* The tingles stopped as Peyton rounded a corner and said "I'm right here, General" Hmmm. General? Definitely something to inquire about.

Christian grabbed him by the throat and pinned him to the wall like a bug. "I'll not ask again." The unspoken threat was crystal clear. Peyton didn't look very happy "Several of the others have concerns about the situation. They wonder if it will be safe to go outside tonight or tomorrow. They wanted to know if they should call in for work or not. I was just trying to reassure them." He spoke like a man who was having his windpipe crushed. Christian dropped his hand from Peyton's throat, and

Peyton nearly landed on his ass. "And what pray tell did you tell them?" Peyton cleared his throat a few times and regained his composure. "I told them to trust that you knew what you were doing and would keep us out of harms way." Oooo talk about a brown noser, I thought that was a very good "Cover Your Ass" speech. Apparently Christian did too.

He nodded and ordered "Lock down the building, no one goes in or out until I say so." In a blur Peyton was gone and we continued or walk towards Christian's office. "Casey, you may take care of your belongings in the conference room at this time." "Huh? Oh! Yeah, I forgot. Umm is there a secure place I can have the C-4 and detonators put?" "Tell Peter to code your "EL" card to Vault room 4, the password is Taipei, like the city." We split up at the turn for the elevator. -Beep beep- "Hey Peter?" I wasn't sure he would answer -beep beep- "Yyes?" -beep beep- "Uh where are you?" -beep beep- "We're in the lair." I went around the elevator to my "lair". I walked in and looked at Travis, crossed my arms over my chest and said "I still need to kick your ass for that. I saw ya'll get into the elevator to go down stairs. What happened?" Travis answered "We decided to come in here and wait." He grinned at me, I couldn't help but grin back, his grin was infectious.

Then my grin changed and so did the look on Travis's face. "Stand up, and take your licks like a man." He was unsure now, tension in the room spiked up. The girls scooted closer to Peter as Travis slowly walked closer to me. He gave a sad, hopeful smile and asked "Is it gonna hurt really bad?" I had a very cold look in my eyes and said "Well, that depends on how much you fight." His face visibly paled, he squeezed his eyes shut, took a deep breath and prepared himself for the worst. "Okay, hit me I'm ready." "Turn around" He did, I looked at the girls and Peter "I'll need your help, please come here." My voice was as cold as my eyes, the girls were scared, so was Peter. I could smell it. Randy asked in a quiet shaky breath "You really are mad at the room name aren't you?" I looked at her and she turned her eyes away. "Yes, I am." Travis gulped. "Travis, lay down on the floor, on your back." He was wide eyed but he did it, no questions asked. I looked to the others "Randy, hold his left arm away from his body and pin it to the floor. Candy, cover the right arm. Pete, pin his ankles down. I don't want him to be able to move." When they had him pinned down, I straddled him and ripped his shirt down the middle, exposing his belly and sides. Then I dropped down on top of him and tickled him until he pissed his pants.

Did you know that "Relief" had a smell? I didn't until I started tickling Travis, then everyone else joined in to help punish him. It was a lot of fun. Once my "piss your pants" mission was successful, we let him up to shower and change. Everyone was relieved I didn't kill him. Randy was laughing so hard she was crying, it sounded like one of those hysterical relief laughs. She looked at me as she wiped tears from her face and said "Oh my God! I thought you were gonna kill him right here in front of us and make us help you. I can't believe you made him pee is pants!" She reached for me and pulled me into a tight hug, then Candy enclosed me on the other side. I was a Casey sandwich. "I understand now, why you were mad. You wanted to keep it a secret didn't you?" I nodded, Candy jumped in "You really are our friend aren't you? Pete said that *you* said you wouldn't hurt him, hurt Pete I mean." I nodded so she'd continue "You wouldn't really hurt any of us would you?"

I gave a small smile and said "Weeelll, my arm reflexes might twitch once in a while, and I might accidentally smack someone upside the back of their heads. Sometimes my arm has Tourette's syndrome and it just kind of does what it wants to." We all giggled at that. I pulled myself out of their arms and scooted over to Pete. I gave him a shoulder bump and a hopeful smile "Hey, are you still upset with me?" "You lied to me." "Well, I might have exaggerated the truth a bit, I didn't want you to freak out. I didn't want to scare you. When you told me you were glad I wasn't a big predator *because* they scare you, I had hoped you would never find out. I like you Pete, I think of you as my friend. Tell me how I can make it up to you." He glanced at me then smiled "I could use a little more groveling maybe some sucking up. A nice meatloaf perhaps." The girls busted out laughing, I had to hand it to him he got me good. "Well, we'll work on the groveling but right now I need help from all of you, if your willing?" they all nodded "Good, Pete I need my "EL" card coded for Vault 4." he froze "Wwwhat? Wwwhy?" Oh hell! "I'm saving the bombs for a friend of mine and I need a safe place to put them. Christian told me to tell you. He gave me the password too." He reached out and clamped a hand over my mouth, nodded at me and said "Let's go to my office."

Once we were in his office I sat down in a chair, and he took his seat behind the desk and ran his fingers through his hair. "I know the password, but you have to confirm it and I'll need your elevator card." I was wondering what an "EL" card was, now I know. I handed it to him and said "The password is Taipei." "Jesus, he really did give it to you." He was stunned and breathing heavy as he coded my card, then handed it back to me. We went back to the Lair collected the gang and headed for conference room one. I wanted everyone to know what we were doing and that it was safe. "Okay, gang, listen up! First I want you to know this is perfectly safe, we are going to take the C-4, and the detonators to a safe room." Randy gasped and clutched her chest "Are you sure they're safe?" I motioned for them to follow me over to one of the bags and opened it up exposing the C-4. "Just think of it as big blocks of clay. Like it is now, that is pretty much all it is. The detonators are separated into other bags, so they aren't together." I pointed to a bag about three feet away. "They have to be joined together and then turned on before they'll work. And we're not gonna do that. I'm not a bomb expert, but I do know that much." The girls and Travis took the bags with the C-4, Peter and I grabbed the bags with the detonators. Peter led the way to vault number four and we followed.

When we got there, I was a bit surprised. There was an alcove about six feet square in front of the door to the vault, complete with security cameras, and we were on the lowest floor of the center. The "private" area. Peter gestured for me to used my "EL" card on the fancy lock, then he walked up and typed in a secret code. A whooshing sound came from the door, It was like a bank vault. The door was about two feet thick, with a big handle on the front. We loaded the stuff inside, locked it up and quickly left the area.

We headed back to the conference room and grabbed the bags of money. I was trying to decide what to do with it when Travis said "This doesn't smell like the bombs, it smells like money." I couldn't help myself "Your observation skills are working in top notch form today. Let's put this in the vault too, that way it's safe." So back to the vault we went. Once the money was safely tucked inside I sent everyone but Pete, on their way. Stopping him from following, we waited in the alcove until we couldn't hear them anymore, then I turned to Pete. "Who all has access to this vault?" "Uh, well, you do, and of course so does Christian and Peyton."

"Can we change the pass code so no one has access to this vault but me?" "Why would you want to do that?"

"Well, I'd feel better for one, that's my money in there, and no offense to anybody, but since there are bombs in there, I'd sleep better knowing I'm the only one who would have access to them." He thought about it a few seconds and said "Well, I guess it will be alright." He turned to the control panel and typed in a code, then had to re-type it "Okay type in whatever code you want." "Does it have to be any certain number of digits?" "Well, at least six if you can, it's harder to break the code the more random, and the more digits." I nodded, I knew that, I opted for old truck numbers of mine and my friends, so I leaned in close so no one would see and I punched in...

775	(for my old truck number,)
1967	(for one of my best friend's truck number,)
1845	(for another of my old truck numbers, and)
73249	(for my other best friend's truck number.)

It was a long code, but one I'd remember, Truck drivers are a weird breed. We remember stupid things like truck numbers, and how far it is from one place to the next. Exactly what mile marker the good truck stops are at and in what state on which freeway. I had to type my code in twice too, then the panel beeped at us and Pete confirmed it was locked.

"Oh, I have pics for you for my son's I.D." I had them on my phone. "Tell me where to forward them." He did.

"Let's get some grub." Slinging an arm over his shoulder, we walked back to the "Lair".

The girls were setting out what they wanted for dinner. I'd have to cook it though, man can these people eat! But oddly enough they weren't very good cooks. I also took advantage of the time I had, and started asking Travis questions. "Question, why did Peyton refer to Christian as General?" Travis replied "because he is one." "Huh?" Travis took a martyred breath and explained "I forget you're new to things in the super natural community. You just fit right in here so well. There are very few things Vampires respect, Rank is one of them. Most vampires are at least twenty five years old, they've seen war, Hell, most have been in wars, or battles throughout time. So, way back in the day, some old head honcho powerful Vamp decided he was a General. As countries were discovered, new Generals popped up. Now it's a regulated Vampire Hierarchy. Take the U.S. for example, one country so one General, but it's divided into three sections. From the New Mexico/ Texas state line straight north is one divider. That would be known as the west coast region. The next divider line is Mobile, Alabama. Just imagine an invisible line from there going north too, but it's a little crooked. Chicago falls in to the central region. Anyway everything east of there is the ???"

"Yeah yeah, lemme guess, the east coast region?"

He laughed "You catch on quick grasshopper." "That doesn't explain about the General thing." "Patients girl, I'm getting there. Now here's the confusing part, but I'll try to keep it simple. Every town or city has a vampire that basically rules all the vampires that live in that area, they are called Majors, every state has a head vamp like a governor that all the Majors report to, they are called Colonels, then every region has a head vamp called Lt. Colonels. Christian basically deals with the

Lt. Colonels and they handle land disputes or what ever and the problems get passed down the line." "So by what you just described it's like a pyramid system, and I'm working with the Big Fang?" He took a bite of his food and nodded, "Yeah your working for the "Big Fang" alright, he's one of the biggest he's a General" Well this was an interesting twist. I thought about that for a few minutes, then I did it again. "Question, what is a life debt? I mean I have a good idea what one is don't get me wrong, but the way Matt said it… gave me Goosebumps."

Everyone stopped in mid-chew, and quit breathing. I can assure you that is not comforting when surrounded by friends. Pete asked, "Matt said he owed you a life debt?" I nodded, "Yeah, why? Your making me nervous here spit it out." They all looked at each other then back at me. Randy and Candy both jumped out of their chairs enfolded me in their arms started jumping up and down and saying things like "Congratulations!" "Oh My God! Your so lucky! He is sooo hot!" "We get to plan the shower!" That was when I snapped "What the Fuck are you girls talking about? A shower?" They didn't even hear me just left the room and their dinner and started making plans, I gave Travis a very pointed look that left no questions. I wanted him to explain. He blew out a long breath and said "Well Crap!" He looked at Pete then me, we were all looking back and forth at each other but no one was talking. "Speak to me, what the hell is going on?" finally he said "There are different types of life debts, for different positions in the pack.

Matt is the leader of the Houston pack. Max rules over all of Texas. Since Matt is a leader of a pack, he has to do several things for a life debt." he started holding up fingers and counting off.

"1. He is supposed to be your guard at all times. Protect you with his life."

Ok that one was a no brainer. Albeit annoying

"2. Since he's a leader who was saved, he has to share all his asset's with you, you now own half of everything he owns."

My jaw had dropped, I was feeling flushed, and a little woozy.

"3. Since he's an unmarried Alfa, he can't sleep with anyone but you. And I mean that both ways. He can't have sex with anyone else either. His girlfriend's gonna flip out."

"Wait! Wait wait wait!" I was waving both hands in the air. "What kind of stupid ass rule is that?" "Well, since you're a female, that's how it works." he shrugged "What if I'd been a male? Would he still have to sleep with me?"

"Nope, then who ever he owed a debt to would be able to pick out a mate for him. Now moving on...

4. He has to take you as a formal mate in front of the pack."

I stopped him again "Are you freaking kidding me? I'm what now? His auxiliary mate? He has a girlfriend! I'm not gonna be a substitute, or second to anyone, this it nucking futs!" I started pacing the floor and mumbling to myself "this can't possibly be happening, it's too fucked up even for me. I have to stop this. I have to…get out of here!" I headed for the door as soon as my hand touched the doorknob Travis closed his hand around mine and stopped me. "We're under lock down, we can't leave. There are snipers outside remember?" "I have to get out of here for a while, I need some air." I was ready to push his butt out of my way. He took a breath and said "Fine, Pete and I will go with you." I started shaking my head "Snipers, remember? I can get out." Travis wouldn't let it drop. "If you go, we go!" I looked at Pete, he stood up and came over by us and nodded to me. Great, just what I need right now babysitters. I shrugged at them "Fine then, let's go." We headed for the exit closest to my Ridgeline. A very big vampire was guarding the door.

Everything about him screamed "Bad Boy", Somehow I could tell he hadn't been a vamp long, he still had a little color to his skin, well, besides the multitude of ink on him. And he just didn't feel that old to me. Somewhere deep down inside me was an inner meter that seemed to register a vamps power. That's the best way to describe it. And he was barely on the meter. He was about six foot two with a bald head and a goatee, brown eyes, and a strong stubborn jaw. He crossed his arms over his chest and stood at the door like we had no chance in hell of getting out. Personally, I was impressed he could cross his arms with all the muscle he had. The closer we got the more tense the vampire got. Travis introduced us "Uh, Hey Harley, these are my friends Pete, and Casey. Are the snipers still out there?"

The Vampire Harley just glared at us. He had been one of the vamps that had been guarding the conference room earlier. Travis and Pete both averted their eyes. Me? I just stared back. He may be a new vamp, but he had the intimidating thing perfected. Did they give Vampire's training classes for that look? I tried to get in his good graces "So, Harley huh? Cool name, how did you get that?" "Do I look like someone who wants to talk to you?" I raised my eyebrows at him "Well, aren't you charming?" He took a step forward to try to intimidate me "You're not getting out this door, so turn around and walk away." I smiled sweetly at him and he flashed fang back at me. "Jeez, you know you could try being a little nicer to people." "I'm only nice at feeding time." His fangs were extended all the way out. "Well, would you mind backing up off of me then? Cause I'm not lunch." He squinted his eyes at me and moved closer until we were a short and curly hair apart. He narrowed his eyes and growled. "Go. Away." Hooboy. "Dude, I've been 5'3 and a half since I was twelve years old. If you think you can intimidate me with your height you've got another thing comin'." I felt a tingle while we stood there. *"Christian, there are people here at my post wanting out."* Christian replied *"Tell them NO."* *"I did, they wont leave."* *"Convince them"* Then the tingles stopped. I held up my hand before he could "Convince us" and said "Whoa there big guy, don't even try it. Not with me, I'll clear it with Christian myself." I got my own mental conversation on then, and made sure Harley was in the loop, so he could hear *"Christian, me, Pete, and Travis are going out for a while, tell your Goon to let us out, or you'll be one Goon short."* I was looking Harley in the eye and had an evil smile on my face. Christian didn't respond right away, he made us wait a minute. *"Let them out."* That's all he said. Harley squinted his eyes at us, scrunched up his face in a mocking manner and then gave us a saccharine sweet smile. He unlocked the door and said "Have fun playing bullet catcher." I turned to the guys and motioned for them to wait a minute, the area needed to be checked out before anyone went outside.

Being invisible is becoming a natural thing for me. Maybe I could just stay that way and live in the shadows. Poking my head out the door had my nerves on edge, I didn't see, smell or hear anything unusual. Moving outside to get a better look, I made a good sweep of the area with every sense I had, and still saw nada. Nothing smelled out of place, no one was hiding in trees, or anything. Better let Christian know what the forecast is like. I went back inside and sent a message to Christian *"I just went outside, I think they left." "Keep me updated."* I motioned for my guys to come on, and we headed for my Ridgeline. So far so good.

Chapter 16

Pulling out of the parking lot had us all antsy, waiting for bullets to come flying at you will do that. My poor Ridgeline wasn't bullet proof. Once on the loop, the tension in the truck lessened. "So where are we going? It's still dark." Travis asked. "Wherever the truck takes us." A serious case of cabin fever had developed after all the information I was just dealt, and the road was calling my name. "I just need to think and driving helps to calm me down. Maybe we'll go to Galveston, feed the seagulls or walk along the wall." Mostly I just wanted to drive, where we went just didn't matter.

As a kid, sometimes my mom and I would just get in the car and drive to the small towns and see what they had going on. When we cleared the town, and by that I mean all hysterical markers (That's what my grandma called them) points of interest, museums, and antique shops were thoroughly examined, we came back home. Usually, it was just a weekend thing. There was a few places I'd like to go back to, and I remembered one of them had a big Gumbo cook off. A last minute decision had me taking the exit for highway fifty nine too fast. The truck handled it with ease, maybe I should get some big gumball mudders, and a lift kit, maybe some flames.

Horns started blaring, and the sound of crunching metal had me checking the rearview, and the guys spinning in their seats. Crap! I hoped I didn't cause an accident with my lane change maneuver. We all saw the same thing at the same time. Three black SUV's with dark tinted windows, followed us, only two were still in pursuit. One of them was playing kissy face with the wall. That had to hurt! Pete was pale when he turned back around "Ththose ttrucks have Gggovernment ppplates on them." Damn! Can't a girl get a break? I just wanted to drive for cripes sake! A leisurely road trip. If it wasn't for bad luck, I wouldn't have any luck at all. How the hell had they found me?

The remaining SUV's were catching back up to us, fast, apparently they were on a mission, and apparently it was me. Kudos's to the Honda corporation on this motor, pushing the gas pedal to the floor, the Ridgeline felt like it took a breath and then jumped forward. It may have been a six banger, but she acted like she had an Interceptor under the hood. It's a good thing I was good at Frogger as a kid, because we were the frog right now. Left around this car, right around that car, and another quick exit. This is my town, Dammit! My stomping grounds, did they think to try to catch me here? Well, if they were working with the local cops they could. You can't outrun a radio, but so far no extra cops, or road blocks. Hmmm. That left only a few possible suspects…

1. One branch from the alphabet soup gang. (CIA, FBI etc.)
2. Military, but they'd use different vehicles right?
3. Mercenaries, but they'd be shooting at us right?
4. A privately funded group maybe?

Hell, there were too many questions in my head and not enough answers. Just too many possibilities. The government tags had me worried. Turning into China town was going to be fun. I delivered here a few times and knew of a place we could go, if we could get to it.

The street was lined with small strip centers, but they were turned sideways. Pull into a driveway and your facing store fronts on both sides. It always reminded me of a big comb, with the teeth being the buildings. The traffic wasn't helping much, too early in the morning. I turned a corner and lost them for about five seconds. That's all I needed, I hit a driveway and pulled to the end of the building, where there was a big dirt lot for big trucks to turn around in. Not every building had that nice feature. Some were dead ends, unless you'd been back here, you wouldn't even know it existed.

The ground had ruts in it, from big trucks turning around when the ground was wet. Travis was holding on to the "Oh Shit" bar to stay in his seat and Pete had one hand braced against the door, and one on the roof.

Maybe I should have a roll cages installed. Just a thought. We hit the grassy part of the lot then went down into a very wide ditch, and up an embankment for a set of railroad tracks. Well, at least I had a new suspension. I wonder if Honda tested their trucks for getaways. Well, we were testing it now.

As soon as we were on the railroad tracks, someone fired at us. Someone in the SUV must have seen us turn to come back here.

"Uh, Casey, problem ahead." The tracks were really rough and we were bouncing more now than when we were in the dirt. "I see it." Never a dull moment, or a break. Can you guess what was coming down the tracks? Right for us? There was no way to see out of the rearview mirror with all the bouncing, it was impossible. When I was up, it was down and vice versa. "Pete, can you see how close they are?" My teeth felt like they were about to rattle out of my head. "I think their closing on us, it's hard to tell." We were racing the train to the closest intersection, it was gonna be close. Shots fired at us again and the train was blaring it's horn, with a repetitive intensity. A soft prayer made it's way to my ears from Travis. I eased my foot off the gas, so the SUV's could get a little closer. "What the hell are you doing?" Travis was as pale as a sheet

"Look up ahead." "Yeah I see it! We're gonna crash!" Travis was screaming from fright. Totally understandable, my adrenaline was pumping through my veins so fast, it felt like there wasn't any blood left, just pure adrenaline. Bullets hit the back of the truck, and the boys ducked down. I could hear the bells of the warning lights and see the cross arms were going down. We hit the intersection at the same time as the train, but we were smaller, faster and more maneuverable. There was at least four feet between us and the cattle guard of the engine when I drove through the cross arm and broke it in half. As soon as we were on solid smooth street again, I came to a screeching halt and looked back for the SUV's.

They hadn't made the intersection, and had to peel off the tracks.

The embankment here by the intersection was steeper than where we all got on this ride. They didn't drive down at the right angle, well one didn't anyway. The SUV we could see had flipped. Men were crawling out of the windows. Since they were okay, I hit the gas and got us the hell out of there.

Five minutes after our little fiasco, we found a Denny's and pulled in. Mandatory bathroom breaks for everyone. Personally I thought a crow bar was going to be needed to get the seat out of my puckered butt. We met back up outside and passed around hugs, it is a very nice feeling to know your alive, and the hugs were definitely a must have. As the adrenaline rushes were wearing off, we all inspected my truck. My truck driver side came out then with flair and fury "Damn those cock suckers! Look at my new truck!" Pete came over and felt the holes in the tailgate, and gave a low whistle "Casey, I don't smell any silver or anything weird." nodding to him "That's good at least." Travis asked, "Now what?"

"Now? Well uh, hmm" My mind was turning over ideas of what needed to be done. Some Government agency knew what I drove now. Would I have to ditch it? Scrap my new truck? Get if fixed? Now would be a good time for some of that armored plating. "Get in, I know where were going."

Explaining my thoughts to them, the guys got all excited. "Have you ever been to the local car shows?" The guys both shook their heads in confusion "Well, it's almost like the brotha's compete with the Vato's. Those guys can do all kinds of shit to a vehicle. Hydraulics, boom boom so loud you wouldn't hear a train if it was right on top of you." They didn't like my analogy "And I know where one of their shops are, we'll just go and hang out there til they open." Between the three of us, we had a really good list of stuff to do to the Ridgeline, by the time we pulled into the parking lot.. It was also a very much needed distraction from the last half hour. Coming up with ideas got us calmed down and excited in a good way.

The shop used to be a gas station, but was now an automotive rebuild shop. The pumps had been removed from the ground, and a three stall metal building had been added to the side of a small office. The ground was stained with old oil, and the side of the parking lot was lined with old tires, like they were using them as a Bridgestone Radial fence. A hand painted wooden sign was hung at the top of the tin building. It read "Casa de El Culebra" House of snakes, homey.

Hispanic men were bringing out beach and lawn chairs to sit in out front. A light smell of burning plastic wafted through the truck, nerves. Travis asked "Did you know this was one of Javier's places?" "Really?" he nodded. "That could be useful as hell." We got out and walked towards the office, but didn't make it.

A Hispanic male about five foot eight, and lanky walked over to us. His face was round giving the illusion he was chubby, he had black hair cut short in to a buzz, and eyes so dark brown they were almost black. A snake tattoo wound around his shoulders and neck. He eyed Travis, and Peter, then looked at me. "Hi, I need some work done to my truck, are you guys real busy today?" He didn't look impressed with us at all "No. We're closed, and no perro's allowed here. Vamoose, go on get out of here." The guys jumped back into the truck, no questions asked, I was insulted. "Hey, show a little respect man, you don't have to scare them. What's your problemo?" "Don' even try it Weda, you need to leave too." "Uh huh, okay, what's your name?" "You don' need my nobre' jus' leave" "Okay, will you tell me where else I can go to get work done, since you won't do it?" "No" He turned then and started to walk away. I'm not usually one to name drop but this time I made an exception. The beaner had pissed me off! "Hey Travis?" He rolled down the window, poked his head out and very nervously said "Yes?" "Can I use your phone to call Javier, he's gonna want to know about this." Travis's eyes got very wide. The Hispanic male called out to me at that. "Weda! What have the dogs been telling you? Huh? I'm sure their pack alpha would want to know they've been talking to humans about us." My smile would have melted butter "They haven't been talking to anyone, Javier owes me. I just meant to do a little collecting." His face clearly said he didn't believe me "Come with me weda." His tone was arrogant.

We both went inside to his office, he picked up the phone and dialed a number. A man answered on the third ring. "Si'?" "Carlos, es Enrique, que paso?" "Nada, what you want?" "There's a weda aqui says she knows Javier and he owes her." Ah speaker phones were a great invention, Enrique had a very smug look on his face "uno momento" finally Javier came on the line "Enrique explain" before he could say anything I opened my mouth "Hello Javier, it's Casey, I had a little trouble with some bullet holes in my new truck. I wanted to get it armored like ya'lls cars, and some other work done to it. I'll pay for it, that's not a problem, but I need someone to do the work and your boy here is being an ass to me and my friends. Since he has made it perfectly clear he doesn't want me or my money here, would you be able to refer me to someone who can do the work?" Yeah I know, a little condescending, but a girl works with what she's got. A soft hiss came over the phone line. "Enrique, pick up the phone." Enrique got an earful then, I can speak some Tex Mex, which is half Spanish and half English. The yelling he was getting was all in Spanish.

I could pick out a few choice words here and there, you always learn the bad words first and there seemed to be a lot of them coming through the phone. He placed the receiver in the cradle, looked at me and said "Drive your truck into the bay and tell us what you want." He didn't look pleased at all.

He didn't smile at me or anything. -beep beep- "Travis, pull it inside please." Travis drove my truck into a bay, and I turned to Enrique "You might want to write this down." "I'll remember jus' tell me." "Okay, I want armored plating and bullet proof windows, a lift kit and oversized wheels. Solid rubber tires, I don't want any blowouts. Off road shocks, three or five point seat belt hook ups, brush guard, roll cage, and some engine modifications if possible. Please make sure my gas tank is completely protected, I don't want to blow up either. If you can, check my tranny, it just got a really good work out. I want a new paint job, no glitter, or Florissant colors, oh and just one more thing. Make it a hard top convertible."

Enrique raised one eyebrow to me and asked "Is there anything else you'd like, maybe some rockets that come out of the head lights, or ejection seats?" The sarcastic toad. With a very serious look and tone I nodded "Okay add that in too, while your at it, slap me some flame throwers on the back okay? Oh and hook up some NOS to my six banger too would ya?" He smiled at me then and shook his head. He wasn't the only one who could be sarcastic. Truck drivers are fonts of sarcasm. "It'll take us a while to do all the modifications to your little truck." "How long?" "I'd say eh, maybe a week."

Travis and Pete got out of the truck and came to stand by us. "Is there a car lot around here where I can buy a good cheap car until you fix my truck?" "A block up is one." He nodded up the street, then walked over to the truck, rubbed his hands gently over the bullet holes in my tailgate, and gave a low whistle, and shook his head. I guess when guys fondle bullet holes the whistle just comes out. "Okay thanks, I just need to get something out of the trunk first." I climbed into the bed of my Ridgeline, opened the hidey hole lid and pulled out the duffle bag that had been stored there. Good thing there was extra money in it.

As the three of us walked down the street we stopped in a Jack in the Box for breakfast. It had been a while since we'd had anything to eat and we hadn't finish our dinner. We found the used car lot. Bright colored flags of red, white, and green waved eagerly in anticipation. The flags were on a white plastic strand that ran from the light poles to the building and back again. Bright colored balloons were taped to some of the wipers on the cars and all of the cars sported plastic static cling Florissant numbers. The year and price of the cars were plastered across the front windshield.

We walked the lot looking for a vehicle big enough to tote our stuff in if we went shopping with the girls again. Then compared those few we liked to cars that had some giddy up and go. Growing up a tomboy I knew a few of the tricks to check and hopefully make sure we didn't drive a lemon off the lot. All the cars were marked "As Is".

A short Hispanic male in a white dress shirt and slacks came out to greet us. He was way to happy, this early in the morning. His hair was a little long to be business cut, and he was thin all over. Middle aged with thin hair on his head and almost feminine features. He introduced himself as Pedro. With an overly exaggerated smile on his face he asked "Which car would you like to see? They are all very fine cars, I promise!"   yeah riiiight. We'll see. "Um, how about that one." I pointed to a "Hello Officer!" red 1975 Oldsmobile Delta 88 convertible. There was real glass in the back window! It had white interior and a white top. The car was a tank, a land yacht! Perfect!

Pedro popped the hood and I started inspecting the 350 Rocket under the hood. Cars may be a "Guy" thing but when I saw the big gas guzzler with the four barrel Holly, I just cooed. If I could have sprouted a woody I would have. The engine was clean, no saw dust in the oil cap or the radiator cap. No oil leaks, nothing strange in the gas cap, then the moment of truth came and I told Travis to "Fire this baby up!" My head was under the hood, so I could listen to the motor. It purred like the well oiled machine it was meant to be. No pings, or misses in the motor. I reached under the Holly carburetor and pulled on the gas lever. It went vroom vroom. Music. Pedro saw the excitement on my face "She's a classic, a real beauty. And the price is good!" Ha! The price was fifty five hundred dollars! I'm not stupid or gullible. It was a sweet ride, but he liked it more than I did. Like he said, it was a classic. A nice way of saying "it's old."

Motioning to Travis to kill the car I turned to Pedro. "I'll give you two grand cash, and not a penny more." he shook his head "I can't let it go for anything less than five thousand." I shrugged "Okay, In this day and age of fuel efficient cars, and everyone wanting to be "Green" do you really think this gas guzzler's gonna sell for that kind of money? How long has it been on this lot?" He thought for a few minutes, gave a deep breath then said "Hold on a minute while I talk to the boss. Maybe she will come down on the price a little bit more." "Tell the boss I have cash" He nodded then left us. The back seat was big enough, I could lay down in it and stretch out completely.

Pedro motioned for us to come inside, so we did. He introduced us to a woman named Elizabeta. She was about five foot five, looked like a grandmother, and she smelled like apple pie and tamales. "Pedro says you have cash for the olds?" My face was a blank mask when I replied "Yes" "Okay, three thousand" "I'm not some dumb shmuck, the blue book value of that car is less than two grand, I'm offering more than it's worth now." Opening the bag of money I pulled out and counted two thousand dollars and held it out in front of her. The choice was hers. She could take it or leave it. She watched me with calculating eyes nodded and said "SOLD!" she snatched the money out of my hands and started giving Pedro orders to do the paperwork and get me the title. An "End Zone" dance almost over took me. We rode with the top down and cruised back to H.Q. The excitement level for the day had been reached and breached. It was nap time.

Chapter 17

How had they found me? And who were they? What Government branch? These thoughts filled my mind when I woke up sandwiched between two wolves. Pete had stayed the night with me and Travis. This was kind of cozy. We were all tangled together, like a big knot. We reluctantly crawled out of bed. The guys headed back to their rooms to get dressed. I put on a new matching pink undies and bra set, faux leather pants and top, then headed to my Lair for breakfast. Today was definitely a leather day, even if it wasn't real leather. My head ached from stress, and my mood was foul. Not being able to get out and drive earlier had upset me more than anything else had so far. Something that always calmed me down was gone, like taking away my favorite toy. Travis made us sausage and biscuits for breakfast, but my stomach just wasn't in it.

    I got a mental knock knock *"Your presence is requested in my office." "on my way"* "Sorry guys gotta go." I gave a tap to my temple so they would know I'd been summoned

"Oh hey Pete, when is the other set of identification gonna be done?" "I should have them tonight." "Ok, Cool. I'll get them later." I felt sick to my stomach, I didn't need this kind of shit right now in my life.

I reached Christian's office and sent him a mental *"I'm here, do you want me to just walk in?"* There was loud arguing coming from the other side of the closed door, someone screamed at the top of her lungs *"Just get in here!"* I opened the door and Max, his brother Matt, five guards, and a woman who was having a conniption fit were all inside. I took a quick look at everyone then took my place at Christian's back. The woman stood up, she had dark auburn hair cut in a pageboy, big green eyes that had thick black smudges around them from where she'd been crying. She reminded me of a raccoon. She had the pale skin of a red head, about five foot nine, and almost model thin. Her features were well defined, mostly because she was so skinny. She pointed a boney, well manicured finger at me and nearly howled. I'm guessing this is the girlfriend.

"YOU! This is all your fault!" Before anyone could react she pulled out a gun and shot at me. What the Hell did I ever do to her? Matt rushed her, and grabbed the gun from her as the guards pinned her to the sofa. Matt turned to me with a look of horror on his face. I just shrugged and swiped a hand across the bullet knocking it on to the floor. "NO, worries" The wolves all looked stunned. They couldn't believe I couldn't be shot. Well not unless I wanted to anyway, like that was ever gonna happen.

Matt, came over to me and ran his hands over me like he owned me already, I was pulling away from him, and the crazy bitch (Yes, pun intended) was trying to pull away from the guards to get to Matt. Max stood up walked over to the woman and slapped the crap out of her. "Paige! That's enough! Control yourself or I will!" Matt turned to watch the spectacle then back to me "I'm sorry about all of this but it is necessary." I gave him the "you've got to be kidding me look" lifted my hand in Paige's direction and asked "Why is this necessary? And why does she look like she wants to boil me oil?" "Didn't you speak with Travis?" "Well, yeah but from what he told me, it's not gonna happen." For some reason that calmed Paige down a little bit. She looked at me then with tears in her eyes and asked "You're not trying to trap him? You don't want him?"

I tried to give a reassuring smile, walked around the desk so I was closer to her and replied "No, I'm not trying to trap him, and I don't know him. So how could I possibly want him?" I turned to Max and Matt, "There has been some confusion here I think." Matt stepped up to me and said "I owe you a life debt, from now on, I am yours to do with as you see fit, until the debt is paid, or we die of natural causes." I was a bit taken back "That's going a bit too far don't you think?" I felt power pushing against my shield and Matt looked me in the eyes and got very serious, and started quoting poetry to me. I didn't think this was the time for that.

"I hunt only for you"

Paige screeched and tried to launch at me and the guards caught her. She was hysterical. Matt went on…

"I protect only you"
"I will claim no other, only you
I give freely my loyalty to only you
I take as my mate only you.
My pack is yours and you are ours.
My blood, my life, my all."

I felt power push at my shield like it was trying to squeeze me to death. I hit my knees trying to breathe past it. Matt held me to him and said "For god's sake drop your shield or it will crush you!" I looked up at him and dropped my shield. My breath was hard and fast, I looked into his beautiful cinnamon flecked brown eyes and wheezed "What did you do to me?" As soon as oxygen hit my brain and it started functioning again, my shields went right back up. "I didn't want there to be any misunderstandings between us. I did what needed to be done." I pushed away from him and stood up. My knees felt like jelly. One of the guards had taken Paige out of the room, after her stunt. I turned to Max. "Whatever he did, undo it."   "I can not." "You said no matter how big or small Max, fix this. I can't be his mate!" My shakes were becoming uncontrollable "Did it ever occur to you people that I might already have a husband? And what about my kids and my family? OH MY GOD! My Mom is gonna skin you alive!" I felt a panic attack coming on, bright spots of light began floating around my vision, like I'd just taken a head shot. Max looked sharply at Christian "You never told us she had a family." Christian shrugged "You didn't ask, doesn't matter either way. I didn't know. She hasn't spoken about her personal life much in the few days I've known her."

My body had had enough, finding my way to Christian's trash can, I dropped to my knees and hurled.

When the dry heaves stopped, I calmly walked out and found a restroom and rinsed out my mouth. Then made my way back to Christians office. I noticed the trash can was outside the door. Max and Matt were questioning Christian about me. "If you have questions about me, then ask me! You might get an answer that way." Matt nodded "Your right, forgive me." He came to me and tried to hold my hand, but I stepped back shaking my head. "What did you do to me Matt?" My voice sounded small, like I just reverted back to being a five year old. "I bound us together." "Didn't it occur to you to ask what I thought about the whole thing?" My finger was moving back and forth between us "How are we supposed to have a relationship if one of us is trapped in it? Do you know how bad I want to beat the hell out of you right now?" "We're bond mates, you can't hurt me." "HA! Wanna bet? So what? Do you expect me to pack up and just move in with you? Play house with you?" "Your choice, you can live with me, or I will move in with you." He couldn't possibly be serious. "You have put yourself in Danger Matt! I'm wanted by the Government, Mercenaries are trying to kill me, I'm trying to help my family and now I have to deal with you!" He splayed his hands in a pleading manor towards me. "We'll solve this together, as a couple." "Your nuts! Certifiably crazy! You don't even know me!" "I have the rest of my life to get to know you. And I will." He was starting to assert his dominance now, power was flowing over me again too, boy was he in for a surprise. Our lips were less than an inch apart when I made my stand "Don't even think about trying to dominate me wolf, I'll yank your beast out of your body, put a collar on your neck and name you fluffy! No one will ever dominate me!"

"I am still pack Alfa, you are considered my second, my mate, but what I say is law!" He growled it at me, pushing his power all over me, trying to make me submit. So I did what any strong willed independent woman would do. "Law this!" My knee came up before he could move, and collided with his nuts. He doubled over but didn't fall, and took several deep breaths before straightening back up. Still growling he said "Never do that again." "Stay far enough away from me and you won't have to worry about it." Max moved between us and raised his hands "Both of you sit down and relax a minute, we need to sort this out. Calmly, like adults." Matt had to follow his brothers orders, since Max ruled the Texas packs, but I didn't have to. Turning to Christian I said "Let me know if *You* need me for anything." At that I walked out. Matt jumped up to try and follow me, so I vanished so he wouldn't be able to see me. This was just too much, too nuts! It was absolutely unbelievable. I am not a piece of meat to be claimed! Yep, definitely a black leather day.

Travis, Pete, and the girls were in the Lair when I opened the door and walked in. "Uh, Casey?" Travis asked "What?" I snapped. He waved his hand in the air in circles at me and I remembered "Oh." becoming visible again in here was fine. These were my friends. My eyes were leaking uncontrollably, I wasn't crying, my emotions were just going every which way, and my body didn't know how to cope with it all. The RC twins came over to me and closed me in a girl hug, took me to the couch and just held me. Candy asked "What's the matter?" My voice sounded very far away when I answered "Matt claimed me there in Christians office, he didn't care how I felt, or about my family. He didn't even ask. It was all about him." "He just took over?" I nodded "What are you gonna do?" This from Pete. My head was shaking back and forth "I don't know, what are my options Travis?" The look on his face said clearly he didn't know either. "I don't have the foggiest idea, if he did claim you though, that makes you our Accalia ." My brows furrowed in confusion "Your Accalia?" " Essentially the male rules, and helps provide for and protects the pack, he's the "Bodolf" and the female rules, nurtures, and protects the pack. The female is the "Accalia" our female Alfa. Usually the Accalia is the one who is supposed to keep the pack stable." I laughed out loud and it wasn't a happy laugh "Yeah riiiight, I'm sooo not qualified for that position! My life is so F.U.B.A.R. right now it's not even funny, and now

I'm supposed to take on the responsibilities of a pack?" He just shrugged, there was no way I'd be able to handle this. "I'm going back to bed, maybe when I wake up this nightmare will be over. If ya'll wanna come with me you can." They knew I needed the support right now, so they all came with me.

We went downstairs and turned down the hall with my room and saw the door open, and Christian standing outside of it. We jumped back around the corner and listened. Christian gave a quick look down the hall and briefly met my eyes before saying. "I do not know where she went or when she'll return, she could be anywhere, the mall, Ireland even a playgirl mansion for all I know." That slick Vampire just gave me permission to go to his other day resting place. I grabbed my friends and herded them out the door as fast as their feet would carry them. Then sent a mental "Thank you" to Christian. *"Sebastian will meet you there."* There were no words for the gratitude I felt at that moment. "Are you guys ready to fly first class?" They all wore expectant faces and watched me shift into a big black Dragon. Travis asked "Do we just climb on?" My big head bobbed up and down.

Chapter 18

Everyone was excited and near to exploding with laughter when we got to Christian's house. They climbed down off my back and I shifted into my regular self. Randy and Candy couldn't quit gawking at me, then at the house. We walked up the steps, and I tried the doorknob. It was unlocked. It shouldn't have been, but we went inside anyway. Once we were all inside and the door was shut several things happened almost simultaneously.

A huge dark haired Vampire stepped out of the salon, turned his body slightly sideways in a fighters stance, brought up his arm and power blew out at us. When I saw him come from the salon, and put up his arm, I put up both of mine. Instinctively to block what ever came at us. I wasn't fast enough. I was hunched over in a tornado wind of power. A loud crash and glass breaking sounded behind me, but I couldn't look back, I was holding the power in place for the moment. Then the power just died like it had been instantly shut off. I looked up and saw a beautiful clear pale yellow wall of power between us and the Vampire. His power was still hitting it, but the wall wasn't moving. I turned to help the others. Pete and Travis were helping Randy up off the floor. The back door was gone and so was Candy.

We rushed out to the backyard and found Candy on top of the door. Blood was everywhere. Several pieces of the stained glass that was in the door window was now sticking up through Candy's body. A big piece pierced her stomach, another through her chest, and a big sliver through the side of her throat.

Randy let out a blood curdling scream. I wish I'd thought to do that. Travis said "If we get her off the glass she may heal it." He didn't look like he believed that anymore than I did. Shifters can heal a lot of damage, but when most of your blood has already flowed out of the body, it could be damn difficult without intervention. My mental S.O.S. to Christian was loud even in my head *"Christian!! We've been attacked! There's a powerful fucking Vampire in your house! Candy is dying HELP US!!"*

I looked at Travis "Okay, put your hand under her hip and shoulder and we'll try to pull her off the glass. On the count of three, ready?" he nodded "One, two, three" We lifted straight up at the same time, but the glass came with her. It had broken off into her body. Jesus Christ. I pulled her into my lap and looked at Travis "Pull out the glass and be careful so it doesn't break." He was wide eyed and crying, we all were. Tears were falling down my face as fast as everyone else's. We were scared, we were watching Candy die right here, in my arms. "Do the chest first Trav." He gripped the glass shard that was sticking an inch out of the front of Candy's chest and pulled it out of her back. I pushed my healing power in at the same time. "Now the neck." Travis didn't question my choice of order. The glass sliver there had gone through and severed her main carotid artery. Blood was pumping out with every heartbeat. As Travis pulled it out, again I pushed in power. Next came the stomach.

The glass was out and I was holding Candy as close as I could. She had very little strength left, but what she had she used to hold onto me. My power flared out of me and into her. I felt the wounds closing and healing. She took a big gasp of air, like she'd been holding her breath to try and hold on while my power healed her. Either way it worked. I pulled back so I could see her face. Now she was crying. Randy, Pete, and Travis all collapsed on top of us. Holding, hugging, petting and crying with relief.

Christian and Sebastian had arrived sometime during the healing. I had been so focused on Candy I never knew when they got there. There wasn't a car in sight but they were there. Christian laid a hand on my shoulder and asked "Casey, is everyone alright?" We all looked up at him and I nodded "Good." He said. My breathing was evening out and the look on my face must have caused Christian concern, he said "Don't do anything rash. I'll take care of this." Through gritted teeth I said. "You won't have to, I'm gonna kill him." I started pushing people of me so I could get up.

My clothes were soaked with Candy's blood. A small whimper escaped my throat when I pulled my shirt away from my body and heard a sticky sucking sound. I turned and started walking towards the steps to the porch. Sebastian came up behind me and wrapped both arms around me and picked me up. Christian said "No! You cannot! Let me handle this." I started kicking and thrashing around in Sebastian's arms like a wild animal. Revenge was the only thing on my mind at the moment. I wanted that Vampire to burn. "Let me go Sebastian, NOW!" I could see right into the house, the Vampire in question was still at the end of the hall watching us. Our eyes met and held. "Let me go Damn it! Let me at him!" The dark haired Vampire was about six foot four and built just like a warrior should be. He had muscles in all the right places, and when he was alive he had an olive complexion. Which kept his skin from being porcelain white. His face looked like it had been carved out of granite.

He was older than Christian and more powerful, my inner meter told me so, but his skin just wasn't as pale as it should have been. Even with my pale yellow wall between us I could just feel his age. You could see the endless centuries in his black eyes. We glared at each other for a few seconds then he said "Control your servant or I will." My jaw dropped and my eyes widened "What?? No the hell he didn't! Let me go Sebastian or your gonna get hurt." "I do not think that is a wise idea." "Okay, you asked for it." My dragon form shot out of me and Sebastian had no choice but to let me go.

Once I was completely shifted I looked down at Sebastian. He was flat on his back between my front legs. In a flash he was gone.

My big head came up to look at the dark haired Vampire, and Christian moved into the doorway between us.

Both of his hands were out in front of him, and he caught my shoulders as I shifted back and tried to push my way in the door. Christian's hand grabbed my face and he turned me so I would look directly at him. "Please Casey, do not do this. I will talk to Ajax." "Talk hell, you ever heard of shoot first ask questions later? I'm out of questions. Move." "No" Power pushed right into me, my shield didn't stop it. A cool calming sensation began to cover my body. My eyes were locked with Christian's and I couldn't look away. He spoke directly into my head then *"Relax, quit acting like a spoiled Qa'Hom! Go back to the center and be with your friends."* My brows furrowed together at what he said and I asked "Did you just call me a titmouse in Klingon?"

As distractions went it was a good one and it worked. I was a Trekky. There are very few things you can say to a true trekky, that we wouldn't understand about the movies. In the early eighties when Star Trek was the shit, all of my friends and I learned Klingon. Mostly so we could cuss in front of the teachers and not get into trouble. It was funny to us.

The current problem I was having was the shock of actually seeing and hearing a centuries old, supposedly refined vampire, using Klingon. Weren't vamps supposed to have some kind of old world charm? Didn't they speak languages that were lost to the world or something? Well, he wasn't gonna call me a titmouse and get away with it. No self respecting trekky would let that slide. "I'll let you handle it for now mu'qaD, but there is another obstacle I need to deal with first, before I can get to the p'taK." Christian's eyebrows shot up now that I had used Klingon, and insulted him, and "Ajax". "What obstacle is that?" "Look at your hallway." Slowly he turned to look down the hall and saw the pale yellow shield there. He turned back to me and asked "What is that?" I shrugged "Uh, something I did. I'm not sure really." He turned back with my hand clasped in his, and pulled me up the hall. I don't think he trusted me. Smart vampire.

Sebastian was at our backs. Both of us raised our empty hand towards the wall of power. Running my fingertips over it felt amazing. A slight warm tingling vibration ran up my arm. Christian dropped his hand away from it and looked at me. "Remove it." My head bobbed up and down "Sure, okay. As soon as I figure out how." I mumbled "Work on this. Sebastian come with me." He turned and started walking for the back door then stopped. "Matt, is on his way here to take you back." Before I could protest they were gone. I turned back around to face my power wall, as Christian and Sebastian walked through the front door.

I placed both hands on the wall of power and tried to visualized it sucking back into me. But nothing happened. I held both hands against the shield and said "Come." It wouldn't go. I rested my forehead against it and very quietly mumbled "Just go back where you belong." I was frustrated and tired. My adrenaline was wearing off and I still wanted to kill me a vamp. The shield wavered and I lifted my head. It started flowing up my hands and arms like pale yellow water until it settled back over the outside of my body. Holy Crap! This was my body shield! No wonder Christian's power hit me like it did, and clamed me down. There had been nothing there to stop it. Next time instead of trying to suck it back into me, I'll try to remember to pull it back ON to me.

Once my shield settled over me, I did a quick check to make sure it would block everything! Then I slowly started walking up the hall towards the salon, and the waiting vampires.

Chapter 19

Sebastian was standing in the doorway to the salon, with his back to the hall, but he heard me approach and half turned towards me. He took a step closer to me and said "Casey, please. If you truly wish us no harm, as you have claimed, then you will remain calm. Ajax doesn't know you. From his point of view, you were the enemy coming to attack him. He just defended himself first." I gave Sebastian an incredulous look. Christian and Ajax had stopped talking and started watching us. Preparing themselves I'm sure for an irate female. "Is that what he said?" I waved my arm at the vamp in question "Cause I'm sure, as an ancient vampire, he was utterly terrified, when five people who were giggling and loud, and not trying to be sneaky in anyway, came up to the door. Oh yeah, I can see it. Laughter as a distraction." I don't think the sarcasm could have been any thicker. I pulled a fake out on Sebastian. I leaned one way and he followed then I whipped around the other side of him.

I stood there five feet from the man I wanted to see burn, in my favorite room. Christian came up to me and flames erupted over my shield. He steeped back. "Don't touch me Christian. Thanks to you I'm still calm, cool and collected." I gave him my most sincere smile. "I can however still think for myself and even though my feelings have been recently altered, again thanks to you, my goals haven't changed." My gaze went to the new Vampire in the room. Ajax. Whatever it was Christian had done to me made me feel warm and fuzzy all over. Almost charitable. "Well Ajax, have you nothing to say, to me or my friends?" His voice was a deep baritone. Like Barry White or James Earl Jones. Like base vibrating through the body.

"I will not apologize for my actions. If that is what you are waiting for, then you will wait along time. And as for you, feel privileged I have even given you my attention. Slaves are beneath me." Here we go again with the slave thing. "I'm not a slave, you antiquated parasite." His arm shot out and he backhanded me. The force of the blow knocked me back through the salon doorway across the hall, and through the banister. Good thing a wall was there to catch me. Neither the hit or the impact hurt me thanks to my protective covering, but I had been jolted. I got up, dusted off the wood splinters from the banister and calmly looked back into the salon. Christian was in front of Ajax talking to him. I'm not sure what he was saying because my head sort of went tunnel vision. My focus was solely on Ajax. I pulled a sai out of my boot, maneuvered it behind my leg, out of sight, and patiently waited.

Christian's power still had me in it's grips. It was like a power shot of valium. Sebastian glanced at me but didn't see the weapon in my hand. A strange sense of vertigo came over me, everything in the room slowed down, then stopped. The vampires looked frozen in place. I could move so it wasn't me. Had I been far enough away that whatever had trapped the vampires, missed me? I leaned forward and looked down the hallway and out the back door. Was someone new on the scene? Candy was in Travis's arms in mid swing just off the porch steps. They were frozen too. My eyeballs bounced around looking for whoever had done this, then settled on Ajax. If someone new was here to cause trouble I'd deal with them after I settled a score.

Very quietly I walked into the salon. I didn't want to attract the attention of whoever had frozen everyone. Getting face to face with Ajax was impossible since Christian was right in front of him. So I moved to stand behind him. Maybe stabbing someone in the back is chickenshit, at the moment I didn't care. I raised my sai when the vertigo hit me again and everyone started moving. At the last second Christian saw the sai, grabbed Ajax and pushed him sideways. My sai slid into Ajax's back but I had missed his heart. Barely, Damn! Maybe I got lucky and nicked it.

Ajax arched his back, turned and hissed at me. The smell of burning Vampire flesh from the silver permeated the air. Small puffs of smoke flowed up Ajax's back and over his shoulders. Now his back was facing the hall and Christian pulled the sai out. Burning his hands in the process. Ajax's hands came up like claws, his eyes glowed red, and he launched himself at me. I vanished, ducked and rolled. Ajax landed on the divan and smashed it. Then he growled out "Only a coward stabs someone in the back. Face me Dragon. You wont be the first Dragon I've killed." I was hovering up by the ceiling now, on a shield platform of sorts. So he couldn't get me, when I realized what he said. There really were other Dragon's? Javier said there weren't, that they didn't exist. As a shape shifter, wouldn't he know? Wouldn't any of them know? I started moving from one side of the room to the other floating along the ceiling and said. "You should respect an eye for an eye. You'll heal. Consider us even. Besides, only a coward hit's a female. You caused Candy pain, now I've caused you pain."

A car pulled up into the driveway and slid to a stop, doors opened and slammed shut. Voices were raised outside, then running came down the hall and Matt stood there with two of his wolf body- guards. Matt was red in the face as he took in the broken furniture and stairs. He growled out through gritted teeth "Where is my mate?" His hands started to change to wolf claws. His skin looked like something was alive under it moving around, soft brown fur pulled out of his skin and his nails grew long and thick, and sharp.

Christian bellowed, his voice carried throughout the house and into the backyard. Power laced every word. Like frostbite. "ENOUGH! CONTROL YOURSELVES! ALL OF YOU! Casey stand down, Ajax, it's over, you didn't kill Candy and Casey didn't kill you."

Ajax wasn't exactly happy at the moment. "I expect you to punish your slave for her actions. I am ...." I didn't let him finish what he was saying "We know what you are. Your someone who likes to hurt innocent girls. You've proven that. AND I'M NOT A GODDAMN SLAVE!" "You are a Dragon, and Christian's familiar. That makes you his SLAVE!" He yelled the last at me.

I floated towards Christian, then down to the floor, and became visible. Matt immediately closed his arms around me in a very protective gesture. My calmness was finally starting to fade, I looked at Christian, and quietly asked "Explain that to me." I pointed a thumb over my shoulder back at Ajax. "What he said. What does that mean exactly? Please tell me it's not what I think it is." My voice might have been pleading there at the end. He looked me directly in the eyes and said "Yes, Dragons do exist. They are the most powerful of the shifters and extremely rare. My familiar is the Dragon." He stared at me, waiting for me to figure it out. "Are you saying that I'm what? Like your base animal? The one and only type of shifter you can lay claim to?" I was starting to get a huge bad feeling in my gut, my blood was starting to run cold. He didn't say anything just gave one small single nod to me. My breathing was coming faster and more shallow. My voice was barely more than a whisper when I asked "Have you? Have you claimed me too?" Tears were working their way out of my eyes at that. Christian reached up to place a hand on my shoulder but Matt pulled me back so Christian wouldn't touch me. At the moment I was grateful for Matt. He was also helping me stand. My knees felt like they wanted to buckle. Christian's hand dropped back to his side, he gave a resigned sigh and said "No, I haven't. Until I saw you shift to protect Matt I wasn't completely sure you were a Dragon." I turned my head to look at Matt, and quietly said "Get me out of here."

Ajax wasn't done yet "If you have not claimed her, then someone else will." I looked at Ajax "Like who you?" He smiled at me then and it wasn't encouraging "Yes exactly like me. Why do you think I'm here?" Christian stepped between me and Ajax "I did not invite you here for that. I wanted answers to questions I had." "And did you not think, that if a Dragon were here an unclaimed that I would not want a familiar for my own?" Oh hell there were two Vampires here who could claim me? I don't think so. "Fuck all ya'll! Let's go Matt." Matt herded me to the back door with his guards bringing up the rear.

All the shifters got in the big dark blue Hummer that sat in the driveway. Randy, Candy, and Pete were in the very back, Matt, me and Travis were in the middle seat and the guards rode up front. I felt numb. I had read books where some Vamps had animals they could call on. And really it makes sense. Some one the Vamp could trust to guard him or her during the day. Someone he or she had claimed that wouldn't turn against them. But why? Why the hell had my luck been so fucking shitty?

The odds of getting picked by aliens is higher than winning the lottery, but I did it. And now, out of all the Vampires in the world I had to be in a city were not one but two were attracted to my Dragon. Well I guess I won't be shifting into a Dragon anymore. I damn sure don't want to be claimed by anyone else. One ball and chain is bad enough.

Chapter 20

We got back to HQ but I really didn't want to go in to a place where Christian might be coming back to. Everyone climbed out of the Hummer but me, I just looked at the door. Matt leaned into the car and said "We don't have to stay here if you don't want to." I looked him in the eyes and was thankful he was there. I didn't really know him, but right now having someone else make some decisions was nice. Being a Libra, it's in my nature to let someone else lead if things go smoothly. It's when they aren't going smoothly that I generally jump up, take charge and put them back the way they need to be. I like my life balanced. Right now my life, hell my world, is anything but balanced. "I don't want to stay here." Great, I sounded like a lost child. He nodded to me and held out his hand "Give me your room card." I did. He turned to Travis and Pete. Since they were his wolves they had to follow his orders.

"Pack her things, quickly, and bring them to my house." Matt snapped his fingers at the guards and got back into the Hummer with me. The guards climbed back in up front. "Can Travis, Pete, and the girls come and stay too?" Matt held my hand, rolled down the window and called to Travis who turned and jogged back to the car. "Pack some things for you and Pete too. Tell the girls they're welcome to come as well if they want." Travis nodded to Matt and smiled at me. Then ran back towards the building.

I was tucked under one of Matt's arms for the trip to his house. We headed up U.S. 59 towards Kingwood. Tall trees, and expensive living. The neighborhood we drove thru had huge lots, all nicely fenced off with brick walls. Tall towering trees, green grass, and mansions tucked back behind electric wrought iron gates. I did a double take when I got my first good look at Matt's house. Then a bad thought occurred to me. "That crazy bitch who tried to kill me isn't here is she?" DUH!! Mental forehead slap moment. "Sorry, I mean your girlfriend?" I got a small smile at that. "No she isn't here. And your right she is a crazy bitch. It's not me she'll miss but my credit card." We parked and got out. "Don't tell me you didn't have feelings for her, and probably still do. Most guys don't like to be used." A very soft chuckle reached my ear and I turned to see one of the guards as he schooled his face. "Am I missing something?" Matt scowled at the guard, wrapped an arm around my shoulder and led me into the house.

He took a deep breathe and said "She was an arrangement. And a pain in the ass. She treated everyone including me, like a rabid stray. I had thought to try and unite the Houston pack, with the Dallas pack more. Have closer ties, and hopefully less arguments. Then you came along." I felt like I had just set the pack back into a troubled situation, and it was all my fault. "I'm sorry, I didn't mean to cause problems." Matt and the guards laughed and he squeezed my shoulder "Welcome home my mate, you didn't cause problems, you saved us from certain misery."

We walked through the entrance from the garage to the kitchen. The kitchen was huge with light grey marble countertops. The appliances were all new looking and industrial brushed steel. White Italian tile with light grey veining covered the floor, and a large skylight circled with recessed lighting graced the ceiling. The center island was big enough to have four stools along one side. Built in cabinets and the trash can. I walked to the pass thru bar and looked out into the sunken living room. It's what is called a great room. My whole old apartment would have fit in there.

In it's own way it was just as fancy as Christian's Victorian. Except this was bigger more contemporary, and plush. Matt reached for my hand and said "Come on, I'll give you the tour." He showed me the game room, which had a pool table and a billiard table. Dart and shuffle boards, several arcade games, and a full bar. The solarium which in my opinion is just a big glassed in deck with lots of greenery, and a hot tub, was just gorgeous . The library was breathtaking, dark wood, rich wine colors on the walls, leather chairs, and a beautiful grandfather clock that actually worked. There was also a private theater with twelve black leather recliners. The whole first floor had either hardwood floors or marble tile. Then we went up the hand carved stair case to the second floor. The carpet was at least an inch thick. The master suite was the biggest bedroom I had ever seen. My nerves shot straight through the roof when I realized Matt was gonna want me to share this high class room with him. The bed itself was an extra large king size sleigh bed. French doors led to a balcony on the far side of the room. His and her walk in closets were on the right. They could have been spare bedrooms. On the left was the master bath. Cream colored marble counter tops, his and her sinks, a glass walled shower with four shower heads and a sunken Jacuzzi garden tub.

My nervousness must have showed on my face, I wasn't trying to hide it. I'm not sure I would have been able to. Matt came up to me and pulled me into his arms and rubbed his hand up and down my back. "It's okay, relax your safe here." My back was stiff, I couldn't relax "You can sleep down the hall if you want time to get used to the idea. But I would rather you slept in here with me. We don't have to do anything. I don't expect anything." I didn't know what to say to that. So I tried something else. "Can Travis or Pete sleep in here with us?" now he stiffened "No, I'm sorry but I don't want another males scent in my bed." I could understand that, but I didn't like it. "I have issues you know? I was starting to get used to Travis and Pete in my bed. I'm not used to having anyone in my bed at all." A soft growl purred at my back. I lifted my head and looked at Matt. He asked "Have you had sex with them?" my eyes went wide "What? Hell no! I just met them a few days ago! What do I look like a lot lizard?" The growling stopped and he took a deep breath "No, I didn't mean anything like that, I'm sorry." I stepped away from him "It's okay, can you show me to my room?" He looked sad but led me down he hall to another master suite. Travis, Pete, and the girls were coming up the stairs with bags full of stuff.

I poked my head out into the hall and yelled "Down here!" They turned towards me and unloaded everything into the middle of the floor.

The guys didn't seem impressed, I guess they'd been here before. But the girls were. Matt stood to the side and watched all of us. The RC twins didn't need a tour guide, they helped themselves. "Hey everybody listen up." They all turned to me. Even the body guards that were standing outside the door. "The closets are big enough for all of us, so help yourselves." Matt stepped up then "The men will sleep in another room." We all turned towards him. The look in his eye pretty much said no man was going to be sleeping in the same bad as me. My eyes shifted between Travis, and Pete. They knew I glowed in the dark, and had become like my personal teddy bears. My head slowly nodded. And very quietly I said "Alright, the girls will stay in here with me then." Travis came up to me and wrapped his arms around me in a hug and Pete came up beside us. We opened our arms and let him in our hug. A low growl echoed throughout the room and the guys stiffened in my arms. I turned us so I was between them and Matt.

Slowly we pulled apart, and Travis and Pete left the room with out a word. I watched them go. Then turned towards Matt "That was uncalled for." I pulled bags off the floor and placed them on the bed and began pulling stuff out and hanging things up. "Don't tell me it was uncalled for, you're my MATE!" We needed to settle a few things, he needed to understand what I had been going through. I crooked a finger at him and said "Come with me." We walked back to his room, and left the girls to unpack. Once he was thru the door I closed it behind him. "Sit down and listen to what I have to say, when I'm done, then you can ask questions." We both sat down in the small sitting area out on his balcony. As I looked into his beautiful cinnamon flecked brown eyes, I gave him the readers digest version of my life, and a more detailed version of the past two weeks. Then ended with "They have become my friends and at night my comfort zone. I'll make you a deal. You can sleep in there with us, at my back, in the dominant position. If they can sleep in there too. That will let me also get accustomed to you." I waited for him to say something. Finally after a few minutes he said "You've had a hell of a life. I find it hard to believe some of the things you've said to me. They are quit outlandish." His tone said he didn't believe most of what I said. I closed my eyes and asked "Is there anything you want to question me about?" He puffed out a disgusted laugh, shook his head and said "No, but I would have liked the truth. It was a good story though." Then he got up and left me there. My shoulders slumped then I said "Ask Travis, and Pete." He stopped with his hand on the door knob, I got up walked to the door pushed his hand off of it and walked out the room. Tears were stinging my eyes. It really bothered me when someone accused me of lying.

I found my way down to the kitchen and rummaged through the cabinets, and refrigerator. Pulled out food and started cooking. It's a great stress reliever for me, I can blank my mind of everything bad and concentrate on adding spices to this, and turning that. Soon the smells of chicken fried pork chops, stuffing with gravy, and mixed veggies floated through the house. I thought my gang was the first to arrive, but Candy pointed over my shoulder and there stood Matt. Watching me from the other side of the pass thru bar. Being in the cooking zone, took all of my concentration. Especially when emotions are running high. I never knew he was there. He could have snuck up on me and killed me. Well, if I could be killed.

I made the come on gesture with my head towards him so he could join us. I wasn't going to deal with his issues right now. I had enough of my own. But I wouldn't exclude him either. It was his house. There was enough food to feed an army. I guess a house of shifters is the same thing. There weren't any leftovers. I was worried there wasn't gonna be enough. But after we finished off dessert, everyone was well satisfied. Mental note : make more next time.

One of the guards approached me, neither of them had come near me before this. He was just over six feet tall and well muscled, with dark brown hair that came to his collar. His eyes were hazel and smiling when he introduced himself. "I'm Jayce, dinner was delicious, thank you for cooking. Paige never stepped foot in the kitchen, and I'm glad. She wouldn't know a frying pan from the dishwasher. Anyway welcome to the pack Accalia, I hope you stick around. I'm getting tired of pizza." I smiled at him as he left and returned to his post, or wherever he was going.

Before the girls and I went to sleep, I warned them about my small night light problem. Candy said "I don't care if sparks fly out of your ass, and you spew pea soup." She put both arms around me in a tight hug. "You saved my life, besides, this way I won't need to turn on a light if I have to pee in the middle of the night." The three of us giggled and prepared ourselves for bed. My relief was almost a solid living thing. I put on a t-shirt with my panties, the girls just stripped down, and climbed into bed. I was standing by the side of the bed and asked "Uh, aren't you gonna put some clothes on?" The RC twins looked at me confused and asked "Why?" at the same time. "Well, what if something happens and we need to run out of the house? You'll be naked." They looked at each other then at me. Again in stereo they asked "So?" My head was shaking back and forth, I'm a prude and I know it. I might even be a bit homophobic. I just wasn't comfortable sleeping in the same bed with two naked women, and they noticed. Randy asked "Do you want us to put on a shirt and shorts?" I chewed my bottom lip and nodded to them.

They both smiled at me, got up and put clothes on. "Thanks, maybe in a decade or two, I'll be more comfortable about it, but not right now." Candy said "It's okay, I was the same way. Society trains us to think certain ways, but you'll come around." I wasn't sure about that, but I let it drop. The girls were on the side of the bed closest to the bathroom, leaving me between them and the door.

A knock sounded and Matt walked in. "May I still stay in here with you?" I was still upset with him, I shrugged my shoulders rolled over and said "Whatever." I heard clothes hitting the floor and said "Keep your drawers on, if you sleep in here." He slid into bed, under the sheets, and aligned his body right up next to mine. He had kept his grippy boxers on. Which was a relief, but it didn't stop what I felt swelling by my butt. He had one arm wrapped around me and the other tucked under me. His face was nestled in my hair. Leaving his mouth and nose by my ear. He was practically on top of me. I hate to admit it, but it felt good. He was warm and smelled like sunshine, fresh cut grass and pine needles. It was a good smell.

The next morning the girls rolled out of bed first. I really didn't want to move, my spot was warm, and I was still cradled in strong arms. After the girls got dressed and left, Matt finally moved and said "I'm sorry for last night. I didn't believe you." He rolled back just enough for me to turn over to face him. When we were eye to eye he continued "You really glow... and you seem really warm, like a banked fire." My face started heating up as

I nodded to him, then looked away embarrassed "Yeah, it's kinda weird, I didn't know I got warmer though." He gently turned my face back towards him and kissed me softly on the lips. No tongue, just a soft, pleasant kiss. He gave me a smile and said "Good morning, my mate." I smiled back "Good morning, to you too. Do you have anything planned for today?"   "Yes, I need to start planning the monthly gathering." My forehead wrinkled in confusion and he explained "Every month the pack gets together for the lunar phase hunt." Ah! Now I get it. "So they can shift." I nodded he responded "Yes, so *WE* can shift, you will be there with us." Hoo boy, this was gonna be interesting.

He lightly ran his fingertips up my arm and made me shiver. Very softly he said "Last night you said you could shift into any animal, so you could shift in to a wolf right?" I nodded to him, his fingers were still making trails from my fingertips to my shoulder and back again. It was very relaxing. "I'd like to see your wolf before then, I want to see you. All of you." From relaxed to stiff in two seconds flat. Now my nerves were on high alert again! His smile was straight up devilish when he said "I'll show you mine, if you show me yours." My eyes got huge and he laughed "Our wolves woman, nothing else." "Oh, umm, okay I guess. When?" "How about right now?" "Now? Uh, I gotta pee first." I rolled out of bed and headed for the bathroom. While I was in there I stalled as long as possible, brushing my teeth and hair. Then finally set my shoulders, because I knew it was time to go back out there.

I decided to shift in the bathroom and just stroll out. I pictured a soft, thick furred wolf, with a white undercoat and grey going darker at the tips of the fur. My wolf resembled my dog Angel. Warm ripples caught me and then I shifted. However, opposable thumbs and hands to open the damn door would have been nice. Wow. This is embarrassing. I whimpered and pawed at the door. Matt opened it and grinned at me. "You should have left it cracked so you could get out." I playfully nipped at him and he jumped back giving me room to get out of the bathroom. He smiled down at me and said "Your beautiful."

Matt started pulling his grippy boxers down, to stand naked in front of me. Even with my wolf eyes, he was a beautiful specimen of a man. Broad shoulders, and a nice even tan. Except where his pants line was. He had the tightest abs I've ever seen on someone who didn't work in a gym. Then he shifted into his wolf right there in front of me. I got to watch the fur ripple over his skin, and heard popping noises of bones realigning. It was gross and fascinating at the same time. His coat is cream colored with chocolate brown tips. And his eyes turned a pure cinnamon color. He was still beautiful. We circled each other sniffing parts most humans wouldn't sniff. Once we were both satisfied, Matt nipped me on the hind quarters. I jumped and ran for the door. A game of chase was officially on.

I ran down the hall and then down the stairs towards the kitchen. As we plowed past Travis, Pete and the girls, they dropped what they were doing to chase and run with us. In their two legged forms. Over couches, under end tables, around the library, the theater, game room, then back to the kitchen. We stopped and stared at the guards who had opened the fridge grabbed some steaks and heated them up for us. Travis, Pete, and the girls, came in laughing. Travis pointed a finger at us and said "You better be thankful we followed you. Do you know how many lamps we saved?" Then Candy said "Not to mention the end tables." We were barely listening to them, cause at that moment our steaks were ready.

Chapter 21

We were sitting in the living room together talking about stuff in general. Listening to the girls mostly.

Then Pete gave me my youngest son's new identification. It had been ready but with everything going on, I just hadn't gotten it yet. "I need to give you your money, wait here." "Actually, here's the money you already gave me." He handed over the Wal-mart bag with the hundred and fifty grand in it and explained. "You're my Accalia now, any services I do for you are free of charge. That's the way it works." I wasn't sure I liked people catering to my needs like that. I wasn't used to it. Having to work hard and pay for everything during my life made me a certain way. "Um, ok, but if you ever need money or anything let me know." He smiled at me, bowed and said "Yes, Accalia" "Oh Hell no! don't do that!" He laughed then and left the room. I checked the new I.D. to make sure everything was correct on it. It was. The RC twins and Travis left to go back to their jobs and I was lonely. I missed them.

Over the next couple of days, I hibernated at Matt's. The internet had become my new best friend. I ordered new phones for me and the whole family so we could talk safely. Next time we were together I'd pass them out. My nerves had finally settled down enough I didn't feel like I was about to explode. I had also been looking for a new residence for my whole family. When Matt saw what I was doing he put a stop to it real quick. "I said you and your son can live here. You're my mate, Casey. That makes him my stepson. Would you take that away from me?" "Oh please, you don't even know him, so don't go there. Besides, the house I'm looking for, is for my family." "Aren't they my family now too?"

I just looked at him, he couldn't possibly be serious. He was. "Matt, you haven't met them, they just learned I'm a shifter, what do you want to do? Introduce them to the pack? Come on, my mom has a job, my sister has her playgroups with my nephew. I'm, trying to keep them in the same general neighborhood. So my crazy ass life doesn't disrupt there lives too much." I turned back to the computer and felt warm hands start massaging my shoulders.

"Please let me in to your world, let me help you Casey, I CAN help you." His tone was almost pleading, and I caved "Okay, fine." We worked together over the next couple of hours, and learning Matt was into real estate was a big bonus. We found a house but didn't buy it. I wanted my family to have the final say so. This was going to be tricky anyway. Making sure the Lions, and the Government didn't get in the way. Then came the moment of truth, I sent mom a message through Matt's face book page to get my son for the weekend, and to be ready to go Saturday morning at 10:00 am. I had to wait three more days to see them. The timing was good since this was the last week of school. Finally something going my way. But tonight was the full moon, and the lunar hunt.

Late afternoon everyone prepared themselves by dressing down. I mean way down. Some of the shorts the people were wearing were lucky they still had buttons and zippers. Most of the women wore bandana's for tops. Quick tie up and just slip out. No need to worry about messing up shirts that way. At least that's what Randy said. The guys didn't bother with shirts and almost everyone was barefoot. A few people wore flip flops but not many. What did I wear to my first lunar hunt? Jeans, t-shirt, and my purple boots.

Matt had said I wouldn't need my weapons here but I felt better with them. My claws were in my hip purse, cell phone on my side. Who knows? We may need to call AAA or something.

We all crammed into various cars and drove north about thirty minutes, then pulled off the freeway onto a county road. Another five miles then into a rock driveway. One of the other wolves got out and opened a metal swing gate, and we all drove through. Once we were all on the property and parked, the same wolf closed the gate. I noticed there were about forty wolf shifters total give or take. We got out of the cars and I started looking around. The trees were thick except where we'd parked, and dusk was about forty five minutes away.

Matt came around to my side of the car and tugged on my hand to get my attention as we walked through the woods. "We have five hundred acres here to run around on, there are a few spots on the property where we set up some equipment to play on. Bridges we built to go from tree to tree to give a height advantage, tunnels both on the ground and dug into the ground, a few slides, things like that. We hunt here so I make sure it's stocked. Sometimes I have deer, pigs, or sheep brought in, but there's plenty of rabbit, and the pond at the back is stocked as well." It was amazing the things a shifter had to go through just to hunt every month. We cleared the dense tree line and came into a clearing. When I looked back I couldn't see the cars. Natural camouflage.

The clearing was about the size of basketball court. On one end was a four tiered dais made of green marble. Each layer was a foot and a half thick. The bottom layer was ten feet across by ten feet long. The second layer was an 8 x 8 foot square piece, the third layer was a 6 x 6 square piece, and the top layer was 4 x 4 square feet. A small green marble pyramid.

Matt climbed to the top of the pyramid and pulled me up with him.

Once we turned back to the clearing all talking just stopped, and everyone was looking at me! I spotted Travis and Pete grinning like they had just won the lottery.

Matt spoke loud and clear so there was no mistaking what was said. "My wolves, the arrangement with Dallas has ended." Cheers went up from everyone. "Paige has gone back to her pack!" Again louder cheers, fist pumps in the air, and howls of joy. "I present you.." he held my arm up in the air "My new mate! Your new Accalia!" Travis and Pete were definitely the loudest, everyone else was more subdued. They didn't know me, or what kind of person I was. I didn't blame them for being nervous, especially after Paige. Matt turned to me and quietly mumbled in my ear. "Speak to them, reassure our wolves." Oh hell. What do you say to a pack of wolves? I cleared my throat and just blurted out what ever came to my mouth.

"This is all very new to me. I've never been an Accalia before. I met Paige once, personally I thought she was bat shit crazy..." Several agreeable chuckles came from that, I glanced at Matt and he gave me the go ahead nod. "I'll do my best to be patient, help with your problems, and in general try to be a good Accalia, but I warn you now. I'm a mother, so don't try to pull any fast ones over on me, you can't scare me. I have teenagers." That earned me more heartfelt chuckles. Then I yelled "Are you ready to get this party started?" Everyone yelled and howled. The look on Matt's face was pure pride, which made me smile. He yelled "Pack, time to hunt!" Power flowed from him and stretched out across the clearing like clear waves. It was like looking through gas fumes, almost tangible. Everyone started changing where they stood. I was real nervous being around a whole pack of shape shifting wolves. Trying to keep my head and not freak out was the best I could do. Werewolves were real and I was fixing to get a first hand look at a whole pack of them. Deep breath in and out, stay calm. My new motto. Matt and I were the first off and running, the newer shifters took a little longer to shift.

The ground was soft under my paws, the air was thick with smells. Pine needles, and prey and the smell of forty other wolves. One thing new I learned was when in wolf form everyone could mentally talk to each other. My head was full of voices, both human and wolf. It was damn distracting. I followed Matt through the woods, with the rest of the pack bringing up the rear. He ran through an obstacle course. He didn't mention everything they had added onto the property. We ran up a ramp then he jumped, caught a knotted rope in his teeth and swung out over a mud pit, to land on the other side. By the time I saw what the deal was, it was too late to stop. If I tried I'd end up face first in the mud. So I jumped and caught another rope and hoped like hell I made it. My back right paw landed in mud, but other than that, I was good.

We all chased each other until we caught the smell of deer. Then it was a race to see who could catch it first. Being with the pack was one of the greatest feelings I'd ever had. A feeling of belonging to more than just one person. Of unity, family. We cornered and trapped the big buck by coming at it from all sides. Then we pounced on it. The submissive wolves held back until the dominants were full. Warm, fresh, wild tasting blood dripped down my throat with each bite. Raw meat never appealed to me before, but as a wolf it was damn tasty. My ears picked up a honking noise and I asked Matt *"What is that?"* *"I hope it's the moose I ordered for our hunt in your honor."* Awww, he got me a moose, how many girls can say that? I nosed his muzzle, then took off after the honking noise. My inner beastie wanted that moose. BAD! I shifted into my Dragon form and left the ground, flying over the land until I spotted it. All the wolves that were behind me came to a crashing halt when I shifted.

I flew low over the moose and caught him in my front claws, then headed back to the pack. They were all crowding Matt so they were easy to spot. Even in the dark. My Dragon form doesn't have a link to the wolves so my head was blissfully quiet. I hovered over them as they watched. Their tails were tucked under and their heads were lowered to the ground. They were trying to make themselves a smaller target. The moose kicked and jerked in my claws, I gave it a good neck snap, then started pulling it apart in hunks and dropping it down to the wolves. I saved a good piece of back strap for me and Matt, landed then went back to wolf form. The chaos in my head started up again, and Matt and I had to howl to get them to shut up a minute. Once they settled down I spoke to them *"Yes I can shift into a Dragon, but you're my pack now and I won't hurt my pack, I know who you are. What you smell like. It doesn't matter what shape I'm in, I'll always know who you are. The moose is torn enough we can all have some, so eat up and enjoy."*

Travis, and Pete came up to me and licked my muzzle, I got *"Thank you Accalia."* (That was gonna take some getting used to) From both of them then they went to find a hunk of moose. Matt came up to me and nosed me. I backed up, picked up the back strap in my teeth and held it out towards him. The other wolves were watching to see if he would take it. He did, but I didn't let go. He gave a low warning growl, and tugged back. We played tug of war with the meat until it ripped. Then we settled down and munched our moose bits. The rest of the pack had finally gone after the bits and pieces I'd thrown down. Matt pinned my head under his, like I was a headrest, and said *"You just fed the pack, only a true leader would do that."* I could hear the pride in his tone in my head. *"Follow me."* We got up and I followed him up a ramp, more slowly this time, and into an open tree house. Mostly is was just a platform around a tree trunk with rails. The vantage point gave us a good view of the pack. We could watch them all from up here.

"What do you mean only a true leader would do that?" *"Well, a lot of the shifter alphas tend to think of themselves first and the pack, pride, or whatever class of shifter they are second, you didn't hesitate. You made sure we were all included."* He nuzzled my muzzle and licked the moose blood off my face while he talked in my head. *"That is a sign of a good leader."* I figured it was a sign of resignation. Being a mother trains you to put others before yourself. It was natural not anything special. But I didn't tell him that.

The wolves played and we watched. The whole thing was surreal. It was no different than going to a park and watching the kids play. Except for the location and the fact they were furry and four legged.

A shadow quickly fell over us and moved on. I looked up to see what it was, but didn't see anything. The night was clear the moon was bright, whatever it was, it was big. Maybe a passing cloud? I was still looking up at the sky when a loud roar broke through my concentration.

Matt jumped up gave two loud barks and a command *"Everyone to the tunnels, NOW!"* My attention was now focused on where the roar came from. Flying above the trees was a huge Dragon. The form I'd been using was one I had seen in pictures. Now I was looking at the real thing. And there were differences. Matt pushed me towards the edge of the play area and towards the underground tunnels. But my attention was behind me not in front of me. *"Go Casey, now. Move.!"* *"I want to see it Matt!"* Besides, my morbid curiosity, I wanted to compare my dragon to that one. *"No! it's dangerous, move!"* I stopped and turned towards him. *"Matt, I am too. Don't forget what I am."* He thought for about two seconds shook his big furry head and said *"It's too risky, come be with the pack. We have to protect them."* *"Well, I can do that better out here. Don't you think?"* I darted around him and headed for the clearing by the lake. *"Casey! Get back here.!"* *"No! go be with the pack, I've got this! Trust me!"* Thankfully he turned and headed back without too much argument. He did keep looking back though, like he couldn't make up his mind where he wanted to be.

Once I was in the clearing I shifted into my Dragon and took to the skies. My link to the wolves was gone, but I had a new link now. To the other dragon.

We flew around each other a few times, sizing each other up. He was bigger than me and had a lot more spikes coming off him. His head looked like it had been crowned in spikes with two long thick horns that followed the curve of his head then gracefully stood up. Instead of one row of spikes going down his neck and back he had three. And it was definitely a he! My dragon sight took in all of his details. Like me he was black scaled with an oily iridescent sheen to him. Unlike me, his underbelly was a solid deep dark red. His wings were longer and wider than mine and segmented four times, where I had segmented mine three times. The muscle definition was impressive. Compared to him I was sleek and petite, but that would change now that I had seen a real one. It was information time.

"Who are you? And what do you want?" A very deep voice responded to me. One I recognized and made we want to run. Ajax. *"I want you!"* At that moment if I could have been half porcupine I would have. I did however sprout two new rows of spindly spines down my neck and back, and more thick spikes on my head. I was gonna need every advantage possible.

I shifted back to human and ran for the tree line. Opened my hip purse and called Christian.

"Hello?" A roar screeched through the woods "Your friend his here. Can I kill him now?" *"Where are you?"* He sounded almost worried. "With the wolves, hunting." *"Stay away from him, Casey. Stay with Matt, we'll be there as soon as possible."* Then he hung up without saying goodbye which left me staring at the phone. How was

he going to find us in the woods? Did he know where the pack hunted? Part of me hoped he knew, the other part wasn't sure it was a good idea if he knew. Ajax the dragon circled over head then landed in the clearing I just ran from. I slipped on my silver claws and mentally prepared myself as best as I could. Which wasn't much. He wanted me? Oh Hell!

I needed the link between us so I could distract him until the cavalry arrived. Ajax watched me with piercing eyes as I walked back into the clearing. My dragon form rippled over my skin in an instant. *"When you said "you wanted me" what exactly did you mean?" "You are a rarity, and so am I. We belong together. Dragon and Dragon Master." "Thanks, but I don't want to be your Master."* Probably not the wisest choices of words, but I wasn't going to be a slave to anyone. If I could help it. He didn't like it. Smoke was streaming out of his nose every breath. He was a fire breathing vampire dragon. That's just weird! *"You're a fire breathing dragon?" "Yes" "You're a vampire, doesn't the fire hurt you?"* Maybe if I pelted him with questions I could stall long enough. *"Not in this form." "Yeah, and speaking of 'this form' how is it you can shape shift?" "I'm old and my familiar is the dragon. To my knowledge our clan is the only clan who can become their base animals."* Hmmm. *"So, other Vamps can't do it? They can't becomes wolves or Leopards? Bats?" "No, Now come to me and let us complete the binding." "HELL NO! You stay over there! You are still on my shit list!"* He stepped forward towards me and I backed up. It almost looked like he was anticipating a chase and capture maneuver. So I quit backing up. Predators like to chase right? I'm not prey Damn it! Changing my route we were now circling each other. His thick black tail whipped close to my nose and I snapped at it. I hoped that let him know that this wasn't going to be as easy as he thought.

He snarled at me then *"Don't make this harder for yourself little one. You will gain from this as well."* *"Ha! What could you possibly give me I might want?"* *"Immortality, power, and station, to name a few."* *"The first one I don't need, The second one I don't care about, and third one, only stuck up yuppies care about. What else you got?"* Another puff of smoke came out *"Hey! That's probably bad for the environment you know?"* *"I don't care, I don't need to breathe in my other form."* *"Don't you have to breathe to talk in your other form?"* Did they? It made sense to me, it seems logical. With a growling tilt to his voice in my head he said *"Let us finish this then. Either you will be mine or you will die."* I remembered him saying I wouldn't be the first dragon he'd killed. Which of course made me more curious. *"Just calm down a minute, you said you'd killed other dragons? Did they not want to join you?"* *"I do not answer to you little one."* *"Well, I'm curious by nature, whoever gets stuck with me, is just going to have to deal with it. If you don't like it, then fly away and don't look back."* *"That can be tamed out."* OH HELL NO!! I laughed at him, and that sound coming out of a dragon's snout is ear piercing, and smoky. *"That's some funny shit. Tame me? Are you into BDSM? Or are you just a glutton for punishment? I'm a woman of the 21st Century not the 11th Century. This bitch bites back, twice as hard! Just like my mamma taught me…"* I saw an object flying in the air towards us, it was coming from behind Ajax. Good! Just a little more distraction and it would be here. *"So... I guess if your feeling froggy then jump."* I flexed my silver claws in his direction. *"Just remember Ajax, I owe you."* *"And I owe you."* As soon as he jumped at me, I launched at him. We hit almost chest to chest. My silver claws slid easily through his scales and into the thick muscle. Then another dragon hit Ajax from behind. Ajax's claws couldn't penetrate my shield. Thank you GOD!

The impact of the new dragon pushed us backwards to the ground. With the weight of two dragons on top of me, it would be difficult to get up. Since I was smaller than the other two dragons, I was being squished. I got a glimpse of the new dragon and his familiar rider. My eyes grew huge as I spotted Sebastian on the back of the other dragon. That meant only one thing. The new dragon was Christian. He had confessed to having dragons as familiars, and Ajax said only the dragon clan could shift. I heard Christian's cultured voice in my head as I sank my teeth into Ajax's ear and tried to tear it off. *"Casey, get out of here NOW!"* *"In case you haven't noticed, I'm stuck!"*

Then suddenly the weight was rolling off of me and to the side. My teeth were still clamped down tight on an ear, and it ripped in half when Ajax was pulled off of me. He let out a fierce roar as I rolled over onto my belly gasped in great gulps of air, and took stock of were they were. Part of an ear just wasn't enough payment in my book. I managed to get to my feet and balance myself. After my first step something landed on my back. My big head swung around to find Sebastian there with both hands up in the "I surrender, I'm unarmed gesture." While he was on my back we could do a mental link so I gave him warning. *"You might want to go find the wolves, I have SO NOT gotten my pound of flesh yet." "I was told to keep you safe." "Whatever, big guy. Hang on then."*

Both dragons' were on their hind legs clawing, biting and whipping their tails at each other. Neither had their backs toward me, but that was ok. Christian's dragon form was a deep amethyst with the same iridescent quality to the scales. His under belly was a dark midnight blue. Size wise they were evenly matched. As Vampires Ajax was taller, but in animal form they were almost the exact same except for their coloring. They were concentrating on each other and not on me which was a good thing and a stupid thing. Depending on the dragon. Ajax's tail whipped around to slam into Christian and I caught it in my front claws. Silver sliding in, past the thick scales and into the muscle. I held on when he tried to pull his tail away from me. Letting my claws slice down half the length of his tail. He pulled back at that, away from both of us.

He sucked in a deep breath and blew fire at us. I jumped in front of Christian and fired back. Waiting to see if the fire would hurt Christian wasn't even an option. Especially since he had come to the rescue. Ajax's fire hit me square in the chest against my shield. My fire cauterized his ear and left soot in his face. *"This isn't over."* Ominous much?

He turn and leapt into the air and we watched him go. Wow, it was over and nobody died. When he was out of sight I turned to face Christian. *"Don't be getting any bright ideas to finish what he started, and thank you for coming to help." "You are most welcome, I won't force you Casey. A master and familiar coupling should be a partnership. Much like what we did tonight. I've lived long enough to learn you can't force true loyalty." "Look, I've already been put in one position I didn't want, I don't mind being your guard still, but let's keep this strictly plutonic. I'm sure some day you find a nice Lady dragon. But I ain't it." "Maybe." "No maybe's. I have too much to deal with right now, if anything else happens to me, I'm going to just explode and let the pieces fall where they will. I appreciate your kindness, and everything you've done for me. I really do, but too much has happened too fast. I'm a strong woman but shit, I have my limits!"* Matt came out of the trees and attacked Christian. Sebastian jumped off my back and wrapped his arms around Matt and held him while we both shifted. Christian back to two legs and me back to wolf. *"Matt! It's okay. The bad Dragon is gone! Matt!"* I damn near had to bite his tail to get his attention. He quit wiggling in Sebastian's arms and looked at me. *"Then who is that?" "Uh, The cavalry. It's Christian." "Then a bad dragon is still here."* He growled at the Vampires. "We only came because Casey asked for help. Be calm wolf, and finish your hunt this night." I turned to see Christian when he started speaking and nearly fell over. Christian was standing in the full light of a full moon butt naked. His skin had a soft glow to it that was mesmerizing. And the rest of him was pure walking sin. Men like him should come with warning signs, and should be outlawed. But thank god their not! God bless eye candy!

Sebastian was given a signal to let Matt go. Matt shook his fur and moved to stand between me and the Vampires. I looked at Christian and shifted to two legs "He's gonna come back sometime, ya know? When he does, next time, I'll be more prepared." I was so proud of myself. My voice sounded steady not breathy like I felt. "*If* he does, call me I'll be here."

I put my hands in the thick fur of Matt's neck and pointed him back towards to our pack. I'm not blind or dead, while we walked back to where the pack was secure. I did look back for one last glimpse of hot Vampire. Unfortunately he caught me looking. Seeing both Christian, in his glorious birthday suit, and Christian standing under the light of the full moon would make any mouth water. The rest of the evening, thankfully, was worry free.

Chapter 22

Saturday finally came around. Matt and I brainstormed for hours until we had a plan that we thought would work. I wanted to see my family, and show them a few houses we found for them. Most likely they were being watched. So we came up with a way for me to see them, and the watchers (whether they were shifter mercs, or government) wouldn't see me. We hoped.

Matt was going to take the Limo and go pick up my family. I had serious reservations about this part. My mom was going to grill him like nobodies business. He was going to give them their phones in the Limo so no one saw. Then go to the first house where I would already be inside waiting for them. The plan was simple really, I would stay invisible outside of the houses and become visible inside the Limo and inside the houses. I gave him a secret word to tell my mom, so she would know he was safe. Growing up, instead of calling her mom, or mommy, when I wanted something, sometimes I called her mawammy. Like "Please mawammy?" and

I'd give her big puppy dog eyes. It worked every time. I told Matt to use it if he had too.

When the Limo pulled up to the first house and the family got out, Matt looked somewhat relieved to get out of the car and away from them. He walked up to the house like he was on a mission, and unlocked the security lock hanging on the door. Once he had the key, he unlocked the door and let everyone in. I popped my head out of the kitchen as soon as the front door closed, and stepped out into the living room. My family was on top of me in an instant.

Questions were coming at me from all sides. Mostly about the man who picked them up. I raised my arms and started shushing them. My mom wasn't going to be shushed. "Alright Cassandra, He said something only you would say to me, and that's the only reason why we're here." I had to smile and give Matt the 'I told you so look' "Now, what is going on, and who is he?" "Well, we're looking for you a house to move into, so you can move out of where you are now. And this is Matt." Introductions went around "He's well, like my husband." That just felt weird saying it. My sister's jaw dropped, my mom's eyes nearly popped out of her head and my son said "Huh?" My mom's tone dropped to icy proportions, "Your married and didn't tell me? He didn't even ask me if he could marry you. I've never even heard of him. Where the hell did he come from?" My son looked as betrayed as my mom. "Alright stop! Calm down, first of all we're not exactly married per se. There hasn't been a wedding. There's a lot to explain."

My mom wouldn't let it go "Well, I suggest you start explaining then." a heavy sigh escaped my mouth. I looked at Matt "Maybe we should go back to the house, nothing is going get done until this is resolved." He nodded to me and I turned back to the family. "Let's get back into the Limo, and I'll explain on the way."

We left the house, and climbed back into the Limo. I had to be invisible from the house to the car. Once we pulled away from the curb, I started spilling the beans. My son was told shifters really existed. Two hours later, in the great room of Matt's house (My house) after I had explained everything, there was total silence. Until my son asked "Am I supposed to believe all of this?" "Yeah baby you are." His head was shaking from side to side "I don't think I can mom, it's freaking me out a little bit here."   "I know sweetie, it's a lot to take in, trust me I know."

The front door opened and Pete came in then with a big grin on his face. He nearly jogged to us and handed me an envelope. I opened it and saw there were new I.D.'s and passports inside. My brow wrinkled when I saw what it was. Before I could say anything Pete said. "Since your our new Accalia you needed an I.D. with Matt's last name. So now you and your son have new Identification with it!" His smile went from ear to ear. He was way to happy about this whole situation. I looked at them again and blew out a big breath. Well now we weren't Ross's anymore. That didn't last long. Now we were Frosts. Apparently I didn't look too excited because Pete was getting nervous "Umm, I I ccan change it if

you dddon't like the name I pppicked out for your sson."
I hadn't really looked at that well, but I did now that Pete
said something. My son was curious too "Okaaayy, so
like what's my new name?" Pete looked at him and said
"Well, um Casey is really strong and outgoing. I thought
you might be like her. She was keeping to Scottish and
Irish names, so um, I uh, thought you'd make a good
Kendrix. It's a strong cool name. Your Kendrix Frost
now. And your mom is Casey Frost. And her mate, your
step dad for lack of a better term is Matt Frost." He was
babbling, ringing his hands together and getting more
nervous waiting for our replies. Leave it to Illiana to be
rude. "Kendrix? What kind of weird ass name is that?"
Pete answered "It's a uh Sscottish name. It mmmeans
Royal Ccheiftain." I wasn't going to let my sister make
Pete feel bad. "Well, I like it! It's strong and powerful just
like my boy. You did a fabulous job on these, and quick
too." That earned me a smile. He walked over to my
son, still ringing his hands and asked him "Do umm, do
you like it? I never was vvery sstrong or powerful. But
I thought it might fit you. Please tell me you like it." He
was getting more nervous by the second. My son tested
the name "Hmm Kendrix, Kendrix Frost." He nodded
gave a slow smile to Pete and said "It's pretty cool, the
chicks should dig it." Pete let out a huge breath he'd been
holding and smiled "Good, I'm glad you like it. I uh
hope it's okay I made you a little bit older too." "Sweet!
I can get a license sooner!" We all smiled at that. "How
much older am I?" he got up to come look at the new
I.D.'s Pete said "Only a couple weeks, not much older."

"Awww man! That's it? That's bunk." Pete was getting uncomfortable again and Matt said. "Well you don't want to be 16 and in the eight grade do you?" My son thought about it and shook his head "Naw, everybody would think I was a douche." Matt nodded his head in agreement.

Everybody was getting along and asking questions when I saw a small red dot appear on my kids forehead, I didn't hesitate I just moved so fast and hard when I hit the couch the whole thing flipped over knocking my mom, sister, son and nephew backwards onto the floor. I yelled "Stay down! Snipers outside!" I gathered everyone close to me and held them there so my shield would cover them. Pete scampered around the couch and huddled with us. Matt and the guards had taken cover too.

Matt used military sign language to instruct his guards to find the sniper. Jayce and another guard moved with preternatural speed out of the great room. On their way out they turned off the lights. My mom and sister squealed. "It'll be okay. We'll be able to see them better this way." Matt said. I reached out to give everyone a reassuring pat. Matt came around to our side of the couch and said "Get ready on three. We're gonna get up and run to the safe room. You'll stay there until we know it's safe, and I come get you. Okay?" silent nods "Okay ready one, two, three." We all got up and ran following Matt through the house to the downstairs bathroom. He opened the closet and pulled on a shelf and the back of the closet opened up. Cool.

Lights came on in the safe room and everyone quickly went inside. Matt tried to push me in too. "Matt, I can help." He shook his head "Stay with your family right now they need you." He kissed me on the cheek pushed me inside and sealed the door. I turned to my boy and held out my arms, he and Pete came to me. The safe room looked like it had everything you could ever want, furniture, food, and books. The room itself should be sound proof, blast and fire proof. I'd seen them on T.V. but I'd never been in one. "It'll be okay don't worry." I didn't like being stuck in here. I hated feeling like I could be helping them but at the same time I was kind of glad someone else was doing the work for once. We all settled down and waited. Hopefully it wouldn't take long.

"I haven't heard you pull the trigger yet!" The Leander's voice growled through Alex's earpiece. "She saw the laser and reacted before I could pull the trigger. Then the lights went out." *"FUCK! Get out of there before they catch you."* Alex started unscrewing the pieces to his sniper rifle and put them in a hard protective case. He stood up, turned around and was looking down the business end of a .45 Desert Eagle. Jayce had him in his sights. "Don't even think about it Alex, and you might live through this. One wrong move and your Swiss cheese." Jayce yelled out "Matt, over here. I have him." Ten seconds later Matt came upon them and belted Alex in the side of his head, knocking him out. He did a quick search and found the earpiece. He put it to his ear and

said "I've got your boy, Marcus. And if we find anymore we'll have them too." He crushed the earpiece under his boot and motioned for Jayce to grab Alex. While he carried the sniper case.

The door to the safe room finally opened and we were all thankful. My family was terrified. I was nervous and antsy. I had done my best to keep them calm and reassure them. When I saw Matt I asked. "Well?" Everyone waited for his response. "Well, he have one sniper in lock up." He had been speaking to everybody then turned to me "It's Alex." "Oh shit, where is he? Was Brett with him?" "He was alone, we didn't pick up any other scents out there." While my family and I had been locked in the safe room, we agreed it would be best for them to stay the night here. They got to ask lot more questions too. I told Matt and we showed them to guest rooms where they could settle down some more.

After my family was settled in I cornered Matt "Take me to him." he placed both of his hands on my shoulders and squeezed. "Calm down, he's being interrogated right now. My best wolf has been called in. We'll get answers. But I know Marcus sent him." My calm cool façade was starting to falter. "He was going after my son." I was starting to shake, and tears were falling down my cheeks. I hated crying. The after effects were never pretty. The Lions had targeted my son. That was the wrong thing to do. I made myself a silent promise to kill Marcus.

Chapter 23

After breakfast the next morning my mom insisted they go back home. I gave them the addresses of the houses to look at and she promised she would, and let me know. We have been living with friends and it really was time to get the hell out of their house. Matt sent them home with two wolf bodyguards.

I kept my son with me. School was officially out for summer break. The problem right now concerning my son besides the obvious ones, were his father didn't know where he was. While he'd slept I stood over him, just watching. If anything happened to him, I'd lose it. On everyone. As I slowly ran my fingers over his cheek I wished my shield to cover him. I'd rather he have it. That way I knew he was safe. I imagined it blocking everything, inanimate objects like bullets, knives, even rocks. Claws, so he wouldn't get scratched up or turned into a shifter, even viruses. The shield may not protect from that, but hell, why not try?

I envisioned it sliding down my arm to cover him. A soft pale yellow glow covered my son and then turned clear. I smiled, it had worked. As I pulled my hand back a thin string of the shield stretched between us. Uh oh what now? It split in the middle and snapped towards both of us. Well did the damn thing stay with me or him? Quietly I opened the bedside drawer and pulled out a pencil, and placed it on his side. I saw a thin stripe of pale moonlight between him and the pencil. Yeah! My boy has a shield! He's safe. Deep breath. Oh, the relief was unbelievable. A ton of bricks off my shoulders.

Around lunchtime Matt found me, Pete and "Kendrix" (Wow, that was gonna take some getting used to) in the game room shooting pool. He whispered in my here "Hey pretty lady" I smiled and blushed "How would you like to take a little trip to the basement with me?" My eyebrows rose up to meet my hairline. "Um, that doesn't sound very romantic." "Well, I thought you might like to talk to the prisoner." My smile faded, I tossed the pool stick to Pete "Take over for me, I'll be back in a bit." Kendrix asked "What's up?" "Nothing to worry about, just show Pete what your momma taught you and kick his butt." I smiled at him and then turned and left with Matt. My son was placing a wager with Pete when we left. Matt led the way through the kitchen and to a door that looked like it was a pantry. He opened it and carpeted stairs led us down to the basement. It was a full basement, with white walls and thick pillars placed here and there for support beams. In the center was a wide open area, towards the right was a hallway with spare bedrooms. Complete with bathrooms. Matt was giving me the bargain basement tour, so to speak. Towards the left was another hallway that Matt led us down. At the end of that hall he opened another door and we went down another set of steps. Geez we were descending into the bowels of hell. These steps weren't carpeted, but dark grey stone. They still had nice sharp edges, so they hadn't been used a lot. The most horrible stench assaulted my nose and got stronger the further down we went. Smells like burned meat, burned hair, urine, blood and shit. Rot and mold just to name a few.

At the bottom on both sides of the aisle were built in jail cells or cages. A freaking dungeon. It was like a big room with vertical bars of silver for walls and doors. Each cage was about the size of a jail cell, eight foot by six foot. No beds or amenities of any kind. Just a concrete floor with a drain in the middle of each cell. I don't think the drain was there for potty breaks. Alex was chained to the back wall of his cell. His arms were stretched high over his head, pulling him up enough his feet were an inch off the floor. Chains were attached to his ankles so he couldn't swing, and he was totally nude. At closer inspection, I realized the chains were silver and had burned the flesh around his wrists and ankles, until they were raw and bleeding. Good I hope it hurt like hell. A lot of the smell was coming from him too.

Matt put his hand on my lower back and guided me to the cell. Another wolf about six foot six with a shiny bald head stood next to the cell door. He had a goatee that was dark with a few pale grey hair stubbles here and there. He wore sunglasses so I couldn't see his eyes. Why wear sunglasses in the basement? Matt introduced us. "Casey, this is Dutch, he's the pack interrogator." Dutch gave me a slight bow and said "Accalia, it is an honor to meet you." "You to Dutch. Have you gotten anything out of him?" my head nodded towards Alex "My apologies Accalia, but he has said very little. He has had interrogation training." "He's ex-military, I figured as much, let me try. Lower him down to the floor." Matt didn't like that idea "No, he stays where he is." "Matt, please."   I gave him my most sincere look and Matt finally nodded to Dutch, but they all came inside the cell with me. It was getting very crowded in here.

Alex looked liked shit, he was beaten black and blue, his face looked broken, both eyes were swollen shut. And his body, GAK and YARK! Burns covered most of his body along with cuts and more bruises. Strips of skin looked like it had been peeled off in some spots. Dutch hit a lever in the wall and a mechanical sound started up. The chains stared lowering Alex to the ground. Slowly I walked over to him, squatted down and lifted his head into my lap. And to think I thought he was a cutie at one point, he's not so cute now.

"Alex, grunt if you can hear me." I checked his pulse it was still strong. Dutch said "Shifters can handle an extraordinary amount of damage and survive." Yeah I had seen that with Candy. As I looked at his face I wondered if the "Rocky" scene in the movie was true. Where they cut his eyelid on top to relieve pressure so he could still see to fight. Only one way to find out.

"Any one have a razor blade?" Dutch handed me one, go figure. Matt looked confused. I turned Alex's face and said "Hold still this is going to hurt." Gently, I placed the corner of the blade at the top of his eyelid and punctured it. Blood and clear goop seeped out. "Hand me a towel, Quick!" Matt was passed a towel then passed it to me. I wiped the gore from Alex's face and slightly pushed on the eyebrow to get some more out and relieve pressure. After I did the other eye, he was able to open both eyes about half way and look at me. Both of his eyes were blood shot. Great.

"Alex, why were you targeting my son?" His eyes fluttered as he stared at me and he visibly clamped his jaw shut. "Was it an order? Were you supposed to kill an innocent child?" A single tear leaked out of his eye and landed on my leg. Was that from pain or remorse? I looked up at Matt and asked "Can't the Vampires do mind control and make him talk or read his mind or something?" "That is only in books." Damn. Could I do it? Hmm. I stared directly into Alex's eyes and imagined pushing into them. I got nothing. Hell, it would have been nice to know if I even could do it. Nothing was happening. "Alex, talk to me, tell me what the fuck is going on." A hard pull hit behind my eyes and Alex started blabbing like he was on speed. "Marcus told me to do it, said to get your attention, take out the boy. Said we'd get you one way or another. If we couldn't have you then someone close to you would do, and we'd trade. It was a drugged dart, not a bullet. I didn't want to hurt the kid, and I wouldn't have. Marcus forced my hand he has my sister. I'm sorry so sorry." He started crying right then and there and closed his eyes. When he did the hard pull I felt stopped and I blinked rapidly several times then looked at Matt. "Check his gun." Jayce moved to the gun case and expertly checked it and nodded to us "It's as he said, darts." Matt and I shared a moment. He turned to Dutch and told him "Release the chains, but keep him in the cell for now." I laid Alex back down while he cried and left the cell. Everyone but Dutch went back up stairs. I would not feel sorry for him. I just wouldn't. Oh hell.

We all sat in the kitchen and I ran my fingers through my hair. "This is a mess, before you know it we'll catch Marcus and he'll tell us someone has someone of his and it'll just keep going on and on." Matt put his arm around my shoulder and said. "Don't worry we'll get this all straightened out." My look was doubtful but he did try to reassure me. "Trust me Casey, we have a few tricks up our sleeves." At that Matt and Jayce left me in the kitchen and went to his office to start making phone calls. Let the planning begin...

Chapter 24

For two days we planned, did some recon, and finally figured out what the hell was going on. We think.

First on the to-do list was pick up my truck.

Enrique came out of the office as soon as Kendrix and I got out of the borrowed black Limo. We nodded towards each other and I asked, "Is she ready yet?" He wiped grease off of his hands with a red rag and gave me a small smile. "Si', she's ready, but I wonder something?" "What?" "Can you handle her?" "Doesn't matter what you did I'll handle her." I couldn't help but be giddy and laugh. "Come on weda, follow me. Dis you Niño?" "Yep." As we followed my Niño tried to be cool and said. "Hey Vato! Que Paso?" Enrique placated him by shrugging and saying "Not much amigo" We went inside and at some unseen signal another of the were snakes pulled off a tarp exposing my Ridgeline. And OOOOO BABY!! Kendrix smiled and said "Sweeeeet!" I totally agreed, my fingers gingerly glided across the new high gloss paint job. She was now black with a dark grey design and chameleon paint. My brow furrowed as I looked at the design. My head tilted one way then the other. My eyes just weren't seeing it, so I back up, looked again, then back up some more. When my eyes finally made out what the design was, I felt like falling over. I looked at Enrique. He smiled at me and said "Javier gave me an idea." I was dumbfounded, speechless. Along the bottom of the truck was the ghost of a Dragon. He was beautifully done. A dark grey wispy smoke outline of a sleeping Dragon, stretched from bumper to bumper, all hand air brushed on. Up close you wouldn't know what you were looking at, but from a distance the Dragon was clear. The details of the scales and spikes were incredible. And only the Dragon had been covered in the chameleon paint. It was fucking cool!

"Come on Weda, lemme show you wat 'chu got." I could see what I didn't get! I still had regular tires, and a very small body lift. He popped the hood to show me the engine first. "Ok, you got a whole new engine. We had to do a lil adjustment to get it in. New motor mounts and stuff. Dis baby es a Ramjet 502. Es fuel injected and puts out 500 horsepower from the crate. But we did a few things to it to give a girl a lil more. We added a wet-flow NOS nitro kit plumbed into the intake runners and a FAST controller." "What's that?" "A FAST controller is a speed density type system that is more programmable." I must have looked confused. "It will run better jus trust us." "What ever. Just keep it simple, I'm not a car junkie." "No problemo, anyways es a big block v8." I understood that! My smile was going to be permanently affixed to my face. "With the NOS at top end you'll have about 900 horsepower if you need it." YEEHAW! "We had to make you a new hood so it would look as close to original as possible but give a little more height under the hood so the engine would fit." The whole engine looked chrome or polished steel. It was clean and shiny. "We put on the step bars, and the brush guard like you wanted, and modified the light covers. The lights and windows are layered ballistic glass and tinted, the body and under carriage has been fitted with ballistic steel. Get up inside." Kendrix and I both climbed inside. And our jaws dropped some more. 3-point hook-ups had been added in along with a chain link steering wheel and my whole dash glowed like the space shuttle. "Look up Weda" my son and I both looked up. Enrique pointed out things as he talked "Roll bar across the top, here at the front are the latches to remove the top so you can have your lil convertible. New purple lights inside all new race gauges, in tank electric fuel pump and as you see there are a few new switches." He touches the first switch which had a red light glowing at the end of it. "This one is for you NOS adjustment, it es preset for street tune. The switch with the blue light activates another preset for qwik tune. There's you power when you need it. Don' use it on city streets, only the highway. And make sure your RPM's are at least 5500." "Got it only on the highway" he nodded and continued "The Green, yellow and purple switches. I let them be a surprise for later. In case you ever chased. But remember as soon as you flip the green switch, wait like two seconds then flip the yellow they work together." I wanted to know NOW!!! "Come on out" We eagerly followed "Tail guard and hitch are as solid as you brush guard." He lowered the tailgate and we all climbed up without him having to tell us. "Your lil' trunk here has been lined with ballistic steel too. Nothing es gonna get through it or the gas tank. These side rails are bolted to the truck and welded so it looks smooth. Everybody out!" We climbed out and he started pointing at the wheels. "Okay these are you standard "no air" tires. Miguel filled them with a hardening gel, they're heavier than regular tires. Anyways, no blow out! Since they are regular tires, you only got a 3 inch body lift, off road shocks and new suspension kit, new rear end and 3 speed Raptor 400 tranney. Es pretty much bullet proof too, and chu won't burn it out with the NOS. As it es this baby is a street/ strip truck. So what chu think? Can you handle her?" "Oh Hells yeah! But uh well, I don't see a rocket launcher, parachute, or expandable wings..." "You think your real funny don't you Weda?" My head bobbed up and down "Yeah sometimes I am." Enrique smiled and asked "So what chu think?" I said "This Bitch rocks!" Kendrix pointed his thumb at me and said "Definitely what she said." "Okay, tell me the figure I owe you for this. And don't go over fifty dollars." Enrique barked out a short laugh and said "Yeah, you real funny. Uh, look Javier said to do the work and he pay for it, but if you want to give a lil someting to me and my boys for the labor dats cool." "What do you consider a little?" "Eh maybe, five thousand?" Hell, I felt it was worth more than that and I showed it. I could tell he was looking for some extra green trying to maybe pull a fast one on me. I pulled out twenty thousand dollars, two stacks of Benjamin's out of my purse and handed them over. His eyes got big and he started scanning his surroundings. "NO! es too much take some back! If Javier find out he kick our butts!" He tried to push it back at me. Leave it to the teenager to come up with a solution. "Hey man, I'll take it" Kendrix had both hands out and I slapped them down "No, you won't, keep the money Enrique. Consider it a donation to the Pizza fund or something, but you guys deserve every penny." He looked torn between taking it or not but finally kept it.

Kendrix and I climbed in and I fired her up. Oh man did she sound bad! Like there was a race car hiding under the hood. Cool. Since it is a Ridgeline, I wasn't expecting her to win any races, but I hoped it got me out of harms way if need be. As we left the parking lot I punched it. Well, a girl has to know what she's working with right? We burned rubber out of the driveway. Maybe I should have asked for wheelie bars?

We pulled into my mom's office so I could show off my new truck. I was so proud of it. We parked and then went inside to get her. She was sitting behind her desk and when she saw us her face lit up and I asked "Hey can you sneak out for a few minutes?" she nodded and followed us out. My mom works inside the office doing billing and appointments and stuff. The building is a 'L' shaped metal building with two big garage doors, that were usually open. Today they were. My mom's boss had seen us pull in and wanted to know who's truck is was or maybe he was just admiring the truck. Could you blame him? Mack is almost six foot tall and has salt and pepper hair. He's not real muscular but trim. And when I see him he's usually in a decent mood. For being the boss. We all walked up to him and the truck. "Hey Mack what's shakin?" His eyebrows raised and said "Hey, not much. Is this your truck?" I nodded with pride and said "Yep. Cool huh?" "Yeah it is? That's a nice paint job." "Thanks." My mom said "Wow!" Kendrix said "Check this out!" He opened the driver door and pulled the latch for the hood. Mack heard the little pop and grabbed for the hood latch, and pushed it up. "Whoa! That's not stock.." mom's eyes got huge "No, it's not." Kendrix started telling them about like he knew what the hell he was talking about. It was so cute. Mack admired for another minute and then had to get back to work. "Later Mack." He waved bye.

Kendrix closed the hood while mom pulled me aside. She gave me an annoyed look and said "Bradley's called me half a dozen times wanting to know where Shane and you are." Shane is my son's real name, and Bradley is his father. "He got nasty with me over the phone, finally I told him to Fuck off. And I'd have you call him. So call him so he'll leave me alone. I'm not happy with him right now."

I replied "Crap, sorry for that. I'll call him when we leave here." a heavy sigh came out and I bolstered myself. "Well, I guess we better let you get back to work, that way I can deal with Bradley." "Be careful. I love you." "You too. Come on Shane let's go." and just like a teenager "Mom? Can I drive?" ha-ha "Nope." My mom went back into work laughing at us. She called over her shoulder "BTW nice truck." I grinned.

I was dreading having to call Bradley or Brad for short. He was going to be pissy and I knew it. He knew I was in a tight spot right now. Unfortunately I understood his position. We drove to the Walgreen's on the corner and I hopped out to use the payphone. Brad was computer savvy, and had found me before by using my family locator on my phone against me. I deposited my quarters and dialed his number. He picked up on the third ring. *"Hello?"* "Hey it's me, what's up?" *"Where the hell are you? And where is my son?"* "Shane's with me, and were over by mom's office. Why?" *"Bring him home now. He doesn't need to be anywhere around you. The last thing he needs is to get caught up in your damned mess."* Well, I couldn't exactly blame him for that one. I was messed up right now. "We're okay, it's not that messy." *"Don't Fuck with me. Bring him home. Your nothing but a wanted criminal."* "I'm not a criminal Brad. Geez, you make it sound like I murdered someone." Ok, I had, but he didn't know that and neither did the Government. "Look, why don't we come over pick you up and we'll have lunch and talk about it?"

"There's nothing to talk about. Bring Shane home now! I'm not changing my mind." I tried to think of something, anything that would help my cause and nothing came

to mind. So, I just told the truth. "I want Shane to stay with me for a little while. If things get too hot I'll get him back to you…" *"GOD! You are such a selfish BITCH! What kind of mother puts her son in danger? Bring him home now! I'm warning you. Don't FUCK.WITH.ME."* Was I just being selfish? Maybe. Then again I didn't like being threatened either. "Look, we'll come by, so Shane can pick up some clothes. But right now things are going pretty smoothly. I can protect him you know?" *"How long til you get here?"* "about thirty minutes?" *"Hurry your ass up. And be here in twenty."* click.

The phone went dead in my hand. I wasn't going to hurry my ass up and be there in twenty minutes. He could damn well wait the thirty.

Well, the call went about as well as a fart in church. Just what I expected. I hung up the dead payphone and climbed back into my truck and hit the road. Shane (Kendrix) asked "Dad's pissed isn't he?" "Yeah baby he is." "Well too bad, he'll get over it." Wow. "Honey he does have the right to be worried ya know?" "yeah riiiight." What could I say? "Maybe you should think about being with me. I mean there are good and bad to both sides." "I don't need to think, I'm staying with you." "You might not want to after I finish my piece here. Just listen. If you stay with your dad, you can still talk to your girlfriends, you know what's gonna happen everyday. You'll be in familiar territory. Those are the good points. The bad points are you wont get to see me, Grandma, Illiana or the baby. If you go with me, you'll have to make huge sacrifices, like your friends…"

"I'm keeping my friends." "Honey, you could be tracked through them, same with your friends on face book. And you might not be able to see your dad very often, but I'd make sure you could. The good points are, a new school, a new beginning, new friends. You'll have me, grandma, Illiana, the baby, Matt all the wolves… it would definitely be interesting at times. You would learn about a whole new underworld basically. And there will still be some boring times too. You need to think about it. If you stay with me or your dad, there will be sacrifices. Your sort of stuck in the middle, and I hate that you have to be there. Just think about it."

We were on I-10 going west towards Katy. Just after the loop we got off and headed south towards Alief. I noticed the gas price at the station and pulled in. The sign showed gas was a couple of cents cheaper than on the other side of town so I might as well fill up. I pulled into the gas station and up to the pump. I handed Kendrix fifty dollars to take in for gas and he asked "Can I get a Monster?" he loved those damned drinks I nodded to him and pulled the pump out of the stand and plunked it into the tank as my son walked in. As I waited for the tank to fill two marked cop cars, two unmarked and four black SUV's with tinted windows raced down the street. In the same direction we'd be going. My stomach drop and I had a dreadful feeling. He wouldn't dare. Brad wouldn't dare turn me in. We had too much history, it had to be a coincidence. Right?

We pulled out of the gas station and followed the cops. They were way ahead of us since they had been going faster and I was doing the speed limit. I told Kendrix about the cops. "Yeah, I saw them go by. But, dad wouldn't call them." I didn't think so either. But I was still rattled. At the corner of Brad's subdivision is a super K-Mart with several restaurants in the outer parking lot. When I looked over I saw one unmarked cop car and one SUV. I said "Shit" Kendrix asked "What?" I nodded in the direction of the cops. When he saw them he let out a deep breath. "Sweetie do me a big favor and climb in the back and lay flat. " "But Mom…" "Just do it! Don't argue, and Hand me your phone." He did. His father had used the family locator to find me before, so I knew he knew how to do it. And probably was. I popped the battery out of the back and set the phone in the passenger seat now that Kendrix was in the back.

Two more turns and we came to the street leading into his dad's subdivision. About three hundred feet from the light on the right was another unmarked cop car and another SUV. I turned left.

There were four apartment complexes in the middle of a housing development. The street we turned on led us right up the middle of them. Two complexes on each side. Halfway down the street the two complexes on the left were bisected with a street that cut back into the neighborhood. On the right was a half cul-de-sac with a marked car sitting in it. Usually a cop sat there watching the kids as they got off the bus.

I didn't like it. My gut was screaming at me. So I turned down the street that led into the neighborhood, slow and easy like I knew where I was going. "Hey baby? Is there a way to get into the complex from back here? A whole you guys cut through?" He sat up to see where we were and said "Yeah, up here turn right, then go to the dead end. There's a whole in the chain link around the corner. Maybe ten feet in the field." I followed his directions an shut off the truck. I needed a minute to think. And catch my breath.

Brad had called the cops, I know he did. If there was any mention of a reward, Brad would be all over that. But I just had to see if first hand. "Wait here babe, I'll be back in a few minutes." "Heck no, I'm going with you." "Son, please wait here." "Forget it mom. I need to know if dad ratted us out." Aww he said "us" not "you" like we were a team. "Alright but you have to hold my hand the whole time and don't let go or say anything! Got it?" "Mom, I'm not a baby. I don't need to hold your hand." "You do if your going to be invisible with me." "Oh, okay since you put it like that." Stubborn teenagers.

Kendrix climbed into the front seat and held out his hand for me. I checked to make sure no one was outside watching and held his hand. Behind tinted windows we became invisible. After we got out, Kendrix led the way to the whole in the fence. One by one we went through and came out behind one of the buildings, at the very back of the complex.

The complex was U shaped. Drive in on the left and drive out on the right. At the back of the complex where the road turns were two more cop cars blocking the driveway so no one would be able to leave. From the front street, they wouldn't be seen. An ambush.

We jogged along the fence, behind he buildings until we were almost inline with Brad's apartment. Then we walked between two buildings and watched. Another black SUV was parked across from Brad's apartment and down a little ways. Subtle.

I had brought Kendrixs' phone with us, so I popped the battery back in and called Brad. Maybe it was a bad move but I felt completely betrayed. He answered on the third ring. I've got five bucks that says we were being recorded and traced.

"Where are you?" "What did you do Brad?" *"I don't know what you mean? When are you bringing my son back?"* "I'm not blind or stupid, was it the reward? Is it just the money?" *"What do you think?"* "I think you just messed up, big time." Click. Hopefully we hadn't talked long enough for them to trace the call. I pulled Kendrix back towards the whole in the fence, popped the battery out of his phone and left them in the grass, then we left.

"I can't believe dad would do that. He really did it didn't he? He turned you in." "Yeah babe, it looks like he did." The ride back to Matt's was very quiet. Except for the occasional sniffle from the passenger seat. And that just solidified me more. Shane was now dead. A memory. Kendrix has officially been born.

When we got back to the house Kendrix was given something to occupy his time and the rest of us started getting phase two in motion.

Chapter 25

The Intel that we had gotten was very thorough. Apparently Marcus wasn't the only one with ex-military in his group. Marcus owned a number of different properties. He had a gun shop, an indoor gun range, his mercenary business, and rental properties. Two duplexes, six single family homes (Each house had between one and five acres of land) and a two hundred and eighty eight unit garden condo complex. The complex was really nice from what we could tell. Area photos had been taken of each property. The gun shop and range were in a big warehouse, the duplexes were in blue collar neighborhoods, the houses were all on the outskirts of town, or surrounding areas and the condo complex was in the heart of the galleria. It consisted of four buildings, eight stories each. The bottom seven floors had ten units each and the top floor of each building had two really big penthouses. Each with a view of beautiful gardens or downtown or both.

Before we left, everyone was fitted with Black BDU's and weapons. We looked like a S.W.A.T team.

We had mobilized our troops close to one of the houses on the south side of Houston in an area called Pearland. The house we were watching had five acres and sat on the edge of a newer neighborhood. The attached lots hadn't been built on yet but they were flagged. It looked like Marcus just bought them before the land had even been cleared. Which was excellent for us.

Several lions had been spotted patrolling around the property. So I was up first. The thick pads on my paws let me move silently through the underbrush and closer to the house. Since there is some kind of mystical mental connection between the Were's when in animal form, I went in as a lioness to listen and try to pick up any info from the patrols. Travis was in wolf form back with the rest of the Wolves and Matt was keeping him by his side. Travis obviously couldn't talk as a wolf but he would be able to signal the troops if something went wrong.

Dutch coordinated snipers around the property to take out the patrols at the same time when given the signal. One shot one kill per Lion. Raised voices came from inside the house. Someone was arguing with Marcus. His voice was the loudest and easy to hear.

Good, maybe there was dissention in the ranks. I was at the edge of the yard and couldn't quite make out what the people yelling were saying, looked like a good time to move to me.

I slipped my lioness skin and became a wolf and sent the "Go Ahead" to Travis. His job was to bark, bounce, paw at the ground and come towards the house.

Some of our wolves would be two-legged and some four-legged.

Not all of our Dominates were ex-military, or were trained in Martial arts, but they did had one thing in common. An aggressive streak from hell. Over the last couple of days it had become very clear that they were spoiling for a fight.

A silent popping noise started the evening invasion. The patrolling Lions fell to the ground and all the wolves rushed to the house. Wolves burst through every door and window at the same time. Tranquilizer darts were flying everywhere. Matt, Bryce, Jayce, and I came through the front door, and were pushed out of the way by Peyton as he was trying to leave. Well what do you know.

The four of us got our bearings and bolted after Peyton. His vampire speed was fast. I shifted into a dragon and took to the skies to keep an eye on him. But he was pulling away from my guys. Matt, Bryce, and Jayce had to track and chase, while Peyton just had to run. As Peyton tried to dart across a street I swooped down and caught him in my claws. Pinning his arms to his sides. I circled back, found the boys and landed.

They came to a halt and looked at my catch. I slung my big head around towards my back and Matt's eyebrows wet up. "Do you want us to get on?" My big head bobbed up and down "How?" I lowered my body to the ground and extended my empty front right arm with the claws digging into the yard, and they climbed onboard. OOFTA! Three big Wolf shifters and a vampire. Damn that's a lot of weight. Good thing we weren't going far. I flew low, just over the tree tops and got us back pretty quick.

I landed in the front yard, and my riders got off. Matt went inside to check on the situation. Two female members of the pack came out with burdens on their backs. One had a drugged and chained Marcus, the other had a drugged and chained female vampire. The one that brought out Marcus had long jet black hair pulled back into a French braid. She was about five foot six and slender build. With big brown eyes. Her name was Megan. The other was a five foot eight inches tall black woman with a spiral hairweave that had been gathered into a loose ponytail a the base of her neck. Her skin and eyes were almost the same dark brown color. Her name was Shasta (Yeah like the drink but don't tease her about it, she gets testy).

I moved out of the shadows at the side of the house and into the front porch light when both girls jumped and started swearing a blue streak as they ran to the other side of the house. Shasta said "Holy Fuck me running!" Meagan said "Son of a Bitch with a crowbar!" I'd never heard that one before. They both slowly poked their heads back around the corner of the house. Dominates might scare and run but they didn't run far. Shasta asked "Um Accalia?" I nodded my head. Both girls cautiously came back into the front as I closed Marcus in my other claw. Both claws were full now. Pissed off Vamp in one and a drugged Leander in the other.

Shasta put her hand to her chest and breathed out a huge gulp of air and started protesting "I know yous our Accalia an all, but Fuck you scared the crap outta me. I thought the big Alien Bitch was gonna get us!" my head tilted sideways in confusion "You know the Big Green acid for blood Alien Bitch who fights the Predator?" awww now I got it and bobbed my head. Yeah that would be scary. Megan said "Yeah I had those same thoughts too. Could you be a little less scary?" My Dragon form chuckled and I became less scary. I changed my coloring until I was mostly lime green with a pink belly and pink spikes.

Matt, Bryce, Jayce and the rest of the wolves were starting to bring drugged Lions out of the house including one hysterical human female. She got one look at me screamed at the top of her lungs then passed out.

Bryce came over to me and asked "Uh, are you supposed to Elliot?" I nodded vigorously "Oh Shit ya'll she's little Pete's dragon!!!" And knowing Pete was definitely a submissive everyone laughed. Matt came up grinning and said "I'm gonna have to have a talk with Pete, I see. Change back to black you look ridiculous." So, I did.

We split into three groups. Group one was the snipers and the bodies. They were going to take two hummers and "Take care of them". Group two took the human girl and the drugged lions back to the house in a military transport truck. When I called it that Dutch quickly corrected me saying "It's a Deuce and a half". Whatever. The POW's were going into cells in the basement for Dutch to interrogate later. Creepy thought that. Group three was me, Matt, Bryce, Jayce, Dutch, Peyton and the female Vampire and Marcus. We were going to Christian's strip center.

Chapter 26

I flew overhead with Marcus and Peyton still in my clutches. Everybody else was in Hummers. What did they do raid the Hummer store? And steal all the dark colored ones? A few of the Hummers even looked like they were sporting military paint jobs. Either desert camo or primer grey.

I linked up with Christian when we got close *"Hey, Playgirl Dude. You real busy?"* *"As a matter of fact I am. Peyton failed to take care of a few things and I'm doing them and coordinating a search for him."* *"Well, if you come out the back door, I just bet you'll find him."* The guys pulled into the parking lot as I landed and Christian and Sebastian came out the back door along with Harley and several other big Vamps. Christian did not look like a happy Vampire.

"Where ever did you find my Major?" Matt answered "We found him when we raided Marcus's hide out. We found this one too." Dutch tossed the very groggy female Vampire at Christians feet. He leaned down grabbed her by the throat with his right hand and pulled her up off the ground like she weighed nothing. "Well Brenna, what do you have to say for yourself?" She gave a choked moan and held onto his wrist in hopes that he wouldn't hang her right there. "Were you plotting? Planning to betray me?" She squirmed in his grip and Peyton replied "Yes, we were. Your unfit for the position. Your weak. A General should not be weak. He should be able to lead properly. You don't!" Then Peyton spit at Christian. I tightened my grip and gave a little snap to shut his dumb ass up. Christian turned his attention back to the dangling female. A paranormal crowd was growing outside in the parking lot. "Do you feel the same way Brenna?" She tried to shake her head "I do not believe you." Then he ripped her throat out. Before she could collapse to the ground his left hand came around and caught the back of her neck where her spine and meaty flesh was showing and he ripped that out too. Completely severing her head with his bare hands. Her body crumbled to the ground and her head rolled a few feet in the parking lot coming to a stop facing the wall. Imagine the last thing to see as your synapses quit firing is your own throat and a brick wall. Then you start to slowly ash away.

In old world form Christian straightened himself and started gently tugging on the ends of his Tailored suit coat sleeves with bloody fingers. Like what he just did was no big deal. Then he turned his attention to Peyton.

"Did you believe that Rochelle would just hand over the throne? Or were you going to be her lackey? She was not the kind of woman to be second at anything." Peyton replied "We were going to rule together." Christian laughed "No you weren't, if the two of you had been able to get me out of the way, she would have killed you too." "No, she wouldn't have." "If you truly believe that then you are a fool." Christian looked up into my face and said "I always liked my fools extra crispy." I nodded at him and pushed Marcus towards Matt and Dutch. They caught him and I backed up farther away from the crowd. Peyton yelled "You can't do this!" He turned his head to look at me and said "Please don't" Well it really wasn't my call. I wasn't his leader or master or whatever. My chest expanded as I took in a huge gulp of air and blew out a stream of bright yellow fire at my own claw and the Vampire in it. He burned like flash paper just whoosh and he was toast. His ashes fell through my claws and small embers floated on the breeze. Next it was our turn with Marcus. Time to be human again.

We all moved into the conference room, and Dutch placed Marcus in a chair. Harley moved up into the room and I had an epiphany. My head went back and forth between the two men. One a Vampire the other a Wolf. Everyone has a look-a-like or a twin out in the world somewhere. If these two weren't related or twins themselves then I'm blind. My forefinger bounced back and forth between the two and I asked "Are ya'll related?" Neither spoke but they shook their heads like trained dolphins. In the exact same way for the exact amount of time. Like they practiced it. Weird. I turned and raised a questioning eyebrow to Matt and Christian. Matt and Christian both gave small shrugs. Shit they were doing it too! Matt realized what they did and smiled at me.

I shook my head to clear it and get back to business and mumbled. "We'll talk about that later. Okay, Marcus you have two choices, you can die quick or long slow and very painful. Basically you tell us what you know or you don't. What's it gonna be?"

"I'm not telling you shit." I smiled and nodded "I didn't think so, allow me to introduce you to Dutch" My thumb pointed over my shoulder to him then to Harley "And that's Harley. Alex didn't want to talk either but he did eventually." I didn't mention that Dutch isn't the one who made him talk. Either way Marcus paled.

Dutch asked "Hey Harley, do you like your Lion blood with or without pain?" Harley cracked his knuckles and said "With, adds a touch of spice to the flavor."

I've learned over the years that there are two kinds of tough guys. The first kind really are tough, can take a licking and keep on ticking. The second kind act tough but really are just big wimps.

Marcus played a good game, he could talk the talk but when it came down to it, I knew he would cave.

Most of us left the room after Marcus's declaration, leaving Harley and Dutch alone with him for about four hours. Most of the vamps had gone back to there nightly activities while the rest of us sat in Christians office. At least the screams were muffled. I asked "How long do you think he'll last?" Christian shrugged and said "I do not know but eventually I may need my conference room back." Another half hour past before Christian got a mental buzz from Harley. I immediately tuned in. *"He says he's ready to talk."* Christian and I got up and headed for the door, everyone else just kind of followed us.

Marcus did NOT look good. The Bad Ass Twins had peeled the skin off the top of his head leaving his skull exposed. Blood was everywhere under his chair. His clothes had been removed in strips, and so had more of his skin. He looked like a medical experiment. A living practice cadaver. But he did talk.

He told us about working with Rochelle, and Peyton to take over the Vampires and each of the animal groups so he would really be king of the jungle. He talked about Alex's sister then he finally got to the part I wanted to hear. "My contact with the Government is a 3 star General who works in the Pentagon. He contacts me. I don't know his name or how to get in touch with him." "How would he know if you had caught me or not? Were you required to turn me in somewhere? Or just sit on me til he called you?" "You were to be taken back to White sands. He has all of your info, even your families info. Your whole history. He'll find you, one way or another." Matt led me into the hall and said "I'd like to speak with him for a bit, clear a few things up. Go take a break get some food, I'll join you later." I didn't want to go, But I nodded. If I stayed I'd end up killing the bastard. Before I left I made it clear to Matt "Save him for me, I want him."

Matt nodded and went back into the room. I beeped my crew and we met in the "Lair".

After our hugs and updates we went in search of Antony. I really needed some good fattening comfort food.

Before we could find him Christian buzzed me *"We are through with him."* "Okay on my way." This was a moment that was over due in coming. I told the gang I'd be back in a bit and made my way to the conference room.

Marcus had healed a lot of the damage Harley and Dutch had caused him. Everyone cleared out but Christian and Matt when I got there. I closed in on him like I had tunnel vision. "You do know I'm gonna kill you right?" He gave one nod "Any last words?" "You've taken everything do you want me to beg too?" "Nope, not really. That won't help you. You deserve it for what you've done to me, my family, and everybody else's family you've destroyed or tried to destroy." My words were softly spoken. Rage at this asshole had put me in a zone of my own. I've fantasized about killing him a thousand different ways over the past week, now I had to pick one. Torch him? Eat him? Break his neck? Pull his head off and pee down his throat? Naw, I told him it would be quick, I never said it would be painless. "Would you guys bring him outside please?" I didn't wait for a response, just turned and headed for the parking lot.

I shifted into my Dragon as Christian and Matt dragged a kicking and screaming Leander outside. They dropped him in front of me. He tried to get up to run but wasn't fast enough. I caught him in my claws. My right claws gripped him tight around his shoulders and my left claws tight around his hips, and I slowly pulled. He stretched like taffy, then his spine snapped and his skin was the only thing holding him together. Then finally that started to tear in half. Right through his stomach. His innards fell out of him and hit the pavement, while he was still alive to see it. Then the light slowly died from his eyes and the blood curdling screams stopped.

Epilogue

Alex was the next highest ranking Lion in the pride and would be acting Leander until another one stepped up, and fought for the position. His sister (Kelly) was still human. They hadn't turned her while she was their captive. She was now in therapy.

Matt agreed to release the remaining lions to Alex. On the condition they didn't try to come after me again. If they did all bets were off, and we'd war. Alex agreed. Brett would be his second in command, if he ever shows up. Right now he's M.I.A.

For the brief time Christian and Matt were alone with Marcus, they got him to sign documents giving control of the condo complex, over to Matt, and Christian got the houses. The remaining assets would stay with Alex and the pride.

It's been two weeks since we invaded Marcus' hide out. A lot has happened since then.

We got my mom, sister, and nephew moved into a really nice penthouse. Over a dozen pack members helped us move them. That was the easiest and fastest move we have ever done. They love it, and it's not listed under any of their names. Not even the bills. So they'll be harder to track down.

Pete, somehow, got school records for one Kendrix Frost. He lives with me and Matt in our big fancy house, and loves taunting the wolves. I can only hope the teen fairy returns some of his common sense. SOON! Now that summer is here, maybe we can enjoy some of it. I spoke to his father to let him know our son was safe. Unfortunately he was livid and started threatening me. I understood why he said the things he said but I didn't have to like it.

As for me, well, I'm still learning what I can and can't do. But now I'm trying to learn it in a controlled environment. Hopefully I won't have to test any theories in stressful situations anymore. Ha!

My luck isn't that good. See previous pages. Kendrix and I have started taking martial arts and, I talked to a few "Physic readers" trying to find a witch. I still wanted to know if the wolf mating bond could be broken. Matt and I figured out that my son does have a shield to protect him, and I still do too. According to my personal power trainer, who still comes and goes as he pleases, my aura split in two. And can be rebuilt by eating fruit and vegetables. Something about the natural life force will replenish my own aura. So I've almost become a vegetarian. I should be back to one hundred percent now, but I'm not taking chances with my Aura.. And no, Kendrix can't use the aura's power.

Since the night the shit went down with the Lions and Vamps, Christian has been fairly quiet, however he did mention something to Matt about some big meetings and he wanted me to be there. I have no idea who the new Major of Houston is. I haven't asked.

Ajax, Thank God, still hasn't come back. I hope he never does. The government is busy scratching theirs heads right now and I'm still numero uno on their list. Maybe the new identities will keep us hidden. I can only hope.

My world has changed, completely flipped upside down and I'm on the roller coaster ride of the century. But I have a feeling eventually something will go F.U.B.A.R. and once again it will be S.N.A.F.U.

Situation normal all fucked up!

Sebastian sat across from Christians desk in a leather chair and smirked at him. "I told you she would bring life to these old bones." "Yes, you did." "Are you going to do it?" "I told her I wouldn't force her." "That didn't answer my question." Christian let out a heavy sigh, out of habit not necessity and said " I want to, you know that, we will just have to wait and see." "She was a good chance." "You were right on that. Except for one thing. She is an excellent chance."

THE END

About the Author

I've read so many books my mind never slows down anymore. Even while I drive, my mind is constantly working, like a movie in my head. I just needed to write some of it down! I tried to put a few actual facts about Truck driving to make it more interesting. I live with my family, a crazy dog named Angel, and a goofy cat named Cinnamon. They are in the book and they are real!!! Enjoy!